The Mighty Pen

edited by Brianne DiMarco

Blue Forge Press

Port Orchard ✿ Washington

Blue Forge Press
7419 Ebbert Drive Southeast
Port Orchard, Washington 98367
360.550.2071 ph.txt

Dedication

To my wife, Jennifer.

Thank you for sharing your stories with me, and telling our stories so the world will know who we are. Being the wife of a writer has been such an unexpected and wonderful joy.

I love you.

Table of Contents

Quill

Fountain Pen

Pencil

Typewriter

Ballpoint Pen

Computer

About the Authors

The Mighty Pen

edited by Brianne DiMarco

Quill

It Is Written

by Lauren Patzer

Father Evan sat nervously on the wooden bench outside Monsignor Trevanche's office. He was a simple junior monk specializing in penmanship; there was no logical reason in his mind to be called to the Monsignor's office. Had he forgotten a line in the nightly rituals? Was his hair too long? He absently raised his hand to the circle of hair around his head. It was short and well maintained. He ran his fingers over the shaved center and found it nearly perfectly smooth.

His feet were in simple leather sandals with nothing ornate on them. Father Evan was meticulous in observing the simplicity of the order. His robes were plain and tied with a simple cotton rope fashioned from white strips of material. His room contained a simple cot, a small table and a wash basin. The single candle and Holy Bible were the only adornments in the room.

Try as he might, Father Evan could not come up with a single thing out of place. Had Father Brian tattled on him as a joke? He wouldn't leave that possibility out considering Father Brian's often childish antics and pranks. Of course, he hadn't seen Father Brian in nearly a fortnight. Perhaps he'd been sent on a mission.

Of course, that's it! Monsignor Trevanche simply needs some food or paper, perhaps, retrieved from the village? That made more sense than Father Evan being in trouble.

Father Anthony emerged from Monsignor Trevanche's office without a word. Father Evan looked up and Father Anthony beckoned him to enter with a simple wave. The less words used in interactions with each other, the better. Silence was golden and allowed the mind to contemplate the holy scripture more easily and without the distraction of needless chatter.

Father Evan entered Monsignor Trevanche's office and his jaw dropped. The room was much larger than he'd imagined it would be. Instead of a simple desk, there was an ornate beast of a desk big enough for four monks sitting in the middle of the room. Bookshelf after bookshelf lined the walls, with oil fueled sconces in between each. The room was awash in light. On the desk, there were multiple quills, sheaves of paper and scrolls. There were two small lanterns, built into the desk no less, bringing an almost daylight shine to the items on the desk. Some items, Father Evan realized, were either ornate decoration or served some purpose for which he had no explanation. Fine rugs covered the floor helping keep the room warm from the fireplace in the west wall.

"Please see to it, Father Anthony," Monsignor Trevanche said. Father Evan turned to see Father Anthony bow and shut the door.

"Please sit, Father Evan," Monsignor Trevanche said and waved at two exquisitely carved chairs with seat cushions. Father Evan quickly looked around the room for simpler furniture. There was none. He walked calmly to one of the chairs and sat down. It gave way to his weight and Father Evan felt himself sink into the cushion.

Monsignor Trevanche wore simple but elegant clothing. As he wrote on a piece of parchment, the long billowing sleeves of his shirt seemed to quiver and flow in the air with each letter emerging from the end of the quill. Each curved letter was accompanied by a light scratching sound as the quill tip moved across the page. When the Monsignor appeared to finish writing, he placed the quill back in its mount next to what appeared to be a solid gold inkwell and pulled open a drawer. After folding the parchment, Monsignor took a small brass cup attached to a handle and poured a small amount of melted wax onto the parchment. After replacing the brass cup, he then sealed the parchment with his signet ring pressed into the melted wax. Father Evan watched this transpire in awe. He wasn't aware his mouth hung open.

"Careful, Father Evan, you'll catch flies with your mouth hanging open like that."

Father Evan quickly closed his mouth and looked down at the rug beneath his feet. It was decorated with what appeared to be a knight slaying a lion in a forest.

"I'm sure you're wondering why I've called you here, yes?"

Father Evan looked and nodded.

"Father Anthony tells me you've grown quite accomplished with the quill," Monsignor Trevanche took the quill he'd been using and held it up. The feather was unusually large and the tip seemed to be gold. "This simple instrument has revolutionized communication and education across the world. You may not be aware of what else can be accomplished."

Monsignor Trevanche put the quill back and stood up. He walked over to a coat rack and pulled on a simple robe, the one Father Evan was more accustomed to seeing him wearing when walking about the monastery.

"It's time to show you the next step in your training, before I send you on your quest."

With that, Monsignor walked to the door and Father Evan quickly followed, nearly tripping on the tasseled edge of the rug.

Without a word, they exited the office. Monsignor Trevanche locked it behind them and they walked in silence through the monastery. Every once in a while, they would pass a junior monk in the hallway and they'd always look up and seemed shocked to see Father Evan walking alongside Monsignor Trevanche. They would then quickly avert their eyes, look at the floor and remain silent.

They approached a hallway nestled behind the kitchen. It was roped off to deter access. Monsignor Trevanche detached the rope from the wall and motioned for Father Evan to enter the hallway, which he did. Monsignor Trevanche replaced the rope and continued down the hallway around a corner and down a curving flight of stairs until they reached what Father Evan estimated to be a full two stories below ground.

They reached a large wooden door with a single image of a quill carved into the thick oak. A brass knocker hung in the center of the door. Monsignor Trevanche raised the knocker and hammered it into the door three time slowly, two quickly, and two slowly. The door swung open slowly to reveal two blind monks in a foyer leading to a large room beyond. Monsignor Trevanche waved at the monks absently as he walked by.

"Brothers Altuvay and Winsop guard the writing room. Any wrong signal and they'll cut the perpetrator down without hesitation," Monsignor Trevanche smiled as he made his way past the two men.

Father Evan observed the men as he walked by. Their eyes had been burned shut, but that seemed to be the only thing wrong with them. Brother Altuvay's nostrils flared as Father Evan passed close.

"It's all right, brothers, Father Evan is a guest and future scribe."

The men bent close and sniffed at Father Evan, then nodded.

"Come along Father Evan, there is so much to show you," Monsignor said and walked forward. Father Evan kept pace.

They entered a vast room. The walls were over one hundred

feet long and reached over three stories high. Brass rails with ladders attached to them ran along the length of the walls. The walls appeared to be a range of colors from very white to dark yellow and even brown. These reflected the colors of the pages laid flat against the walls, each behind a glass cover.

"These parchments are recouped every year to keep the world in order," Monsignor Trevanche waved at the walls. "Everything we know in the world is written on these walls. A special quill is used to create these documents. The Magic quill, however, has been stolen! If it is not returned soon, the world as we know it will cease to exist."

"Surely, you're kidding," Father Evan said. "There's no such thing as magic, Monsignor."

Monsignor Trevanche walked to the middle of the room where two tables with chairs at them sat.

"Sit," Monsignor Trevanche told Father Evan. He sat as he was told and Monsignor Trevanche stood next to him and pointed at the tilted writing surface with an inkwell on one side and a pen mount on the other.

"Father William sat at this very desk and did this work. You remember when the Lake of Wonder ran dry? That was Father William's doing."

Father Evan frowned. He thought back to everything that father William had taught him in the monastery. He'd brought Father Evan up from a cowering child in the monastery orphanage to nearly where he was now. But Father William had been absent for over a year. He'd seen nothing of his old mentor, nor heard mention of him until now.

"Why would Father William do such a thing?" Father Evan wondered out loud.

"Evil had taken over him, I'm afraid,' Monsignor Trevanche replied. "He was greedy and covetous of what others had so he planned to use the power given him here to enrich himself. A travesty of betrayal. I've been personally hurt by his obstinacy and lies."

Monsignor Trevanche held his hand to his heart and sat down in the other chair. Father Evan looked down in shame and noticed some scratches on the left leg of the table, as if a metal band had once been there but was bow gone. The table leg was thick and intricately carved for both longevity and beauty.

"Father Evan?"

Father Evan realized he'd been staring at the table leg trying to figure out why the damage was on the leg. He quickly looked up.

"Yes, Monsignor?"

"Will you save the world?"

"Well," Father Evan said. "If it's within my power to do so, of course."

"Father William saw promise in you. Your talent with the quill is not merely a mechanical aptitude, Father Evan. There is something special within you that allows you to use the magic in the quill to keep our world alive. You were blessed when you were born. This," Monsignor Trevanche waved his arms at the walls. "Is your destiny."

"What do I need to do?" Father Evan said as he looked around the room. All the glass panes had latches, but no locks. Access to the room was all the security needed and that was controlled through the single hallway and being underground. Father Evan thought it was very effective for what was, quite simply, the fate of the world.

"Retrieve the quill, bring it back here and make the world anew as generations before you have done," Monsignor Trevanche said.

"Monsignor, I noticed that there are two tables. Is there not a second magic quill?"

Monsignor Trevanche lowered his eyes to the floor. He clasped his hands together and took a big breath.

"Birthed in fire, so it was destroyed. Long ago, a foolish man wished for sole power over creation and destroyed the second quill so only he would be able to bring about change or keep things as they were. In the process, he lost his gift. He didn't know it was tied to the quill he destroyed," Monsignor Trevanche sniffed away a tear and gave Father Evan a grim smile. "It has been my life's work to preserve that which is, the single quill's power over everything and to see it used correctly."

"I understand, Monsignor. Where shall I begin my search?"

"Down the mountain, there is a single town. The refuse there may be hiding Father William or they may know where he has gone. There are cities beyond. It may be your search must go further than the village. I would hope not as there are parts of the world already on the verge of crumbling to dust." Monsignor Trevanche pointed at a single page on the wall closest to him. It was brown with age. Father Evan moved closer to it and recognized Father William's hand in the writing. It was a description of a grove of trees far away in the distant moors. The animals and insects that called the grove home where enveloped in the writing. The wind, the rain, the soil conditions – everything there was to know about a place and time was faithfully captured there. Intuitively, Father Evan realized the grove and everything with it would disappear into dust when this page crumbled.

"This page, how old is it?"

"Just over a year. The magic wears away the vitality of the parchment. We've tried adjusting the parchment composition to no avail. Everything must be renewed within a year or risk it disappearing forever."

"What was here before the parchments, the monastery?"

"A dark, cold world," Monsignor Trevanche said as they walked toward the entrance. "Many toiled around a newly birthed mountain of fire, experimenting with spells and materials to bring about the first magic quill and the parchments that began the creation of this world. The grand creator, as we call him, successfully replicated the quill before the effort consumed his body and mind. Over time, they created this place and the secrets within have been a time honored responsibility of the monastery for eons before even I was born."

"Amazing."

They passed through the unlocked door and walked by the brothers guarding the single entrance. Father Evan noticed their nostrils flaring as the two walked by, but they said nothing this time. They walked on in silence until they reached the front door of the monastery. Monsignor Trevanche pointed at a bag of provisions on the floor next to the door.

"You may find need of nourishment along the way. The farmers, hunters and gatherers below do not spend the proper time worshipping to get the fullest fruits of their labors."

He also handed a small bag of coins to Father Evan.

"This may help loosen the tongues of the heathen below. Be wary. They will lie, cheat and steal emulating Father William to a certain degree. I school our brethren on compassion, but there must be no mistake – do everything necessary to retrieve that quill. All of life depends on your success."

"I will do what I must, your Excellency," Father Evan bowed one final time and opened the door to the great beyond outside the wall.

As the door closed behind him, Father Evan felt the weight of his burden upon him. He looked at the path heading down the mountain and shivered. He'd been outside the monastery only to gather provisions from nature and worship amongst the trees. He'd never been down the mountain.

He squared his shoulders and began the journey. It took several hours of walking before he reached the first settlements at the lower elevations. Tilled ground showed the efforts of a few to grow and control their food supply. The fields became more and more vast, but as he went on, it appeared the harvests were smaller and smaller. He marveled at how people could survive on so little food grown at such a huge investment of energy. He only saw the largest of fruits and vegetables in the small planters at the monastery. Not big, by any means, but the flowering plants were much easier maintained in and around their mountain compound.

In time, he came upon the first people of the fields. They were scrawny and malnourished. When they saw him, they scurried away, clearly frightened. The path down the mountain became little more than barely perceptible lines of pressed grass. Eventually, the path disappeared altogether. He looked back up the mountain to get his bearings so he could find his way back. As he got further down the mountain, Father Evan noticed the fields were burned away. Vast tracts of land where forests had once been now showed little more than a wasteland of burned out tree trunks. The cycle of life appeared to have stopped here.

When he came over a rise, he looked down the mountain and saw an enormous wasteland as far as the eye could see. What had once been buildings and settlements were now still smouldering ruins. He went to the buildings and wrinkled his nose against the stench of death. Inside he could see the still smoking remains of bodies, large and small. Tears came to his eyes as he realized these people were being decimated in an instant. This was unlike a normal fire that starts and spreads. He looked to the skies to see if dragons flew overhead, but there was nothing in the air. No birds or insects flittered about in this Armageddon. Even the beasts that scavenged appeared to have abandoned this place.

After a day of travel, Father Evan rested beneath the stars, leaning against an older tree that survived the devastation better than most. His dreams were troubled by images of fire and death. Father William appeared in his dream.

"You're on the right path should you choose to take it," Father William said to him in his dream.

Father Evan awoke with a start.

"Of course, I'm on the right path. I need to retrieve the quiil from you."

Father Evan got up and began walking again. After another

half day's journey, Father Evan glimpsed the first signs of life. A meager settlement nestled in a grove at the edge of the dull grey landscape. As he approached the small outcrop of buildings, he passed some people in the field trying to clear the burned remains of some buildings. When they saw him, they ran, screaming, in the other direction.

When he entered the small town, he turned the corner and several people saw him. They all immediately fell to their knees, prostrate before him.

"Please, don't hurt us!" One man whimpered. A child and what Father Evan assumed to be his wife by prostrated themselves next to the man.

"I'm not here to harm anyone," Father Evan said. "Have you seen Father William?"

"No! I'm sorry, please! Don't burn us like the others!" The man said. He shook with fear as did everyone else who lay on the ground before him.

"Unbelievable," Father Evan murmured and walked further into town. He noticed a building with a single small donkey tied up outside it. He walked to the door and heard conversation inside, punctuated by nervous laughter every once in a while.

"Maybe someone in here will have answers for me," Father Evan said. He opened the door and walked inside.

There was a hush as Father Evan entered the tavern. The monk looked around and saw all eyes on him. He smiled and waved. A group groan erupted from the crowd and muted conversation resumed, but wary eyes glanced his way periodically.

So much fear and suspicion, Father Evan thought. From where did the masses come upon this collective despair? What had happened here?

A small gnome, looking emaciated, walked up to the monk and kicked him in the shin.

"Ow!" Father Evan cried out.

"That's for what you bastards did to my family. Kill me if you want to. I don't care anymore." The little gnome walked away.

Father Evan limped after him. "Please, wait! Allow me to buy you a drink and a meal."

The gnome paused. He was little more than skin and bones at this point.

"What kind of sick joke is that?! You murderers burned the fields and slaughtered the animals! There's nothing left to eat in this town."

Father Evan looked around the room. He noticed no one had food, though there was plenty of drink.

"A drink then," Father Evan said. "I need to know what's happened here."

"You did it! What more do you need to know?" The gnome glared at Father Evan.

Father Evan swallowed and got on his knees, down at the gnome's level. "I've never been here before. This is my first time out of the monastery. None of this makes sense."

The gnome sized up the monk. He walked up to him and sniffed.

"Well, you don't have the overpowering stink of death on you. That'll buy you a few minutes. Come on." The gnome said and walked to a small table in the corner. Father Evan accompanied him. He felt all eyes in the room upon him, but when he looked up, they would quickly look away.

The bartender brought them two mugs filled with ale.

"Do you have any wine?" Father Evan asked. The bartender face went white.

"No sir, I'm sorry. This is all we have left, please, I beg of you."

"It's all right. I'll just drink the ale. How much for the drinks?"

"On the house, Father, please just don't burn the place down. It's all I have left," the bartender bowed his head and had almost gotten down on his knees.

"I'm not going to burn the place, I just want to pay my way. How much for the drinks?"

"Of course, sir. I didn't mean any disrespect. Two coppers will do it."

The gnome scowled at the bartender. The bartender gave him a pleading look. The gnome sighed and looked at Father Evan. Father Evan took out his bag of coins and dug through it. He only found silver and gold coins. He took out a silver and gave it to the bartender.

"Keep the change," Father Evan said and smiled.

"Yes, your grace," the bartender said, turned and walked quickly away.

"He gave you a discount," the gnome grumbled as he picked up the ale and drank it down. He had trouble swallowing. Father Evan noticed that his lips were chapped and the hair on his head had burned in places, leaving his skin scarred. It was bright red in places.

"Well, perhaps he wants me as a repeat customer," Father Evan said.

The gnome bust out laughing and everyone in the room went silent. After a few moments, the gnome gathered his breath and waved to the crowd.

"Its fine, he told a joke. Nothing to worry about," the gnome said and resumed drinking the ale.

"You don't think he'd want me as a repeat customer."

"I think he'll go change his drawers that he's cleared pissed in when you walked in the tavern, is what I think. No one wants you as a customer."

Father Evan sat back in the chair. He looked around the room, again getting the quick action from everyone of looking away.

"Fine. What do you know of Father William?"

The gnome snorted. He took a drink of his ale.

"Well, I've had a good drink now, so I don't care if you kill me. I don't know where the Wanderer went. You can burn me just like you did the others now."

"The Wanderer?"

"Yeah, that's what we call him. The one who appeared before everything went to hell. I curse the day he set foot in this town," the gnome took a long drink, set the cup down and belched.

"Did he burn everything?"

"No. Your brethren who came looking for him did. Anyone who told them they didn't know was burned and their lands with it. When no one came forth with his location, and believe me, some even said they knew when they didn't, they just burned everything and everyone."

Father Evan shook his head.

"No. I don't believe it. The Monsignor said you would lie," Father Evan folded his arms.

The gnome stopped drinking and went pale. Everyone in the room whispered "Monsignor" and left without finishing their drink or talking to anyone else. Some of them left so fast, they didn't even take all their belongings. No one looked back. The bartender ran forward, fell prostrate before Father Evan and held up a shaking handful of gold, silver and copper coins.

"Please, take it all. Just tell the Monsignor I was cooperative and never lied," the bartender said. Father Evan saw tears falling to the ground below the bartender, darkening the gray ash that dusted the floor.

Father Evan's mouth hung open. He looked around the room. He looked at the gnome who now bowed his head.

"Please, just kill me now. Be merciful. Don't give me over to the Monsignor," the gnome begged. "Haven't I suffered enough? Please be merciful!"

Father Evan stood up.

"For the last time, I'm not here to kill anyone! I'm just here to find Father William!"

The little gnome squeaked, pissed himself and passed out. The smell rose to Father Evan's nose letting him know the bartender had lost control of his bowels. Father Evan got down on his hands and knees and looked up into the bartender's face.

"Can you at least tell me the direction he went?"

The bartender lowered his hands and held the coins under Father Evans face.

"All I know is he kept going away from the mountain," the bartender whispered.

"Thank you," Father Evan said and stood up, leaving the coins in the bartender's hands. The bartender turned on his knees and held up the coins.

"Please, have mercy!" He said. His hands shook so badly some of the coins fell out of his hands.

Father Evan picked up the coins, took them from the bartender's hands and walked over to the bar. He placed the coins there. He walked back to the bartender and got back on his hands and knees.

"Mercy has been placed upon you, good barkeep," Father Evan said. "Go forth and do good for the rest of your days."

"Yes, Father. Thank you, Father," the bartender said.

"When's the last time you ate?" Father Evan said.

"The coffers are nearly depleted. I stopped selling food a week ago. I'll have to leave soon if no traders come from afar with supplies."

"All the fields?"

"Burned as far as the eye can see and the mule can walk. The farmers and their families as well."

"Take heart, barkeep. From the ashes will arise new life. These fields will be fruitful and harvested again some day. This danger shall pass," Father Evan said, He stood and surveyed the room once more. He walked out and heard the bartender sobbing his thanks behind him.

Father Evan walked away from the mountain for the remainder of the day. Along the way, he passed more burned out fields and settlements. At some of the locations, he saw bodies strung up on posts and splayed out like a butchered animal. The bodies had not been burned, but rather tortured beyond all comprehension. Father Evan took it all in, even when the bile threatened to surface from his stomach.

Another day's travel brought Father Evan to a small cabin near a sprawling green forest. Smoke rose from the chimney and father Evan was relieved. At least there might be someone who hadn't seen the horrors of the last settlements and might give him some answers. Before he could approach the door, an arrow flew out from somewhere in the forest beyond and struck the tree just behind Father Evan, slightly above his head. Father Evan quickly ducked behind the tree and heard two more arrows strike the trunk.

"Hello?" Father Evan called out. "I mean you no harm."

"Fat chance dressed like that!" A man's voice called out. "But then, I suppose you would've magicked me by now if you had it in you."

"I don't do magic," Father Evan shouted.

""So," the voice sound closer. "As foretold, a simple man with no magical powers would come forth and lead the way."

"I'm not leading anything. I'm just looking for a friend," Father Evan said. He looked around the tree and saw no one.

"Well, you just might've found one," the voice said directly behind Father Evan, making him jump. Father Evan turned around to see a man dressed in a simple, plain brown tunic and trousers with sandals on his feet similar to the one's Father Evan wore.

"Finally, someone who isn't frightened to see me," Father Evan said.

The man held out his hand. Father Evan grasped it warmly.

"Name's Eothur," he said. Eothur closed his eyes and reached his other hand to touch Father Evans chest over his heart. "Pure of heart, but a bit of magical sensitivity in the hands. Just like Father William, of course."

"You know Father William?"

"Well, of course I do. That's why you're here, of course. And quite alone, I've seen to that." Eothur let go of Father Evan's hand and walked toward the building. "Care for some soup?"

"Yes, I would. And, yes, I'm alone. I came with no one," Father Evan said as he followed Eothur.

"Hmm, I'm sure you weren't aware of them," Eothur said as he opened the door.

Father Evan walked through the door into a simple cabin. A cot with several blankets sat at one end of the room and a table with two chairs sat in the middle of the room. Eothur tended to a pot hung over the fire at the rear of the building. The aroma was delicious. Father Evan closed his eyes and took a big whiff.

"Oh, that smells wonderful! So much better than the death and destruction I've encountered most of my journey," Father Evan sat at the small table as Eothur brought two crude wooden bowls and spoons to the it.

"Dig in," Eothur said. "You'll need your strength for the journey ahead."

"You'll take me to Father William, then?"

"Certainly," Eothur said as he slurped the soup into his mouth. "That's why I killed everything that was following you."

Father Evan set down his spoon reluctantly.

"There's been quite enough death and destruction. No more people have to die," Father Evan said.

"Oh, I completely agree," Eothur said as he drank down the last of his bowl. "Would you like another bowl?"

Eothru got up before Father Evan answered and helped himself to another bowl.

"Well, couldn't you have chased the people off instead of killing them?"

"People?" Eothur sat back down and started eating his second bowl. Father Evan noted that Eothur wasn't suffering from hunger and malnutrition like the people closer to the mountain. "I never said I killed people. I said every *thing*."

"I don't understand," Father Evan said. He began eating his soup again.

"Let's start from the beginning and work our way to you being trailed here by creatures of dark evil, OK?"

"I suppose this is where the lying starts," Father Evan said as he dug into the soup.

"Ah yes, the monsignor's tag line – everyone's a liar and a cheat! It's called projection," Eothur said.

"Projection?"

"Yes, accuse others of the things you do. Tell me, don't you find it odd that a man who should embody charity and good faith is arrayed by all the accoutrements of wealth possible in this corner of the world?"

Father Evan looked down. The extravagant wealth displayed in Monsignor Trevanche's office had seemed very out of place. He'd been taught that vows of poverty and charity were among the highest of God's principles.

"I was confused by the trappings of the Monsignor, but I thought perhaps they were gifts or something nobles offered in tribute, so that they might receive the blessing s of his Excellency."

"Monsignor Trevanche has been continually amassing wealth over the centuries he's been in power," Eothur said.

"Centuries!" Father Evan said. "The Monsignor doesn't look a day over forty! I mean, he's been the head of the monastery since I can remember, but he certainly isn't centuries old!"

"Since you were born," Eothur said. "Look, this may come as a shock to you, but you weren't born."

Father Evan sat back and looked incredulous. "This is the tallest tale yet! First, you accuse Monsignor Trevanche of being immortal and now you say I was never born, yet here I am in front of you, plain as day!"

Eothur grunted and stood up. He walked over to a cupboard, opened it and took out a loaf of bread. He brought it over to the table, broke off a piece and set it down on the table. He sat down and dipped his bread into the bowl of soup. He then ate the soaked part of the bread and chewed it thoughtfully.

"Would you like some bread?" Eothur said.

"Yes. If it's as good as your soup, that would be amazing."

"Thank you."

Father Evan broke off a piece of bread and dipped it into the soup. He bit into the soaked bread and nodded appreciatively.

"So," Eothur started again. "When did you first hear about the magic quill?"

"Three days ago, just before I left the monastery."

"The room of creation?"

"With all the parchments, yes, also three days ago," Father Evan dipped his bread into the soup and munched on it again, though he frowned at Eothur.

"When," Eothur held his bread up and took a bite. "Did you first find out magic was real?"

"I-" Father Evan hesitated. "I have taken Monsignor Trevanche's word for the existence of magic, although I've seen no actual evidence of it."

"Is it fair to say you doubt the existence of magic and think this may all be a fairy tale?"

"People have been burned, carved up and tortured! You cannot tell me that has been for nothing!" Father Evan stood up. "If this is some kind of loyalty test for the Monsignor's pleasure, I don't appreciate the lengths..."

Father Evan walked out of the small cottage and pace in the clearing in front of it.

"None of this makes sense! Why all the death and destruction? Why the pain and suffering of those poor people?"

Eothur walked out into the clearing.

"You know there is evil in this world," Eothur said.

"I've seen more than enough evidence of that in my travels," Father Evan said glaring at Eothur.

"That," Eothur said. "Is the mountain of fire Monsignor Trevanhce no doubt mentioned in his creation story."

"How do you know that?"

"I know it because Father William told me of the story he was told when he first began his tutelage and service to the creation room. Before he learned of the evil and the lies. Before he was shackled to the table and forced to continue the at times wonderful, at times evil work there. He slept on the floor and never left the room after his confinement. A chamber pot his only company outside of Father Anthony coming in to change it out."

"How do I know what you're telling me isn't lies?"

"You know Father William was a man of integrity, truth and compassion while he helped raise you?"

"Yes."

"Everything I'm telling you, he told me. He discovered all of it and that's what led him to escape with the quill."

"When you were growing up, how many kids were in the orphanage?"

"Well, that varied some would come, some would go," father Evan folded his arms and stood still. He didn't like where this was going.

"What age did they arrive?"

"They were always babies. I never saw anyone even as old as a toddler come in."

"How many other children your age, now grown of course, are still at the orphanage?"

Father Evan looked at the ground. He knew for some reason that he was never wanted. All the other children were adopted, but he remained forever at the monastery. He'd come to peace with it, buit it still stung to think about.

"None. I'm the alone one that wasn't adopted."

"In a sense, Father Evan, you were the fortunate one."

"Oh, I'm sure the other monks at the monastery made a game of slaughtering children and telling the rest of us they'd been adopted," Father Evan looked at the sky. "This is ridiculous."

"Their pages were burned and they ceased to exist in the Room of Dust," Eothur said.

"There's no room of dust!"

"When did you find out about the creation room?"

Father Evan glared at Eothur. He tapped his finger on his arm.

"Clearly I'm not made of dust!"

Faster than Father Evan could believe, Eothur pulled out a sword and cut off the hand Father Evan had been tapping on his arm with. Father Evan howled in pain and fell to his knees as blood spurted from his bloody stump.

"Why did you do that?" Father Evan shouted.

"Look at your hand!" Eothur shouted back and pointed to the severed appendage on the ground. Slowly, over a matter of minutes, it shriveled up and turned to dust. Meanwhile, Father Evan's wrist had healed and a new hand was growing back where the other had been.

Father Evan sat on the ground looking at his hand in wonder and dismay.

"Right, so I'm going to go finish my lunch. You're free to join me when you wish or go howling off into the forest like a madman, whichever you like," Eothur said and walked back into the cottage.

The sun had moved perceptibly by the time Father Evan walked back into the cottage. His new hand was fully formed and hand grown back. He sat down at the table and picked up the bread. He bit a piece off. Eothur picked up Father Evan's bowl and refilled it with soup. They both ate in silence until the sun went down.

"Take me to him," Father Evan said.

"In the morning, he's resting now. You'll feel it tomorrow when we travel further away from the mountain."

"Feel what?"

"Your mortality," Eothur said.

The next morning, Father Evan was up with the sunrise while Eothur slept in as if his world hadn't changed overnight. The birds chirped, the bugs crawled and flew and various animals darted about in the forest nearby. He watched it all with a new sense of wonder. He looked at his hand again and couldn't believe it had been chopped off yesterday. Even the burn scar he'd gotten when he was a boy from falling in the fireplace was still there.

Eothur walked out of the cottage and stretched. He walked to father Evan and handed him some more bread.

"For the journey," Eothur said as he hefted a small backpack full of other provisions. They walked away from the cottage and toward another mountain range in the distance.

"I still have a scar from falling in the fireplace, a burn mark right here," Father Evan said as he pointed to the back of his hand near the knuckle of his ring finger.

"Do you remember falling in the fireplace?"

Father Evan thought about it for a moment." They said I passed out from the pain and I woke up the next day with a burning pain and the wound on my hand. It hurt for several days. The salve they applied eventually made the pain go away and it healed, leaving the scar behind. But, no, I don't remember the actual incident."

"Your page was rewritten that day to add the scar," Eothur said. "A similar incident happened to Father William. He has that jagged scar on his left temple from when he fell from the top of the wall at the monastery. No memory of the incident, but a wound and then a scar permanently etched on his forehead. It helps keep the lie alive. You believe the lie, you're given evidence to prove the lie and you have no reason to question it. But, in another day's journey, we'll reach Father William. What happens to you then will be very permanent. If I had cut off your hand a day from now, you'd be handless until you returned to the boundaries of the magic of the mountain of fire. AT least, that's the theory. I haven't tested it, do you want to?"

"No!" Father Evan said. "Thank you anyway."

They walked on a bit farther. They passed another settlement with children playing in the yard. They looked healthy and vibrant. The farmlands looked lush and well kept. A farmer and older children toiled in the fields, harvesting grain.

"Why do the fields grow so poorly near the mountain of fire?" Father Evan asked.

"Monsignor Trevanche likes the emaciated look of the people. It adds to his sense of power over them."

"Are they all magic as well?"

"No," Eothur hopped on some rocks as he passed over a stream. "The way things grow in the wild is affected by the magic at his whim, but he hasn't created anything that actually lives outside the monastery. Of course the harvest near the monastery is unaffected and bountiful. He doesn't want to suffer. He just enjoys it when others do."

"I'm not feeling well," Father Evan said.

"Yeah, get used to that," Eothur said. He pointed at the mountain range ahead. The foot of the mountains is only an hour away. Well outside the boundary. It's where Father William has chosen to... end his time. Monsignor Trevanche would be vulnerable and sickly here. He'd probably survive the trip, but he wouldn't enjoy it, so he'll never make the trip. That's why he sent the youngest and healthiest scribe who could make the journey."

"There are others?" Father Evan said.

"Yes," Eothur nodded. "However, none of them are old enough to understand or make the journey. Only a scribe can carry the magic quill or use it."

"So, I'm literally the only one who could make the journey. Monsignor Trevanche is no longer a scribe."

"Not with this quill," Eothur said. "If he hadn't been so impetuous and greedy in his youth, he may have truly learned the error of his ways. Or, perhaps, someone switched the pens on him just before he destroyed it. No one really knows. He's the only one who's lived through the eons. According to legend anyway."

"Legend?"

"Over the centuries, people have visited the monastery and

come away with tales. The stories go back before Monsignor Trevanche's time there. The positive ones end with his reign however."

"So if he traveled all the way out here?"

Eothur laughed.

"He may look every day of his 437 years of age. It's all conjecture, of course. He's only ventured as far as the burn marks you saw on the landscape," Eothru stopped and looked at Father Evan. "I watched him create fire from his fingertips, burning whole families alive. I stayed far from his range and kept hidden with other magics outside his expertise, but I didn't have what it takes to kill him. Believe me, I would've killed that butcher if I had the ability."

They reached a small outcropping of rocks. A path from the rocks led to a small cave in the foothills. Father Evan reached out and steadied himself on a boulder. He bent over and wretched. After a few minutes of dry heaving, he stood up again. Eothur handed him a waterskin. Father Evan rinsed his mouth out and then drank a bit.

"How does Father William stand it? I feel horrible," Father Evan stumbled along the path next to Eothur.

"He came here to die on his own terms," Eothur said. "He didn't want Monsignor Trevanche dictating the way he lived or died anymore."

They made their way to the mouth of the cave. Eothur steadied Father Evan as they stopped before entering.

"Prepare yourself, my friend. This will not be easy to see."

Father Evan nodded and they entered the cave. Father Evan's eyes took a moment to adjust to the darkness of the torch lights along the wall. The smoke disappeared into holes in the ceiling. The ground was a roughly carved out surface with nothing to trip over. The air smelled of fire and lavender. At points in the cave, they passed rooms that looked vaguely like a kitchen and a bathroom. At a fork in the passage, Eothur pointed to the left. They moved left and went another hundred or so steps into the darkness until they reach a small room where a nurse that Father Evan realized was an elven maiden sat at a bedside. She looked up at them and then patted her hand on a wrinkled, liver spotted hand that rested on the bed. She got up and Father Evan gasped.

Father William had aged more than anyone Father Evan had met in his lifetime. As such, he couldn't even begin to gauge how much his mentor had withered so far from the magic that supported his life force.

"Thank you, Callista," Eothur said to the elf. She nodded.

"He's very near the end now," Callista said. "I was able to preserve his energies for a while, but it is time for him to find peace."

Eothur nodded. Father Evan looked at Callista with tears in his eyes.

"You too will start to wither away so far from the energies that give you life. Tarry not more than a day or two," she said to him. Father Evan nodded.

Callista left the room and father Evan sat down at Father William's side. The face was pale and wrinkled, but Father Evan recognized the bone structure and the glistening blue eyes that opened to see him. Father William smiled.

"It's good you came," Father William said in a voice that sounded like it was being pushed through a leafy barrier.

"Eothur has said-"

"What Eothur has said is true," Father William interrupted him. "He is trustworthy and good. Believe in his counsel."

"But, the Monsignor is the leader of our faith," Father Evan said.

"He's is the leader of his own avarice," Father William said. "He hijacked another faith and disguises his evil under its pretenses. The teachings you received as a boy are still true up until the part where you should respect Monsignor Trevanche." The last part came out with a bitterness Fatehr Evan had never heard from his old teacher before.

"Look upon my right leg," Father William said.

Father Evan looked and found a ring of blackened flesh there just above the ankle.

"The manacle he left on me for two weeks burned my flesh every day as a reminder to be obedient to his will," Father William said. "He forced me to create it with a parchment and the magic quill, but I tricked him with words and it fell off in less than the two weeks he had wanted. That's how I escaped."

"Why did you do his bidding," Father Evan said. "If you knew he was evil?"

"Not all the parchments were evil, of course. Maintaining the monastery, the children and the bounty of the earth were not hard to write. He gave me these when I refused to recharge the magicks extending his life, giving him the power over flame."

Father William raised a shaky arm to pull back his sleeve, revealing burned scars in the shape of Monsignor Trevanche's signet ring. There were dozens of scars. Father Evan pulled back the sleeve on Father William's other arm revealing dozens more.

"They never healed fully," Father Evan said.

"Part of the parchment giving Monsignor Trevanche the power of flame – his mark would always be upon you, never fully healed, always painful."

Father William coughed and each cough seemed to weaken him further. Father Evan looked at Eothur.

"It won't be long now," Eothur said.

"Eothur!" Father William called out. "You have everything in place?"

"As we agreed, Father William."

Father William nodded and closed his eyes for a moment, taking a deep breath. He opened his eyes again and they had gotten grayer.

"Oh, I appear to be blind," Father William said almost as if he'd opened a present. His hand reached out to Father Evan. Father Evan grasped his hand.

"I'm still here, Father William."

"The parchments if destroyed will be replaced by newer ones written about them. I've prepared a few that must be survive the destruction of the others until they too must be destroyed. Eothru can instruct you further. Listen to his counsel. He's not tainted by the evil Monsignor Trevanche has grown around the mountain of fire."

"I understand."

Father William sat up and looked to where he thought Father Evan was.

"You must stop him. This evil must end."

"I will, Father William."

Father William lay back down.

"This," he said and grabbed Father Evan's arm. "This is our true purpose in life. It's why we were created. You are the good the world needs."

""The brothers at the entrance to the creation room, they're my biggest concern."

"Use your wits. They're not infallible. They have weaknesses you can use to your advantage. Remember, their creation was directed by a madman. Monsignor Trevanche doesn't think everything through very clearly."

"I wish you could be there with me," Father Evan said. Father William grabbed his arm, his sleeve falling free so Father Evan could clearly see the burn marks from Monsignor Trevanche's signet ring etched over and over again on his arms.

"I was strong enough to run," Father William said. "I wasn't strong enough to fight."

"I'm so sorry this happened to you," Father Evan said as tears fell from his eyes.

"You're strong enough for this, son. I know you are," Father William said and shivered. "It's so cold. Can you get me another blanket?"

Father William closed his eyes and lay back on the pillow. He gave a final breath and died. Within moments, he dissolved before Father Evan's eyes into dust.

Father Evan sat there for a while, he didn't know how long. He stared at the outline of dust that used to be Father William. There was no breeze, so it remained in place, undisturbed.

"So this is my fate," Father Evan said.

"It is the fate of us all," Eothur said. "Eventually, we all turn to dust."

"I may not have been born from a mother and father, but he was the closest thing to family I ever had."

"That is to your advantage. You both formed a bond Monsignor Trevanche will never understand."

Father Evan stood up.

"What do you have for me?"

Eothur pointed at the bed.

"The quill, in its case. No one else can move it even outside the boundary. It carries its own magic."

Father Evan kneeled down and retrieved the case. To him, it was light as a feather.

"It's not heavy," Father Evan said as he opened the case and looked upon the quill. He looked at the sleek design, from its gold tip to the ebony feather.

"Well, it obviously doesn't burn your hand with the fire of a thousand suns when you try to move it, so I'd say you're properly attuned to it," Eothur said. "Everything else we need is close to the entrance."

In the first room that Father Evan considered the kitchen, Eothur walked to a cabinet and opened it, taking out a single scroll. He handed it to Father Evan.

"Is this it?" Father Evan asked.

"Father William spent several years crafting parchments. This is his finest work, condensed into a single document. Makes it easier to smuggle in nestled in a pile of blank parchments. Those brothers have a very keen sense of smell."

"That's what worries me."

"A meal strong in garlic will keep their attention. So it was written," Eothur said.

"They're magic too?"

"Indeed. Father William has been working on this plan for a while, setting up everything you need to succeed."

"He never spoke of it."

"He helped raise you. He knew your values. He knew you'd do the right thing. He didn't need to tell you anything. You would be inserted in this at the Monsignor's insistence sicne he really has not other choice."

"Oh, I almost forgot," Eothur took out a necklace and placed it over Father Evan's head. "This will allow you to effect the replacement in seconds instead of the days it would otherwise take. A single twist on the medallion face and it will do the task."

They walked back toward the mountain of fire. The trip would take days, but Father Evan would finally get to his final task.

At the cottage, Eothur took his leave.

"You're not coming with?" Father Evan asked.

"This is your task alone, not mine. Besides, if I was with you, it would set off a few alarm bells, wouldn't it?"

Father Evan nodded and looked toward the mountain of fire.

"Will death hurt?"

"Dying may, but death is actually the end of pain. That's true for all," Eothur said. "Come have supper with me one last time."

They spent the evening chatting about Father William's quirks and eccentricities, his warmth and generosity, and all the things that made him the amazing man he was. It was a fitting tribute to the only real family Father Evan ever knew. The next morning, he was at ease with his mission.

As Father Evan traveled back to the monastery alone, he reveled in the small signs of life along the way. He acknowledged the tragedies and horrors. With the knowledge the evil would be felled in this area for a time, he was happy in his task.

As he passed by the tavern, he went inside to see the

patrons from before, gathered and still in fear.

"All will be set right," Father Evan said to the crowd. "I found Father William. Spread the word."

The relief that set in on the faces of those gathered made Father Evan smile. Even if he never saw them again, if nothing pleasant happened to him from this moment forward, at least he had that brief moment of joy he shared with the townfolk.

As he rested that night against the burned out tree trunk, he noticed the flickers of movement around him in the night. Dark things moved about the landscape. Monsignor Trevanche would know he was near and would be expecting him. Luckily, it wasn't protocol for the Monsignor to meet visitors or returning monks at the door, but rather they would seek him out for an audience.

As he approached the monastery entrance, the huge oaken door creaked open and Father Anthony waved at him. Father Evan waved back, smiled and maintained a jovial mood as he entered the building.

"The task, is it done?" Father Anthony asked.

"It is," Father Evan said and held aloft the case with the magic quill in it. "The magic will soon be restored."

"Excellent, excellent," Father Anthony said. "Let us go to Monsignor Trevanche at once."

"May we stop by the kitchen first?" Father Evan said. "You can carry this to Mosignor, if you wish." He held out the case and Father Anthony blanched.

"Oh no, that's quite all right. We'll stop by the kitchen and you can deliver the quill yourself after a quick bite."

They walked quickly to the kitchen. Father Evan used his nose to find the most garlic smelling meal being prepared.

"Could I get two bowls of it, lest I have to stop for even a moment in eating," Father Evan said.

The cook obliged and got back to the task of preparing the evening meal.

"Father Anthony, could you fetch me some wine. I'm

parched and it will help this wonderful meal go down so much faster."

"Of course," Father Anthony rushed out to go the wine cellar.

After a few moments, Father Evan grabbed the two bowls and headed for the creation room.

When he reached the large oaken door, he raised the knocker and hammered it into the door three time slowly, two quickly, and two slowly just as Monsignor Trevanche had done before. The door swung open slowly and revealed Brothers Altuvay and Winsop.

"Father Evan and the quill," Brother Altuvay said sniffing the air. Some extra ink, wait, is that garlic soup?"

"It is," Father Evan said. "I thought you two could use a snack while I got started to work."

"I don't smell any ink," Brother Winsop said. "But I will have some of that soup, thank you."

The Brothers held out their hands and Father Evan supplied them each with a thick wooden bowl and spoon. Father William has adjusted their updated parchments to read "and they shall value garlic above all else including duty."

Father Evan rushed into the creation room. He removed the single scroll and placed it on the table.

In the kitchen, Father Anthony returned with the bottle of wine, looked around the kitchen for a moment and realized Father Evan was gone.

"Oh dear," Father Anthony said. He rushed to Monsignor Trevanche's office, bottle of wine still in hand.

Monsignor Trevanche rose as the door opened and smiled.

"Father Evan so glad you could-" Monsignor stopped speaking and his face went dark. "Father Anthony, where is he?"

"I don't-"

Monsignor held up his hand. "Never mind." He twirled his garments around him and vanished.

Father Anthony stood looking at where Monsignor

Trevanche had been, his mouth hung open in shock.

At the large oaken door below, Monsignor Trevanche reappeared. He swung the knocker as required and Brother Altuvay opened the door with one hand, a hot bowl of garlic soup in the other.

"Good day, Monsignor," Brother Altuvay said.

"Idiots!" Monsignor Trevanche shouted and knocked the bowl of soup from Brother Altuvay's hand. He rushed by the Brothers to the room beyond. Brother Altuvay sniffed at the spilled bowl and then sniffed at Brother Winsop's bowl.

"Give it," Brother Altuvay said.

"Over my dead body!" Brother Winsop roared. The Brothers both pulled out deadly long, sharp blades from behind them and began to cut at each other. Moments later, they both fell, fatally wounded by each other. The other bowl spilled out upon the floor.

Monsignor Trevanche ran into the creation room and glanced around. He didn't see father Evan.

"Come out! I know you're here!"

Father Evan emerged from behind a pillar, holding a large stack of brand new parchments.

"You're too late," Father Evan said. "As the old documents fail, they'll be restored with these new ones. Your power is broken."

Monsignor Trevanche looked at the documents on the walls and recognized the old ones that had been there over the last year. He smiled.

"It is you who is the fool!" Monsignor Trevanche hurled flame from his fingertips, enveloping the parchments and Father Evan. "I'll just force the child to write them if I have to now that we have the quill again!"

Father Evan screamed in agony as the parchments went up in flames and ash exploded from his hands. An eerie purple flame rose from between father Evan's hands and rose to the ceiling spreading flame all along the walls.

Monsignor Trevanche fell to his knees. "The quill? You hid it in the parchments?"

Father Evan lay on the floor, his robes smoking and his flesh burned.

"Birthed in fire, so it was destroyed," Father Evan said, his voice cracking in pain.

"No, I still have time. I'll find a way to make another! This was not where my final parchment lay hidden, you fool!"

"You mean this parchment?" Father Anthony said. Monsignor Trevanche turned around to see father Anthony holding a jeweled case in one hand and a torch in the other. He dropped the case and a single sheet of parchment fluttered out. Father Anthony dropped the torch on the paper.

"No!" Monsignor Trevanche screamed in agony and clutched his chest.

Father Anthony slowly transformed into Eothur.

"What have you done to me?"

"Put a hole where your heart should be," Father Evan said.

Monsignor looked around the room and all the parchments disappeared from the glass cases, illusions everyone except for a single parchment. He grabbed a piece of flaming debris and ran to the glass case, flung it open and burned it.

It was a last defiant attempt. As his heart healed, the magicks keeping him alive faded. Age crept along his flesh and withered him from the outside in. He screamed one last time and then fell to his knees, disintegrating in a puff of dust.

Father Evan sat up, fully healed in tattered, burnt robes.

"What?" He said as he felt his body still intact. "I should be dead."

"Father William thought you deserved a real chance at life. Monsignor Trevanche hasn't kept up with magic in the outside world, so he didn't see my subterfuge today until I dropped it. He also didn't know we can make parchments much longer lasting today. With the other parchments destroyed, the final one Father William created is your new reality. You'll be alive for many years to come."

"But do I deserve to be?" Father Evan said as he approached Eothur.

"Why don't you make it worth Father William's last act?" Eothur clasped father Evan's hands in his own.

"I shall," father Evan said. They walked out of the room into the future.

The Magic Quill

by Amber Rainey

crich, scrich, scrich. Katalena smiled to herself as she listened to her Papa writing. It was always the best part of her day. She would curl up behind his desk in the cozy little corner made between it and the fireplace and let the scratch of the quill across the parchment lull her into a sense of peace. The heat from the fireplace kept her toes toasty, especially in winter, and she could often be found sound asleep if her Mama did not come looking for her first. Mama was in a perpetual state of concern over Katalena and her propensity for the hobby.

Katalena was sure that her Papa was writing something very important today. He barely registered the kiss she had placed on his cheek, merely grunting and continuing to write. The Empress had given her father a magnificent peacock feather quill pen and it was this quill with which he wrote today. He only used the quill for very important correspondence concerning the Empress' business. The quill was the most luxurious things Katalena had ever seen. It came in a rectangular mahogany box, polished to shine when the candlelight caught it. When her Papa opened the box, there lie the quill in purple silk. The feather must have been at least as long as her Papa's arm. It's brilliant green vanes surrounded an eye of the brightest blue. She'd gasped in wonder when she had seen it. Papa had explained that she was never to touch this quill and Mama had scoffed at the very idea of Katalena even learning to write.

"Who wants a wife more concerned with reading and writing than cooking and sewing. She won't have time for such pursuits when she is married. It is not for girls," Mama said.

Papa just nodded his head in agreement and Mama went back to her cooking. Then Papa gave Katalena a wink and went to his writing desk, carefully setting the box on the desk and proceeding to go about his work. Katalena had sat in her corner, enjoying the fact that Mama had forgotten about the embroidery project Katalena was supposed to be doing. Papa was very good at distracting Mama from concerning herself with her youngest daughter's wife-training.

Now, Katalena started to dose when she heard her Mama calling for her. Katalena closed her eyes quickly and pretended to be asleep as her father leaned around the desk to glance at her. She knew that her Papa could tell she was awake but she hoped that she was convincing enough for Mama. Mama came into the house and spied Katalena in the corner.

"Shh," Papa said.

Mama spoked insistently but quietly, "That girl is always sitting about with her head in the clouds."

"Mmm," Papa agreed.

"She needs to help me run to the market. It will make the trip faster," Mama insisted.

"Natalya, it is turning cold outside and Katalena just recovered from her illness. Perhaps let her sleep and take Anna?" Papa suggested kindly.

Katalena tried not to smile. Papa was always keen on helping her escape her Mama's plans. She could hear the slight humor in his voice. She also knew the sound of her Mama's reply. Mama would put her hands on her hips and lean closer to Papa. He would wink at her and then Mama would surrender to his suggestions and chuckle. Katalena heard the sound of Mama placing a kiss on her Papa's lips.

"You are too soft on her," Mama chided. "What will become of her if she can't find a husband?"

"Ah, well, perhaps I am not yet ready to think of that," Papa admitted.

Mama hummed in agreement and gathered her shawl, then she went out the door.

"You can come out now, my little Kat," Papa said.

Katalena opened her eyes and stretched just like the cat her father often accused her of being. She smiled at her Papa and then jumped up, throwing herself at him for a big hug. Papa laughed and hugged her back, squeezing so tight Katalena thought she might never breathe again. However, she would never complain as she quite enjoyed the feeling of being held by her father in such a massive hug. Papa stopped hugging her and took her hands in his own.

"Kat, why must you vex your mother so much?" he gently scolded her.

Katalena shrugged. "It's not that I want to vex Mama... it's just..." she hesitated.

Katalena lowered her eyes and bit her lip. She was afraid to talk to her Papa, not because he would begrudge her feelings but because she was embarrassed to be having these particular feelings. Papa put a finger under her chin and lifted her face to meet his. She looked into his eyes and only saw his love for her shining through.

"You may tell me anything," he encouraged.

Katalena nodded and took a deep breath. "I don't want to be a wife, Papa. I want to be a writer, like you."

Papa smiled. "Ahh, I see."

"Mama will be furious with me if I tell her. Please don't tell her Papa," Katalena begged.

"Kat, why do you want to be a writer?" he asked.

Katalena thought a moment. She had never shared anything so intimate with anyone for fear her Mama would find out and ban her from the corner by her father's desk. She had longed to share her dreams with her Papa but tried to be a proper young lady and follow her Mama's teaching.

"Papa, if I tell you, promise you won't laugh?" Katalena pleaded.

Papa nodded and crossed his heart for good measure. He waited patiently for her to continue speaking. She lowered her eyes, closing them to think about how she should begin.

Katalena took a deep breath. "When I sit in the corner and listen to you write, it transports me to new worlds, as if by magic. Sometimes, I can see myself sitting on the hills near the summer palace, watching horses frolicking in the fields. Then the Empress comes and joins me for a picnic and we laugh and watch the clouds passing in the sky until dusk. Other times, you and I are skating on the Neva and it is if I can feel the cold winter air nipping at my cheeks. I can see our breath coming out in white swirls of smoke and hear the branches of the trees on the bank snapping under the weight of the ice. We skate and skate until our cheeks are rosy red and our legs feel heavy. Then we lie in the snow and stare at the stars."

Papa didn't say anything and Katalena was terrified of looking up. She didn't want to see the disappointment she knew must be lingering in his eyes. She didn't want to know that her Papa might think her dreams as useless as she would be to a husband. Her sister, Anna, would be married soon and she knew that her Papa would be looking to her future. She had most likely just ruined all his plans for his youngest child.

"Katalena, why did you not tell me any of this before?" he asked in wonder.

The tone of his voice made Katalena look up at him. Instead of disapproval or disgust, she still saw only love, now tinged with wonder, in his eyes. She cocked her head to the side, studying the look on his face. As she did so, she began to smile. Her Papa seemed almost proud of her. It was not something she had expected.

"I... I thought it would disappoint you, Papa," she admitted.

Papa shook his head. "Nonsense. You could never disappoint me. I had no idea there was such magic in your head, child."

Katalena laughed. "It isn't magic, Papa."

Papa winked at her. "It will be when I show you how to get it out of your head and onto parchment."

Katalena gasped. She never thought she would ever be allowed to learn to read and write. Although the Empress was very enlightened and had begun advocating the education of men and women, she left the decision up to each family within her court. Mama had declared it nonsense and Papa had agreed only because none of his daughters had shown any interest in sitting still long enough to learn. His work for the Empress demanded many hours and most days the girls finished the last of their chores in time for bed. As the girls grew and married, it slipped his mind to even broach the subject again with Mama and so it had never been revisited.

"You will teach me, Papa?" Katalena whispered for fear that she had only been dreaming his answer.

He nodded. Katalena through her arms around him again and he laughed. She could hear the laugh resonating through his chest. A million thoughts raced through her head, all the stories that had been bottled up inside her, keeping her awake at night working them out while her family slept.

"Can we start now, Papa?" she asked hopefully.

"Da, but we must keep it a secret from Mama, just for a time," Papa said.

Katalena nodded, then frowned.

"Why so glum now?" Papa asked.

"When will we have time, Papa? Mama keeps me very busy. Once Anna is gone, I will have even more work to do. I will never get time with you." Katalena choked back a tear as she mentally watched all her hopes wither.

Papa grasped her hands again. "Leave Mama to me."

Katalena nodded.

"Now, sit next to me and pick up the quill."

Papa scooted over on the bench and Katalena sat next to him. She reached for Papa's old quill, a black goose feather quill that had definitely seen better days. Its feathers were matted from years and years of use and the shaft was nearly gone from sharpening. Papa was very particular about the things he liked and often wore clothes until they were so holey, Mama threw them out when he was at the palace. Quills and ink pots were no exception.

"No, no," Papa said, "such a special occasion demands a special instrument."

Katalena's eyes widened as her Papa picked up the peacock quill and handed it to her. She reached out with a shaky and took it, the breath she expelled sent the wispy vanes fluttering. She looked between the quill and her father with awe. He nodded and she gripped it, imitating the position she had seen her father use so many times when writing.

"Here, let me," Papa said.

He corrected her grasp on the quill very slightly, but it did feel much more natural. Then Papa positioned a piece of parchment in front of her and one in front of himself. He picked up the old goose feather quill and dipped it slightly in the ink, nodding for her to do the same. Katalena copied the motion and stared in wonder at the black ink now ready to make a mark on the parchment.

"First," Papa began, "you must learn the alphabet we use. Only then will you be able to put together the words swimming around in your head. Understand?"

Katalena nodded.

"Good, let's begin," Papa smiled and started writing the first letter.

Katalena and Papa practiced writing every day. Some days their lessons would take place when Mama was away at the market. Other days, Papa would make an excuse to Mama, which usually involved him needing her transporting supplies to the palace. Mama would mumble under breath but would not argue with Papa. He would hurry Katalena along to his office at the palace and teach her as quickly as he could in the time that was allotted for her disappearance from home. Katalena got very good at the alphabet quickly and could write her own name within a week. Then, Papa began showing her how the letters formed words and it was if a whole new world opened up in her head. The missing link had been connected and now she could walk the bridge to her imaginative destinations.

After several months, Katalena no longer needed instruction. Papa gave her a box full of parchment and her own quill. Although he had let her use the peacock quill the first time, it was both impossible and impractical for her to use it every day. Besides, Papa needed it for his own work for the Empress. It was expected that he use it, especially when writing in her presence. Therefore, the quill had to be preserved as much as possible. Katalena hid the box, along with her writings, in a loose board under her bed. Anna had finally married and it was now her duty to clean the house, therefore, she never had to worry that Mama would find the box and question its contents.

Occasionally, Papa would ask to read the stories Katalena wrote. She would fetch them from the box and hand them over with trepidation. She never knew why she was so terrified but each time she just knew would be the time her Papa would be disappointed in her and regret teaching her to write. Of course, this never happened. The most Papa would do was correct her grammar in some part of a story or suggest improvements. Katalena would nod, look over the notes he made, and run off to make the edits he suggested. He told her he was proud of her more than once and each time it brought a smile to her face that lasted so many days, she thought her face might be stuck in the silly grin. Mama thought Katalena had finally found a suitor and Katalena was happy to let her continue in this belief.

One day, Papa had just finished reading Katalena's creation when the door to the house opened suddenly and Mama, who was not due to return from the palace for another hour, walked in. Papa quickly hid Katalena's parchment under his own papers and Katalena schooled her features. Mama looked between the two of them as if she had caught them plotting to assassinate the Empress. Katalena swallowed heavily and Papa put a steadying hand on her arm. She calmed somewhat at the gesture and waited for him to speak.

"Natalya, we were not expecting you home so soon," Papa said casually.

Mama nodded, "Da, but I have a surprise for Katalena."

Katalena looked alarmed. Usually, when Mama wanted to surprise her, it meant Mama was trying to marry her off to some Count or other courtier. A sense of dread filled her stomach. Papa squeezed her arm to try and calm her once more.

Mama continued without noticing the change in her. "Aleksei Vasiliev, please come in," Mama said to the person standing behind her.

Aleksei Vasiliev walked through the door. He was very tall and towered over Mama. Katalena had met him a handful of times at the parties held at the palace for special occasions. Her Papa worked with his and they were very close in age. Aleksei had dark, short hair, almost raven black in color. His eyes were the color of a stormy sea on a cloudy day yet they had such depth to them as if two colors warred within them. His face was peppered with a few days of stubble as if he did not care to make a decision between actually shaving or growing his facial hair. Katalena mentally chided herself for complimenting his looks in her head and attempted to harden her heart against yet another of her Mama's machinations to see her youngest daughter married and a housewife.

Aleksei bowed and reached for Katalena's hand. He kissed above it in the French manner favored by the Empress. Katalena jerked her hand back as quickly as possible and then straightened when she heard her Mama clear her throat. Katalena must remember her manners and it was the only warning she would get. Katalena put her hands behind her back and rubbed at the spot where Aleksei had touched her. The touch had sent a shock up her arm but rather than being unpleasant, it had warmed her and this concerned her.

"Aleksei Vasiliev, it is a pleasure to have you visit our home. Would you like some refreshments?" Katalena asked.

She tried to affect a neutral tone but winced inwardly when it came out pleasant and inviting. She did not understand what was happening. Why was this man affecting her so much? She would refuse to give into her Mama's wishes. She had done so before and she would do so now.

"Katalena Aleksandrova, I am pleased to be welcome. Refreshments would be most appreciated," Aleksei responded with a smile and another bow of his head.

Katalena swallowed hard at the smile and then stood there for a moment, staring at Aleksei. She did not know how much time passed before her father gave her a gentle nudge and then she was jolted out of her trance. She blushed and turned to get the offered refreshments. Her Mama followed her into the kitchen, watching her with a big grin on her face.

"Stop it, Mama," Katalena growled under her breath so as not to allow her father or Aleksei to hear her.

Mama came over and gave her a hug. "I'm just so happy for you."

Katalena huffed. She closed her eyes. Mama already thought she had won and Katalena hated to admit that she was quickly softening to Aleksei's charms. She wanted to be a writer, not a wife.

"Mama..." Katalena tried to assuage Mama's enthusiasm.

"Just give him a chance, Katalena," Mama said and patted

her on the arm.

Katalena nodded. She guessed it was the least she could do. Letting Aleksei court her would keep Mama from any more meddling and it could also be an excuse to get in some more writing. She could tell Mama she was going to any one of a number of palace events with him and then hide in Papa's office and write to her heart's content. Mama gave a hushed squeal of delight and Katalena rolled her eyes. Mama hurried her off to serve the refreshments.

Aleksei and Katalena had been courting for three months when he found out her secret. Katalena had told Mama she was going to the garden party being held at the palace for the first signs of spring. In truth, she had snuck out of the party and found her Papa in his office. He winked at her and got up from his desk, excusing himself to a meeting with a visiting dignitary. He'd left out some parchment and a quill for her use and she had jumped into writing down her latest fantasy. She did not know how much time had passed when suddenly, the door flew open and Aleksei rushed into the room. He froze when he saw Katalena at the desk and she froze, quill in mid-air when she saw him. Aleksei looked at her, down at her hands, and back up at her face. The look of shock on his face jolted her out of her stupor and she quickly jumped up, hiding the quill behind her back.

"Aleksei, I..." Katalena stammered.

Aleksei quickly shut the door and walked over to her. He gently reached toward her and for a moment she shied away from him. He paused and waited for her to give him permission to touch her. She gulped and nodded. Aleksei pulled her hands out from behind her back. He grasped the quill and she let go. Then he set the quill on the desk and looked at her hands, turning them over in his and examining the ink stains on her writing hand.

"Turn around," he said.

"Wh...what?" she asked quizzically.

"Trust me," he said.

Katalena studied his face a moment. She did not see the anger or disgust she thought might be there upon him first finding her. She nodded and turned around. She felt his hand on the small of her back and then he spoke.

"You got ink on your dress. Let me help you."

Aleksei moved away from her. She glanced over her shoulder and saw him dousing a handkerchief in some of her father's vodka. She quickly looked forward again as he returned to her side. She felt him dabbing at her dress. After what felt like an agonizing number of minutes, he finished.

"There. You will have to tell your mother someone spilled their drink on you at the party."

Katalena nodded and turned back around. She studied his face again, watching him struggling to keep laughter from boiling up, the amusement in the situation clearly evident. He glanced down at the desk and she instinctively tried to hide her writing. He backed away a step and Katalena looked up with guilt.

"I won't pry if you don't want me to," Aleksei said with sincerity. "Now, I know where you hide all the times you are too busy."

"You aren't angry?" Katalena asked with some confusion.

"Nyet, why would I be angry?" he asked, perplexed.

Katalena shrugged. "Mama always says that a husband does not want a wife concerned with reading and writing. They want strong Russian women who can care for the house and have plenty of children to fill it with joy."

Aleksei thought a moment before he replied. Katalena watched emotions cross his face with interest. The real question she has was what all the emotions meant. Did he want to have children? Did he even want to get married? She had learned there was no end of eligible women ready to marry him and it seemed like he had left behind a string of broken hearts without even meaning to do so. She was subjected to no small amount of jealous looks each time she was seen with him. She was sure he could have the pick of anyone he chose. He looked down at the desk again.

"Could I read what you have written?" he asked suddenly.

Katalena hesitated. "It is not yet finished."

Aleksei nodded. Katalena looked at the parchment. It was a fanciful piece about a courageous young woman fighting a dragon to save the man she loved from becoming its next meal. She blushed, realizing that the descriptions of both the woman and the man had very similar descriptions to those of the two people standing in Papa's office. She could tell him no and run from the room or she could be the courageous woman and let another person she cared for read her work. Katalena swallowed and picked up the parchment, holding it out to Aleksei without meeting his eyes. He took the papers gently and walked to the chair across the desk from her. He sat in the chair and she mirrored his action, sitting in her father's chair. She tried to pretend to be disinterested in his reading but found herself watching him and trying to determine the meaning behind each facial expression or sound he made. Finally, he finished reading and lowered the papers. His face was now neutral and she gulped and looked down at the desk.

"You have a gift, Katalena," he said with awe.

Katalena's head whipped up. She was sure she had not heard him correctly.

"I mean it," he reaffirmed. "This story is impressive. Are there more?"

Katalena nodded her head.

"I would very much like to read them, if you will permit me to do so, of course," Aleksei said.

"I can show them to you if you promise not to tell Mama. She wouldn't understand," Katalena said.

"Agreed," Aleksei said and stood. "Now, would you like me to walk you home? The party ended and I am sure your mother will be waiting for you."

Katalena nodded. "Thank you. Perhaps you can explain just who exactly spilled their drink on me."

Aleksei laughed and offered his arm. Katalena took it and he escorted her from the office.

Many months later, Aleksei asked Papa for permission to marry Katalena. Aleksei was enthusiastically granted permission then asked her to marry him and she had agreed. Aleksei admitted to her that he figured she would say yes, given that he was the model for many of the men in her most recent writings, something Katalena vehemently denied while blushing all the way to her toes. Aleksei let the matter drop and Katalena was relieved. She often drew inspiration for her characters from those she knew and, of course, Aleksei figured prominently in her stories as she became more fond of him.

They married and settled into life together easily. Katalena no longer had to hide her writing and Aleksei made sure she had the finest writing desk he could afford. He also built her a trunk in which to store her parchments and several quill pens so she never had to sharpen one if he was not at home. She made sure to keep the house tidy and fulfill her duties as the wife of a prominent court member. She shared every story with Aleksei and he was always enthusiastic and ready to read one as soon as she told him the latest one was complete.

One afternoon, Katalena was baking Aleksei's favorite pie and dreaming up a new story when an urgent knock interrupted her thoughts. Katalena frowned, not expecting visitors. She quickly removed her apron and straightened her skirts then opened the door. Her sister, Anna, was standing at the door, tear marks trailing down her face.

"Katalena, come quickly," Anna urged.

Katalena nodded. She removed the pie from the oven and then followed her sister to her parent's house. When they arrived, Mama was sobbing. Katalena gulped back tears and looked at Anna, who just pointed to her parent's bedroom.

Katalena walked into the room, the scent of sickly sweet incense burning her nostrils. Papa lay on the bed, deathly pale, and the Archbishop saying a prayer over him. Katalena recognized it as last rites. She rushed to Papa's side and grasped his hand, kissing it and pleading with him.

"Papa, don't go," she wailed.

Papa opened his eyes and smiled kindly at her. He squeezed her hand and gestured for her to come closer. Katalena swiped angrily at her tears and bent over Papa's head.

"My little Kat, do not fear. I go with visions of your stories preparing the way to paradise."

"No, Papa," Katalena pleaded.

"Be kind to your mother. She will need understanding. I know you do not think so, but she too can dream and imagine magical places. You are more alike than you think," he said.

Katalena nodded, "I promise, Papa."

Papa sighed and smiled. He seemed to doze off and Katalena stayed and held his hand. Eventually, Aleksei came and sat by Katalena, holding her hand. Several hours later, her Papa was gone and Katalena felt as if the light in the whole world had gone out. Aleksei took charge and looked after both Katalena and Mama. Katalena held her Mama tight while she sobbed. Mama finally fell asleep from exhaustion.

After Papa was laid to rest, Katalena mourned. She continued to be a housewife but would sit and stare at the frozen Neva instead of writing. Her desk began to collect dust. This habit persisted for weeks until one evening, Aleksei came home with her Mama. Katalena jumped up and dusted off her dress. Mama smiled kindly at her and Aleksei offered to gather refreshments.

"Katalena, sit with me, please," Mama requested.

Katalena nodded and sat next to her mother. Mama reached into her bag and pulled out a piece of parchment. Katalena watched Mama caress the letters on the front of the parchment, like she used to caress Papa's fingers when she thought no one was looking. Then, Mama kissed the parchment and handed it to Katalena. She took it with hesitance and looked at her Mama.

"Go ahead, I know you can read it," Mama said.

Katalena gulped, "But... how?"

Mama smiled fondly. "Your Papa told me. He could never keep a secret."

"How long have you known?" Katalena asked.

"Since the day after you started learning your letters," Mama said.

Katalena's eyes widened and she gasped. How had Mama known for so long? Why didn't she say anything? Why wasn't she angry with Katalena?

"Don't look so shocked, dear one. Your father always knew what was best. He let you girls think I alone made the decisions in the house, so as not to undermine my authority as your mother, but we made decisions together. You had such a love for the writing, I did not wish to quell your joy."

Katalena nodded, "Thank you, Mama."

"I have something else for you," Mama said.

Once again, she reached down into her bag and pulled out the mahogany quill box. She held it out to Katalena, who reached for it with shaky hands. Katalena caressed the top of the case, the letters of Papa's monogram engraved in it.

"He wanted you to have this," Mama said.

"His most precious possession," Katalena said in awe.

Mama shook her head. Katalena looked at her with confusion.

"His family was his most precious possession. He would have traded everything we had for one ounce of your happiness." Mama choked on her words.

Katalena hugged Mama and they both let tears flow. After holding her Mama for many moments, Katalena leaned back and wiped her eyes. She looked down at the parchment sitting on her lap. She picked it up and began to read.

My little Kat,

I am sorry to have left you but we must all go in the end. I have led a very blessed life and I could not think having shared my life with a better family. Your Mama was the love of my life and I am only disappointed that we do not have more years together. I die, knowing I will see her again in the afterlife.

I want you to have the quill Empress Ekaterina presented to me when I became a senior adviser. It has brought me very good luck and now it will bring your stories to life with magic never before seen in this world. You have a gift, child. Your words have transported me to places I never believed I would see and have left me with a full heart and a hopeful parting.

Please take care of your Aleksei. Your Mama and I knew he was the right man for you and I could not be happier in your choice of husband. The day you shared your writing with him was the day I knew he would take care of you and nourish your desires instead of squash them. Talk to him. He has many ideas about your writing and I am sure they will increase your appreciation of his strengths and his love for you.

Never stop writing, little Kat. Your soul would not rest and would eat at you if you let my death keep you from your true purpose. I will be with you in your heart forever. Do not mourn my passing too long for we will be together once again. Until then, let this quill help you. I love you more than the stars could recount.

Papa

Katalena wiped at the fresh tears on her face. She smiled at her mother and then gave a loving look to Aleksei as he entered the room with the refreshments. Later that evening, when Aleksei returned from escorting her mother home, he and Katalena snuggled under the heavy winter blankets. Aleksei stroked her hair, as he did every night, and she drew circles on his chest with her finger.

"Aleksei?" Katalena raised her head and looked at him.

"Hmm?" he asked.

"Papa said in his letter you had ideas about my writing," she said.

Aleksei nodded. "I think you should compile your stories into a book and publish them."

"Are you mad? Russians would never buy a book published by a woman," she scoffed.

Aleksei shrugged. "Don't put a woman's name on them."

Katalena opened and shut her mouth as the idea slowly gained traction in her brain. It was an insane idea but it could work. Aleksei could take it to a publisher. They would never know she wrote the words. She shook her head, trying to clear out the idea and then lay back against his chest. She kept mulling the idea over and over until she fell asleep.

After several days of warring with herself, she finally agreed that Aleksei's idea would work. Aleksei took it to the publisher, who accepted it without question after reading the first few stories. They published her anthology with the title *The Magic Quill* and under the name K. Aleksandr. Katalena had to drop the feminine form of her patronymic name but she felt like then she was honoring Papa anyway, for it was his given name on her book. The anthology was a success and she published two more in the following years.

Katalena sat at her writing desk, another story coming to life on the parchment. Her granddaughter, Tatiana, sat with her feet to the fire and hummed along to the sound of the *scrich, scrich, scrich* the peacock quill made as Katalena wrote. Tatiana always made a song out of the sounds around her. Katalena had written a story about a young princess who could make magical music with the snow falling outside her castle window. She often read it to Tatiana when the thunderstorms frightened the child.

"Babushka, why does it make that sound?" Tatiana asked.

"Ah, you see, the quill is very sharp and the parchment is not very smooth, so the two war with each other but then neither wins. In the end, the ink is the only winner," Katalena replied with a laugh.

Tatiana giggled. She was only six and she adored her grandmother. Tatiana walked over to Katalena and crawled into her lap. She blew lightly at the peacock quill and watched in fascination as the vanes fluttered. She gently reached out and rubbed her finger down the edge of one side of the feather.

"Babushka, why does this quill have an eye?" Tatiana inquired.

Katalena smiled. "It can see far away worlds."

"Is it magic?" Tatiana's eyes grew wide with wonder.

Katalena nodded, "It is very magic. Would you like me to show you?"

Tatiana nodded enthusiastically. Katalena smiled and showed her granddaughter how to hold the quill. She guided the child's hand in making her first letters. Aleksei stopped behind her and kissed the top of her head while encouraging Tatiana. Katalena smiled when a breeze made the candle on her desk flicker. She knew it was a sign from her Papa. Tatiana would be the next generation to wield the magic quill.

Prick of the Quill

By Mark Robyn

Paris in late spring is a beautiful, magical place. Brightly colored flowers bloom and a warmth fills the air with the promise of summer. Ladies don dresses in cheerful shades of blue and magenta and don the latest hats with feathers and silk. Among the aristocracy the most anticipated herald of summer begins as well, the wild and extravagant garden parties, each one bigger and more expensive then the last. Romance also blooms, and plans are made for elaborate and magical weddings.

The spring of 1789, however, found the joy of Spring tempered with the darker emotions of anger and fear. The streets, which occasionally still endured an occasional shower, also faced angry riots full of starving peasants and soldiers with rifles marching in rows and using the butts of their rifles to quell the rebellion. The King's involvement in the war for Independence in America had all but drained the country's resources, and had done something even worse for him, it had set the mind of many in favor of the idea of more freedom in

France as well. Calls went out for more representation in government and the King had been forced to make concessions. The King and Queen rarely ventured out of the palace anymore but seemed like a country of their own, besieged.

Even though the country roiled with fear and uncertainty, some in aristocracy stubbornly tried their best to pretend nothing was wrong, that everything would always remain as it was. They continued to throw their parties and plan their cotillions and ignore the misery of the starving peasants.

Pierre Dumont was such a man. One of the rich burgios, he desperately wanted to work his way into the upper levels of the aristocracy and into the intimacy of the King. And so, the party he threw at his lavish mansion would be the most elaborate and extravagant of them all. Everyone who was influential and important was expected to attend, for they all longed for a distraction to take their mind off the country's woes. It was rumored even the King Louis XVI and Queen Marie Antoinette might attend, though they rarely ventured out of the palace anymore.

On the street in front of M. Dumont's mansion, soldiers in crisp blue uniforms, their muskets gripped tightly in both hands, guarded the gate to assure angry peasants did not dampen the mood by trying to sneak in and disrupt the party. Beautiful carriages rolled up pulled by tall white horses to disgorge ladies and gentlemen in their finest dresses and costumes.

In the large, circular ballroom on the main floor, a full orchestra in wigs and fancy dress played as the party goers wearing elaborate masks danced, as if the world belonged to them and only them. Servants in gilded coats of red and blue with white gloves moved throughout the room offering glasses of wine and fine chocolates. The open French doors led to the elaborate gardens where men and women enjoyed the beautiful flowers or played croquet.

John Charles was on who attended the party. The wealthy son of Andre', the clothier to the king, he was twenty years old and considered to be a young man of great promise as well as one of the most sought after and eligible bachelors in Paris. This night he seemed distracted, however. He stood near the wall in the ballroom and gazed around, as if waiting for someone to appear. When a member of the party, typically a young lady, engaged him in conversation he would smile and seems interested then simply look off into the distance, until the other person finally gave up and left in disappointment. Then when the part seemed to be in full bloom, he suddenly took French Leave and slipped from the ballroom. Once in the hallway he quietly made his way to M. Dumont's study. Glancing about to ensure he wasn't seen, he quietly opened the door and entered.

M. Dumont's study was sumptuously adorned, another example of his wealth and status. A circular room, the walls were filled with bookcases. French doors led to the garden, but filmy white curtains hid the room from outside view. In the middle of the room, a large sunken floor held a huge dark oak desk and chair upholstered in dark green leather.

John Charles did not waste any time admiring the room but went right to the desk and sat down. On the desk next to a golden statue of Aphordite lay a sheaf of blank writing papers. On the corner of the desk there was a black square ink well with four holes in the top. And in one of the holes sat a long, beautiful white feather. Elegant and majestic, it started with a sharp black stalk and blossomed up to a height of two feet, looking as if it might take flight at any moment. Not an ordinary goose quill, this came from a swan, more evidence of Mr. Dumont's status. John Charles couldn't help but stop and gaze at its natural beauty. He picked it up and held it in the air, feeling how light it was and how it seemed to catch the air as floating. Then finally coming out of his reverie, he glanced at the point at the end and was pleased to see it had been cut and sharpened to make a good point for writing. A good writing instrument, cut and heated in coals, could keep its edge for quite a time if taken care of, and this one was no exception. He wouldn't have to use the sharpening stone on the desk before he could use it.

He dipped the quill in the ink bottle on the desk and held it just above the bottle to let the excess ink drip off. Then satisfied it was ready, he grabbed a sheet of the expensive paper, placed it in front of himself and began to write.

My dearest Marguerite,

I love you! From the deepest depths of my soul, with every waking moment and every breath my mind repeats it to myself and dwells on your exquisite beauty. How my heart dreams of holding you in my arms, feeling your soft cheek pressed against mine, and your breast pressed against mine, so I can hear your heart beat.

And yet, despite my undying affection for you, we will never be able to consummate our love. Don't think this is because of a lack of affection for you. I could love no one more and will be yours forever. No, alas, it is the times in which we live and Fate who has doomed our union.

As you know, the King has bankrupted the country and most of the people live in poverty without a crust of bread to eat. Now that the country's coffers are empty, the poor and powerless starve to death in the streets, most with no clothes or wood to heat their homes. Children die from malnutrition and the elderly die off like flies, and yet the King and his aristocracy go on, pretending that the problems don't exist or simply not caring.

I know that I am from a wealthy family and could join the aristocracy if I simply turned a blind eye to the poor and destitute and became one of them, the rich and unfeeling. But you know that I can't do that. You know my heart and how deeply I care for France and its people. I believe it is the reason you fell in love with me in the first place. France is ripe for revolution. We long for and deserve the freedom that the Americans now enjoy. It is what is best for France.

With this goal in mind, I will soon be involved with men of

like mind who seek change. The days of the monarchy are coming to an end, and the bells of freedom ring all over Paris. However it will not come without danger, and even some sacrifice of lives

So, you see why I cannot in good conscience take you as my wife. I won't put you in danger. Possibly, when the course of revolution has run its course and we are all free I can once again seek your hand. I have no idea how long it will be until this happens or if it ever will. I don't expect you to wait for me. Even though I will always love you, I free you to pursue a more suitable companion, one who will give you the life you deserve.

I bid you adieu, my love. I will always love you, but the times and circumstances have doomed our love.

Yours forever,
John Charles

With the look of a man with a broken heart, Charles placed the feather back in its holder and blew gently on the letter. When he was sure it was dry, he carefully folded the letter into thirds. He then took an envelope and slipped the letter inside.

He picked up one of the long, rectangular blocks of wax on the desk for sealing letters. Lighting a match, he lit the wick in the heating plate. Then when the plate was hot, he pushed the wax onto it, leaving a pool of hot wax. He picked up M. Dumont's seal from the table and placed it in the wax. Then he transferred the wax to the back of the envelope, sealing it.

Placing the letter in his pocket, he stood up. He stroked the swan feather one more time, for a moment wishing he and Marguerite were swans who could simply live in peace together on a beautiful lake. How simple and pleasant that would be! He walked out of the study and made his way back to the ballroom. When he arrived, he handed the letter to a servant and asked them to see it was delivered.

The party continued, and the study remained empty for a while. Soft sounds of music and conversation drifted in from outside. Then the door opened again. This time a young lady with long brown curls in a flowing green gown slipped inside. She peeked down the hallway and looked about, as if concerned her actions might be witnessed. Then she closed the door and hurried over to the desk, just as John Charles had.

She sat down and grabbed a sheet of writing paper. But unlike John Charles, she did not give a second glance to the quill but simply grabbed it without looking up, dipped it in the ink well and began writing at a fast pace.

Dear John Charles,

Must I once again profess my love for you? You already know it is true, for how many times when we are alone have you asked me, and I have said I did? Still, I will do it again, to make certain you know it's true. I love you with all my heart and will never love another. If you did not know it before, you should now. And yet I despair, wondering if somehow you have lost your affection for me. It has been a week since you made any attempt to see me, and I have waited in the agony of impatience.

And then I heard a rumor which shed some light on your possible reluctance, but also filled me with fear for your safety. It seems the Captain of the King's soldiers has been arresting anyone suspected of being a Jacobite, those plotting revolution and the overthrow of the King. I heard your name was brought up as possibly one of them!

Be assured, dear John, the thought that you are involved in this cause does not dissuade me from loving you but has the complete opposite effect. I know how much you care for your fellow countrymen and what a big heart you have, and how enraged you become when you think of the poor common folk starving while the aristocracy feast and live without care. It makes me love you even more and admire your courage as well.

But I urge you to be careful, my dear love. If the rumors have come to my simple ears, surely it has reached other more dangerous ones. As you know Cardinal Jean-Sifrein Maury, the King's vulture, has made it his personal mission to root out any rebels and have them executed. He is watching everyone, looking for any reason to have someone arrested. I don't think he even needs to have proof, for his word is enough to send someone to the gallows. It is a very dangerous time and I fear for your safety.

And now I come to the real reason for this letter. Please, John Charles, do not fear to take me as your wife. I want to stand by your side, no matter where it leads me. If it is in the to the Bastille or even to the gallows. I only want to be with you. I will gladly share your fate, whatever it may be. Losing you would be worse than any torture, or even death.

You told me you loved me and would someday marry me. Please fulfill your promise, for I will never marry another and will only waste away alone for the rest of my days if you do not.

With undying love,
Your Marguerite

Marguerite waved the letter about in the air to dry it and then stuffed it into an envelope. Taking a quick glance towards the door to be sure no one had noticed her absence and looked for her, she turned to the wax seal. Surprised to see the candled in the warmer lit and a pool of wax already melted, she pressed the seal into the wax and sealed the envelope. Slipping it into a pocket in her jacket, she hurried out, leaving the quill laying on the desk.

The party continued as the moon rose into the clear night sky. Torches were lit, and their cheery glow shone through the curtains of the study. Fireworks were set off, and the sound of their explosions shattered the stillness in the room. Then the door to the study once again opened and new person entered. Dressed in the red robes of the Catholic priesthood it was none other than Cardinal Jean-Seifren Maury himself.

Cardinal Maury did not bother to conceal himself, but simply walked in a very businesslike manner to the desk. He sat down in the chair and picked up a sheet of paper, his face a death mask of darkness and cruelty. He noticed the quill lying on its side on the desk and it gave him a moment of mild irritation. A good quill could be ruined by being left out to dry. He mentally chided M. Dumont on his carelessness.

He picked up the quill with its long, white feather. Smiling at it, he stroked the plumes with his fingers. He thought how innocent and pure a creature the swan was, a beautiful example of God's perfection. How wonderful it would be one day when only the holy and righteous would exist, and all others would burn in a lake of fire in abject misery. The thought of the Lake of Fire particularly pleased him, putting him in a cheerful mood. It reminded him of the tortures he'd inflicted on men, and even women, in the Bastille.

He gripped the feather with his thumb and finger and moved it towards the ink well, but then he stopped, looking at with a frown. The quill was dull! He would have to sharpen it before he could write. A dislike for M. Dumont grew inside him, quickly growing into the decision to investigate the man for treason. It would teach him for having such an untidy desk.

He found a sharpening stone sitting on the corner of the desk. In fast impatient strokes, he scraped the quill against the stone, first one side and then the other until it grew sharp again.

Finally satisfied, he dipped the quill carefully into the ink bottle. He began to write swiftly, the swan feather moving in the air almost as once again in flight.

To the Captain of the Royal Guard:

It has come to my attention that there is a certain young man, a member of a very influential family who in fact may be a Jacobite, right here in our midst. His name is John Charles Baptiste. You will arrest him immediately and transport him to the Bastille. There we will discuss the matter with him and discover the truth. He will confess his sins, of that you can be sure, and if he is indeed a revolutionary, he will tell us who his co-conspirators are, or wish he had never been born. We will see he understands the consequences of being a traitor to the King, even if it costs him his life.

Cardinal Jean-Sifrein Maury
On authority from His Majesty King Louis XVI

The Cardinal put the feather back in the ink well and gazed at the letter with dark pleasure. He folded it in half and placed it in an envelope. In his haste he didn't notice that the candle of the wax heater was lit, but simply placed a new tube of wax on the heater and waited for it to melt. Then placing his personal ring in the wax he sealed the back of the envelope. He rose, placed the envelope in his pocket and left the study.

The party continued into the early morning hours. Sometime during the night, a servant handed Marguerite a letter. Another handed a letter to John Charles Baptiste. The two met in the garden and it was there they were found when the party was disrupted by the arrival of soldiers, who promptly arrested John Charles and led him away. until it was broken up by the arrival of soldiers who arrested John Charles, placed him in chains and led him away. The rest of the guests, alarmed and frightened by the turn of events, left soon after and the party ended. Marguerite, upset and crying for some unknown reason, was taken home by her parents. It was later determined that she had a mental illness. She was taken to a mental hospital for treatment.

Fountain Pen

Not So Gentle Men

By Carrie Avery Moriarty

Evening was falling fast, a chill coming through the pane next to his desk. He'd hoped to finish the draft before supper, but that was not going to happen.

"Louis," Kate called.

"In here, dear," he replied. He placed his fountain pen on the desk, then pulled the spectacles from his nose.

"Have you finished?" she asked upon entering.

"Nearly," he replied. "Is supper on?"

"In a moment," Kate said. "Shall I wait to serve?"

"Oh, no," Louis replied. "I'm going to have to come back to this." He stood, embracing his wife. "You smell divine."

"Pshaw," she replied, slapping his arm. "You tease."

"And how is my dear son?" he asked, patting her extended stomach.

"Or daughter," Kate replied.

"I would be happy about that, too," Louis responded.

"He's growing tiresome of the cramped conditions, I'm afraid," she replied.

"I'm growing tiresome of waiting for him to arrive," he said.

"What has the doctor said about when we should expect him?"

"You know it's too early," Kate admonished. "He'll be too small if he's born now. Come and eat, then you can finish your project."

Louis followed his wife into their small kitchen, enjoying the smell of the stew she'd prepared. They dined in comfortable silence, simply enjoying time together.

"I've a surprise for you," Kate said as she removed the dishes from the table. She made her way to the sideboard after placing the dishes on the counter. With great flourish she removed a cloth, releasing the delicious scent of apples and cinnamon.

"Pie," Louis exclaimed. "You spoil me too much, dear."

"'Tis a pleasure to do so," she replied. "Soon enough I'll be busy with more than just your needs. You need to appreciate it while you've got me all to yourself."

"I am more than willing to share you with our son," he replied.

Kate brought the pie to the table, sliced it, then served them each a generous portion.

It was late when Louis finally finished his draft. He left it on the desk, a stone atop it to keep it still until morning. He replaced his fountain pen in its slot at the top of the desk, then turned down the lamp. He would need to be at the office before the sun was up to present it. As he climbed in bed, his wife didn't stir. Gently he cozied up to her, wrapping his arm around her as much as possible. He marveled in the fact he would soon be a father.

"You've finished, then," Kate said in the close quiet.

"Just," he replied. "Sleep now. You'll not get much more when the baby arrives."

"Mmm," she responded.

Louis was not nearly the scholar as his father, but hoped that his request for inclusion in the Society would be granted. It was the final step in his assignment.

"Sleep, dear," Louis said as Kate stirred.

"Let me make you tea," she insisted.

"No, just rest," he replied. "They'll have tea at the office."

Kate reached out to her husband and he came to her, kissing her softly.

"I'll be home mid-day for a meal," he said as he tucked her in. "No need for anything fancy. Leftover stew is perfect."

"Good luck," she replied as her eyes closed.

Startled, she bolted up in bed, unsure what had awakened her. Then she heard the sound again, a rapping on the door. She climbed from the bed, donned her robe, and made her way to the front. Opening the door, she found a police officer standing on her stoop.

"Mrs. Kent?" he asked.

"I am," she replied.

"I'm afraid there's been an accident, Ma'am," he said. "Is there a family member or friend we can call on?"

"My husband is at his office…" she began.

"That's why I'm here," the officer interrupted. "He's been killed."

Kate wasn't sure she heard correctly. Louis just left for the office, he would be back mid-day. Suddenly, without warning, her world shifted and she found herself falling, darkness consuming her vision.

A pungent odor brought her round and she slowly opened her eyes. It was nearly noon, much later than she wanted. Needing to fix a meal for Louis when he returned from the office, she turned to rise. Startled, she asked, "Who are you?"

"Afraid I'm the bearer of unwelcome news," the man said. "Are you feeling better?"

Sitting, Kate assessed herself. She still wore her robe but was in bed. Suddenly the conversation returned, a police officer had told her that Louis was dead.

"It can't be true," she implored, looking straight into this stranger's eyes. "Tell me it was a nightmare and that my Louis is coming soon."

The man turned his head away, but she saw the answer in his countenance. She was on her own, left adrift in this large city without a man to help and guide her.

"Arrangements will be made," the man said as he stood. "You will be taken care of as well. Mr. Kent was a well-liked fellow, and his entrance into the Society has been granted, posthumously."

"I... I don't understand," Kate stuttered.

"His letter was on him when the accident occurred," the man explained. "It was a well thought out and presented argument, and the Guild determined, unanimously, that he should be granted the full weight of a fledgling member of the Society, with all the benefits that entails. Thus, your comforts will be ensured, as well as those of your child."

"Society? Guild? I'm afraid I don't know what you're speaking of," she said.

"Of course," the man said. He came back to the bed and set upon its edge. "The Society of Gentlemen is an establishment for those who rise above the average in both intellect and stature. One must petition entrance, then go before the Guild to present their case. This can take months, but once you're a member, you and your family are protected.

"Your husband," he continued. "Petitioned entrance a few weeks ago and was set to present his case before the Guild this morning. Unfortunately, the fates saw to it that he never arrived. I was sent to investigate and found he had been killed in an accident. His letter was on him, and I took it to the Guild in his stead."

"And that all happened this morning?" Kate asked.

"Indeed," he replied. "When I came to call upon you I found you on the ground. Apparently, the police had just arrived with the news of your husband's untimely demise. When you wouldn't rouse, I resorted to an old trick to wake you."

"What was that smell?" Kate asked.

"I'd rather not tell," the man replied. "Suffice it to say, it worked."

Kate nodded, understanding some of what she'd been told. Still, she had questions. "What happens now?"

"Now," the man said. "You dress in your mourning attire and meet me in the front. I will take you to the Guild and present you as Louis Kent's widow. They will then grant you the full amenities of the Society, allowing you full access to all the benefits available. Do you require help? I can call for an attendant."

"I can manage," Kate replied.

"Fine," the man said. "I await your company."

"What is your name?" she asked before he could leave the room.

"Reginald," he replied. "Reginald Grant. Now, please be quick. We are expected presently."

Kate had scarcely gotten herself together when the man had rapped on her door, begging her leave. She'd donned her one black gown, foregoing the many trappings she usually added, and had simply put her hair in a twist at the top of her head. She'd gathered her cloak at the door when they left. Ever the gentleman, Mr. Grant offered her his arm as they made their way to a large building near the center of town.

He'd kept her attention with explanations as to what would be expected once they arrived, how she was to act, what she should and should not say, and things of the like. She'd been around enough aristocrats to understand the mannerisms required, but had been out of practice since her pregnancy began. Louis had always insisted that she be well read and versed in numbers, assuring her that it would be a good habit to have and would serve her well in the future. She silently thanked him for that insistence as she stood before several gentlemen who appeared nearly twice her age, and more.

"Gentlemen," Mr. Grant said. "I present to you Ms. Catherine Kent, widow to our newly acquired member, Louis Kent."

"Widow Kent," one of the more robust men near the end of the table said. Kate inclined her head in acknowledgement as he continued. "What do you know of our Society of Gentlemen?"

"I'm afraid not much, sir," she whispered.

"Speak up, woman," another of the men said.

"Not much, sir," Kate repeated a little louder. "Mr. Grant has given me some information, but I'm afraid it is out of my realm of knowledge."

"Good, good," the first man said in response.

"All you need to know," a third man groused, "is that Louis has membership. This means that you do as well."

"Thank you, sir," Kate said.

"Reginald," the first man said, clearly dismissing Kate's presence. "What arrangements need to be made?"

"The burial is being handled," he said. "We will need to find a suitable home for Widow Kent soon, though. She is nearly to term with her child, and a move at a later date may not be practical."

"Move?" Kate whispered.

"Yes," Mr. Grant replied for her ears only.

"Very good," one of the other men said. "Has a house been selected?"

"Unfortunately," Mr. Grant said. "With the immediacy of this situation, I have not, as of yet, been able to investigate that."

"What is the next available location?" another man asked. "Had one been selected prior to Mr. Kent's meeting today?"

"That was to be my assignment today," Mr. Grant said. "The change in circumstances made that impossible until the immediate issue was handled."

"Then find someone to stay with her and help her prepare while you find a suitable location," one of the men demanded.

"Yes sir," Mr. Grant replied. Gripping Kate's elbow, he

steered her from the room. Once they were outside he asked, "Do you have family close that would be able to help you pack?"

"Why must I move?" Kate asked. "Is there something wrong with my house?"

"The Society has enemies," Mr. Grant said. "Because of that, all members are kept in secure locations. It is the way it must be."

Kate felt near tears but pushed them down. "I have no family," she finally said. "The only family I have is Louis, and now he's gone."

"I'll have my sister help you," he said as they made their way out of the building. "We'll stop on the way back to your place."

"I still don't understand why I need to move," Kate said.

"You will," Mr. Grant said. "My sister can explain the Society and its rules to you while you pack. Please keep up."

Kate wasn't sure what was worse, the non-answers or the insistence that she do as she was told, without asking her opinion.

"I still don't understand," Kate said for what seemed like the hundredth time.

"They just want to make sure that everyone is safe," Renee said.

Mr. Grant's sister seemed bright and open once he'd left them at Kate's house. Kate would almost describe her as vivacious. They'd begun in the bedroom, packing all of Kate's clothing into a small chest. She also kept a couple of Louis' best shirts as a memento. It didn't seem possible that he'd been there that morning and now, just a few hours later, she was being expected to change everything.

"It'll all work out fine," Renee said. "Just keep your head down for the next few weeks. Once the newness has worn off, they'll stop being so meddling."

"But what do I do in the meantime?"

"Just what I said," Renee replied. "Keep your head down

and don't make waves. Now, shall we get started in the kitchen?"

Kate led the way, leaving the trunk near the door of the bedroom where some men would come to gather it later. She showed Renee what she wanted to keep and what she felt she could do without, then made her way to Louis' study. This was going to be the hardest room to pack. Some of his things she knew she needed to keep, but others she wasn't so sure about.

Sitting at his desk, the one he vacated merely hours ago, she was moved to tears. They came slowly at first, but rapidly moved to gut wrenching sobs she was unsure she would be able to stop. That's where Renee found her.

"There, there," Renee cooed. "You'll get through this. I'll be right beside you the whole way."

Once she'd gained some composure, Kate confided, "I don't know how I'm supposed to go on without him."

"One day at a time," Renee said. "You get up, go through the day, then go to bed. Every action the same as when he was here. Eventually you grow to accept it."

"And when my child asks about his father?" Kate asked. "What do I do then?"

"By the time he's old enough to question that, you'll have a new husband," Renee said.

"I don't want a new husband," Kate sobbed.

"Oh," Renee replied. "The Society won't allow for that. You'll be expected to remarry after a respectable time of mourning."

"I want my Louis," Kate said, sent to tears again.

"Would you like me to pack this room?" Renee asked.

"No," Kate blustered through her tears. "This is where Louis spent most of his time. I need to find what he would want me to take. You can't do that."

"I'll continue in the kitchen," Renee said, then left.

Once again, Kate was alone in Louis' space. Looking at the desk, she saw his prized pen near the top. Picking it up, she turned its shiny wood surface in the filtered sunlight from the window. Never again would he use it, bringing out the worlds within his mind, setting them to permanence on the page. No, he was now growing cold, waiting to be laid in the ground. He would never see his child's face, never hold him, teach him the way to bring life from nothing but a dream. Instead, she'd be forced to take the hand of another man, allow that stranger to use her body for his pleasures, and be unable to enjoy the simple things that had become so precious to her.

The pen clattered to the floor as Kate gripped her abdomen, a pain like none she'd experienced taking root there. She screamed out in agony and Renee came running.

"What is it?" Renee asked. Kate was unable to answer as another pain gripped her. "It must be time for the wee one to arrive," Renee said.

"Too soon," Kate ground out. "Too soon."

"I'm afraid you are not in charge of that decision," Renee admonished. She helped Kate to her feet, guiding her in slow steps to the bedroom. "Lay back," she said as she helped her to the bed.

Kate gripped the quilt on the bed in firm fists as yet another pain shot through her. She screamed out in agony, both at the physical pain and the thought of losing her child, the last link she had to her Louis.

"Breathe through the pain," Renee said.

Kate tried, but couldn't seem to catch a breath, the pains coming rapidly. Suddenly, without warning, she felt warm liquid rushing from her body, soaking the bed and its coverings. She began to sob as the pains continued to come, her body ejecting the only piece she had left of her dear, sweet husband.

"Let's have a look," Renee said as she lifted Kate's skirts and shoved them back to gain access to the coming child. Swiftly she removed the undergarments left on her new friend, allowing her to see the head of the child right at the entrance to the world. "You're going to need to push," she said in encouragement. "It won't take but a moment, and then you'll be able to hold your child."

Renee was right. Kate bore down, pushing with her muscles. The silence broke with a small cry that grew in volume.

"Here we are," Renee said as she wrapped the babe in a cloth that she found. "Meet your daughter."

"What do you mean, a delay?" Reginald asked.

"The child arrived unexpectedly," Renee replied. "Between the stress of her husband's death and the packing, it doesn't surprise me."

"Is he well?"

"She," Renee corrected, "is small but sturdy. Kate is doing well, and the child is feeding just fine."

Scrubbing his face, Reginald asked, "Can she be moved today?"

"She's insistent upon packing Mr. Kent's study herself," Renee replied. "She said that she isn't sure what all is in there, but will know if something is important when she sees it."

"She'll need to pack it today," Reginald insisted. "This move must happen without delay."

"Everything else is packed," Renee said. "I'll check to see if she thinks she'll be up to finishing."

"I'll go," Reginald said. "You need to remain the nice Grant family member."

With that, he walked back to the bedroom to find her sitting in a rocker, the babe wrapped in cloth, nursing. He cleared his throat and Kate looked up, smiling. There were tears in her eyes, but they seemed to make them glow with joy rather than sorrow.

"I'm sorry to rush you," he began. "But we need to finish packing. I understand you don't want anyone else in the study."

"It was Louis' space," she whispered. "I feel like I'll lose him altogether if I let someone else decide what needs to go with me."

"What if I were to pack everything," he suggested. "Move it all to the new house, then set it up exactly as it is here. Would that be acceptable?"

Her eyes widened as she asked, "You'd do that for me?"

"My job is to move you in the most expedient manner," he said. "If that means I pack every sheet of parchment, every quill, every ink well, and every book, then that is what I will do. Now, do you accept this offer?"

Kate looked past him to her new friend who was standing in the doorway. Renee nodded, indicating that she would see to it that Reginald was as good as his word. Finally, she looked him in the eye and nodded her assent.

"Fine," he said, then turned and left.

"He's a good man," Renee said after he'd gone. "He understands what you are going through all too well, I'm afraid. He'll not disappoint you."

"Thank you," Kate said.

"I'd better go and help," she replied. "I'll see how much longer you have to wait before we take the rest of your things to your new house."

Kate nodded, not trusting her voice. She watched Renee leave, then looked at her daughter. How much the baby looked like Louis. Unable to contain her emotions any longer, the tears began to fall once again.

"Just one more thing," Kate said, handing her daughter to Renee. She stepped back into the home she'd shared with Louis and made her way to the study. She turned to be sure she wasn't followed, then went to where the desk once sat.

As good as his word, Mr. Grant had packed everything in the room. From the furniture to the papers and books, all of it was now on its way to the new house. Looking around she took a deep breath and held it, closing her eyes. She could still smell him, even over the scent of the other men who had been in here to take the items out. It was a smell she would miss, having had it near her for nearly two years.

Opening her eyes, she looked down and noticed Louis' fountain pen on the floor. Gingerly she stooped to pick it up.

"What did you find?" he asked.

"Just Louis' pen," she replied. "It is his favorite, and I'd hate to lose it." Standing, she smiled at the man. "Are we ready, then?"

"One more thing," he replied. Reaching into the bag at his hip. "I knew Louis before," he said. "He asked that I give this to you should the unimaginable happen."

Kate took the small box, turning it around in her hands. There was a lock on it, but it was otherwise unadorned. "Thank you," she said, failing to hold back her tears.

"Shall we?" he asked.

Kate nodded and stepped to the door, giving one final sweep of the room. Turning, she left with Mr. Grant behind her, and made her way to the wagon. He helped her into the seat, then Renee handed the baby to her. They both got on and he snapped the reins, the wagon moving with a lurch. The trip was short, and they quickly arrived at the house he had chosen for her.

"After you," he said as he opened the door.

Kate stepped inside and turned to look around. The place was enormous, much larger than any house she'd ever lived in. She turned to Mr. Grant and asked, "Am I to live here alone?"

"You will be afforded staff," he said. "Otherwise it will just be you and your daughter."

Blinking, Kate looked from him to the entrance, turning in awe at the splendor surrounding her.

"Let's get you settled," Renee said. "Then we can discuss your daughter's name."

"Bridgette Louise," Kate said.

"I'm sorry?" Mr. Grant asked.

"Her name is Bridgette Louise," Kate replied. "After her father's mother and her father."

"What a beautiful name," Renee said.

"Fine," Mr. Grant said. "I'll leave you two alone to get settled. I have further things to take care of for the Society. I shall call again this evening to take you home, Renee."

"We'll be fine," Renee replied, shooing him out the door.

Turning she watched Kate take in the surroundings, walking from the entryway toward the lounge and beyond. Following, not wanting to interrupt her exploration, she saw many emotions cross her new friend's face. Having gone through the transition from a modest home to one that was supplied by the Society, she knew it would take some time for Kate to grow accustomed to her new place.

"Oh," Kate said in surprise as she stepped into the kitchen. "I didn't realize anyone was here."

"Just Mags," the woman said. "Need an evening respite? I can put something together right quick."

"Oh, no," Kate replied. "No need to go to any trouble."

"No trouble at all, Miss," the woman said. "Happy to serve ye."

Kate looked back at Renee, confusion on her face.

"Let's find your room," she said. "We'll get you settled and let Bridgette nap. You look like you could use a nap as well."

Renee steered Kate from the kitchen, making their way back to the foyer and up the staircase to the residential section of the house. She found the master suite, the bed made and a bassinet next to it for the baby. Placing Bridgette into the cradle, she then helped Kate undress and climb under the covers.

"Rest now," she said. "You've had a long and busy day. I'll wake you if anything needs your immediate attention."

"Will you hand me my satchel?" Kate asked.

Renee picked it up and laid it on the bed next to her, then turned and left, closing the door behind her. Kate was exhausted, but wanted to look in the box Mr. Grant had given her. She pulled it out of the bag, turning the clasp to herself. She then pulled a pin from her hair and set to work on the lock, a trick Louis had showed her just last summer. Quickly she succeeded in releasing the lock. When she opened the box she was surprised at what she found.

"Has she settled in?" Reginald asked his sister.

"She's adjusting," Renee replied. "The day has taken its toll on her."

"And the baby?" he asked.

"Doing just fine," Renee said. "I tried to get her to eat, but she simply won't."

"I'll talk to her," he said.

Taking the steps to the second level, he found his way to her room. "Mrs. Kent?" he asked as he opened the door. When he got no answer, he tried again. "Kate?" he questioned as he entered, making his way to the curtained window. Again, there was no response. Pulling aside the drape he saw Kate curled on the bed, the box he'd given her in her arms, and the babe tucked beside her. She was sound asleep.

Quietly he let the drape fall back in place, blanketing the room in darkness. He closed the door behind him when he left, then found his way to the foyer where his sister waited.

"She's sleeping," he said. "I'll ask Mags to fix up a meal and keep an eye on her."

My Darling Kate,

You must have such sadness in your heart if you are reading this note. I had expected to have time to explain everything to you, but that obviously hasn't happened. I trust Reg with your safety. He will ensure everything goes according to the plan. I need you to help him complete this task. There is a secret compartment in the bottom left drawer of my desk, only accessible with the key you wear around your neck. I don't know if you remember what I said when I gave it to you. That you would need it to get all my secrets.

Make sure that no one sees you access the secret

compartment. *That is imperative, as there are those in the city who would cause you harm if they knew my true nature. Once you've had the chance to read the contents of the files, you will know what to do. You are one of the cleverest women I know, and I trust that you will be discrete with these things.*

My heart has always been yours, and our child holds a large piece as well, even though I haven't met him, yet. Know that I have never meant to hurt you in any way, and that you are more precious than anything I could ever hope to attain in this life.

Forever yours,

Louis

Kate hadn't been able to stop the tears after reading the letter. Why had he felt the need to keep this Society a secret from her was something she couldn't fathom. They'd shared everything together, both the good and the bad. A decision like this, entering the Society, was something that would affect her as well, and he felt the need to keep it a secret.

Not only that, but he'd entrusted her safety to a man she'd never met. He knew that she would be uprooted, moved from her home, and thrust into a life she was ill prepared to cope with. All of this while she was awaiting the birth of their first child. The more she thought on it, the more distraught she became.

The housemaid brought trays of food, but she simply couldn't eat. Even the smell brought on a bought of nausea. She simply stayed in her room, lantern low and drapes drawn.

"She simply won't eat," Mags said to Renee.

"She must," Renee implored. "How is Bridgette doing?"

"The babe seems fine," the housemaid said. "I'm just worried about her mum."

"I'll talk to her," Renee said, making her way up the stairs. "Get a bath ready."

"As you wish," Mags replied.

"Kate," Renee said as she opened the door to the bedroom.

Darkness engulfed the space and she could barely make out the shape of her friend on the bed. Walking to the window, she pulled the drape wide.

"Stop," Kate cried.

"I will not," Renee said. "Mags said you haven't eaten."

"I'm not hungry," Kate replied.

"But the baby is," she said. "I know this is hard, but you must eat. Do you want to lose Bridgette, too?"

"She's fine," Kate said. "I've been feeding her fine."

"Here," Renee said, pulling the blankets from her friend. "Get up. Let's get you a bath."

"I don't need one," Kate said, pulling the covers back on her.

"Yes," Renee said, "you do. You smell, and you haven't been out of this room in days. Now, give me the baby and go to the bath."

Renee took the baby from her friend without a fight, then pushed Kate out the door and down the hall. Kate didn't put up much of a fight after that, and Renee was able to get the bedding changed and air out the room, all while Kate was in the bath.

"Now," she said as Kate returned. "Don't you feel better?" Kate just glared at her friend. "Mags has made us a lunch, and we're going down to the dining room to eat it."

After Renee left, Kate found her way to the study where all of Louis' things were. She sat on a small settee with her daughter, simply holding her as she slept. Looking around the room, she was surprised that it looked nearly identical to the one at her other house. Mr. Grant had been as good as his word in moving everything and setting it up. Knowing Bridgette would need to eat soon, she didn't want to bother putting her down. Instead, she used the time to marvel at the locket she'd found in the box with the letter that Mr. Grant had given her. Turning it, she saw more than just diamonds were imbedded. There were stones of all colors, reds, greens, blues, yellow, and so many more. It had to be worth a fortune, and how Louis had found the money to pay for it was beyond Kate's knowledge.

Bridgette began to fuss, so Kate went in search of a change. Once that was complete, she fed her daughter. The baby was a good eater, even at such a small size. Kate had been worried that if she were born too soon, she wouldn't survive. Bridgette proved to be a fighter, though, stronger than she'd expected. Thankful for this miracle, she finished feeding her child, then put her in the cradle that had been placed in this room for convenience. It seemed there was a cradle in every room in the house, something she hadn't been prepared for, but was thankful of, nonetheless.

Listening, she heard the housemaid and her son in the kitchen, so went to the desk. Opening the drawer Louis indicated in his letter, she pulled out the papers within. Sure enough, in the bottom, she found a small hole, just big enough for her to place the key she wore around her neck. She'd thought the small key was a sweet gesture from her husband when he'd given it to her on their wedding night. He'd said it was the key to all his treasures. Little did she know those treasures were right there all along and had nothing to do with his heart.

She walked to the door and closed it. Then, returning to the desk, she inserted the key into the slot. Shifting it, she heard the lock give way. The cover slid back easily, and she found a leather pouch. Pulling it out, she opened the tie to remove a stack of parchment.

There were copies of documents of all kinds, none of which made any sense to her. Then she found a hand-written letter to Louis. She pulled that out and began to read.

L.K.

I understand a storm is coming. Winds are shifting rapidly, so I suggest you plan accordingly. The gods are ruthless but can be abated with the right gifts. Remember your gear and bring currency.

R.G.

Kate was confused by the note, but figured she'd understand once she'd had a chance to read more of the documents. Another letter, then another, caught her eye. All in the same writing as the first, all signed R.G. She gathered all the letters together, then put the rest of the paperwork back into the satchel. She tied it up, then put it back in the secret compartment, locking it tight before putting the other documents on top. She replaced the key around her neck, put the letters into her pocket, then picked up Bridgette to head to her bed. There would be plenty of time to read these in the wee hours of the morning when she would be up with the baby.

Days ran together as she learned her new routine with her daughter and the household. Renee stopped in to visit a few times, but she had not seen either her or Mr. Grant in nearly a week. Between her continued grief, and the adjustments as a new mother, she'd only read the correspondence, but had not taken the time to pull any of the other paperwork from the drawer.

"Mrs. Kent," Mags called from the entry.

Kate moved from the study to the front of the house.

"Mr. Grant," she said. "What a pleasant surprise. What brings you to my door?"

"We need to discuss your husband's service," he stated.

"I thought he'd already been laid to rest," Kate responded.

"The Society must be allowed to show their condolences for your loss," Mr. Grant said.

"Won't you join me in the study? Mags, will you bring us tea?" Kate asked.

"Of course, Miss," Mags replied.

Kate moved to the study, the gentleman following. Once

they were settled, Mags arrived with a tray of tea and all the accoutrements. She was swift in her placement, then was gone quickly, leaving the other two to discuss their business.

"How have you managed?" the gentleman asked.

"I've been getting by," Kate replied. "Still learning the running of the house, along with the demands of motherhood."

"You look well," he said.

Kate smiled at the compliment, then asked, "What do you need from me as far as the arrangements?"

"If it's all right with you," he began. "I'd like to plan for the service to take place the day after tomorrow. This will give the Society time to get the word out. Will that work for you?"

"Of course," she replied. "Where will the service take place?

"It will be held here, of course," he said.

"Here?" Kate asked. "Not in a Society hall?"

"They like to come to the home of the deceased," he said. "It makes them feel they aren't putting the aggrieved out."

"So instead, they'll come to my home and disrupt it," she muttered.

"I apologize," he said. "It is the way things are."

"That will be fine," she replied. "Is there anything I need to do? Anything I can help with?"

"I'll take care of everything," he said. "I'll be sure that Renee is here to help you dress and care for the baby."

"I appreciate that," Kate said. "Bridgette has demanded much of my attention. Between caring for her and trying to get enough rest, my days have been fairly full."

"Do you need more help?" he asked. "Perhaps a nanny?"

"Oh, no," Kate said. "I just think it's the newness of it all. I'm managing, and Mags has been a godsend."

"Good, good," he said.

"I did find a note in Louis' desk," she began. "It was signed R.G., and I wondered if that was you."

"Do you have the letter?" he asked, unsure which letter she may have found.

"In my room," she said. "Will you wait while I get it?"

"Of course," he replied.

She rose, left the room, and climbed the stairs. Reginald watched her go, wondering what he would say if she showed him something he couldn't readily discuss. He knew Louis had kept her in the dark about their true nature, as well as the need to infiltrate the Society, but also knew that he trusted his wife implicitly.

"Here it is," Kate said as she returned. She'd pulled the most innocent of the letters from her collection, the note saying something about the weather and a storm coming.

Reginald looked the letter over, then glanced to Kate. He could tell she was not being completely forthcoming with her information, and he didn't blame her. Perhaps she'd found Louis' documents, the ones he'd yet to uncover. He looked at the letter again, realizing it was one of the earliest ones he'd written.

"This does appear to be my hand," he admitted. "Although I'm not sure why he would have kept this particular letter."

"I just thought it interesting that someone would be writing to Louis to discuss storms," she said. "He never really showed any interest in the seasons."

"Perhaps he was anticipating a shipment of something and was worried that the weather would delay it," Reginald offered.

"That is likely it," she said with a smile.

"Well," he said, standing. "I shall take my leave now to get things moving. Plan for Renee to be here first thing. She'll have all of the details for the gathering."

"I'll show you out," she said, standing.

They walked to the door and he opened it. "Until later," he said, then swept out into the night.

Kate was left a bit confused. She was sure that the letters had been from him, but he seemed to dismiss it as nothing. She wondered if the storm was about something else, not the weather but another type of storm. Bridgette began to fuss, so she went to her. Her mind was still on the man who'd helped her, unsure what role he would play in her future.

"Thank you," Kate said to another stranger who had come to give their condolences.

She knew that the Society was important, simply by the fact that they'd arranged so much since Louis died. She was not prepared for the inundation of new people she would need to meet.

"How are you holding up?" Renee asked. She held Bridgette in her arms, the babe dressed in a christening gown befitting her place in this new society.

"Ready to be finished with this," Kate confided.

"It will be over soon," she said. "Then you and Bridgette can resume a more normal schedule."

"I'm not sure what normal is going to look like," she said. "Nothing is as it was."

The day ground on, her meeting and thanking strangers for their condolences of a man they likely never met. It was all very formal, and by the time evening rolled around, Kate was thankful the last of the guests had left.

"Thank you for all you have done," Kate said to Reginald.

"It was my honor," he replied. "Do you mind if we talk for a bit?"

"Certainly," she replied.

He led the way to the study, which surprised Kate. When she was inside, he shut the door.

"May I speak frankly," he asked.

"But of course," she replied. "What is it?"

He opened the door and looked around, then, apparently satisfied, he shut it once again, turning the lock. "Please," he said, indicating the sofa.

She sat and he took the place next to her, much closer than proper etiquette allowed.

"Mrs. Kent," he began. "You showed me a letter a few days

ago." Kate nodded so he continued. "I did, indeed, write that letter to your husband. It was not, however, about the weather as you surmised. I'm not sure how much you know of your husband's work, but we have been working to gain access to this Society for a few years. They are not as they might appear, benevolent as it seems."

"Why are you telling me this?" she asked.

"I have been watching you," he replied. "And I feel that you are trustworthy and should know the truth about what is going on, as much as I can say. I would hate to see you hurt by anything the Society might do, or because of what may become of them once they are exposed."

"I'm not sure what you're getting at," she said, confused.

"Louis told me that you were an honest and trustworthy woman," he continued. "He said that, should anything ever happen to him, that I was to ensure that you were kept safe from any fall out of the destruction of this sect."

"Sect?" she asked.

"Yes," he replied. "They are run, in part, by corrupt and unlawful businessmen. In fact, some of the members have also made their way to our government, serving as representatives, governors, senators, and judges."

"Oh," Kate said, shocked to hear that this was an issue. Louis never discussed politics with her, though she was aware of some things.

"We were asked by the government to seek entry into the Society," he continued. "I was able to get in at a lower position because of my background. Louis wanted to try to gain access as an actual member. This is why he took the position with the Hutchinson company. It afforded him the higher profile necessary for entry into the Society as a fledgling member.

"He had completed most of the requirements," Mr. Grant continued. "The last task was to present his case to the Guild, which he was on his way to doing when he was struck. I'm not sure how the accident happened, and no one seems concerned within the Society. Nonetheless, I do need you to be vigilant in who you speak with and what you say to them."

"Of course," Kate replied. She wasn't sure what to do with all the information she'd just gained, but one thing seemed clear. "Would you like to see the other paperwork I found?"

"You have his papers?" he asked.

"I have yet to read them," she said, standing. "But they are all in his desk."

"Leave them," he said, pulling her back to the sofa. "If you get the chance to read them, please let me know what they say. Did he give you a cipher?"

It was Kate's turn to look confused. "I'm not sure what you mean."

"We always wrote in code to each other," he began. "Louis was a master with cryptography. He could make a letter sound as benign as the one you showed me, talking of the weather. The truth of the letter, however, was much more detailed, if you knew how to read it."

"I may have it somewhere," she said. "Where should I look?"

Mr. Grant scratched his head, remembering conversations he'd had with his friend. "He had a pen he used all the time," he finally said. "Something he cherished nearly as much as you."

"I have that," she replied. "It was the one that was almost left behind in his study."

"Check to see if you can take it apart," he suggested. "I don't mean break it, but open it. If you can, there might be a cypher inside." He stood, bringing Kate to her feet with him. "I must be going now. But I'll check on you in a day or two. Should you find something, please keep it secret. My sister is somewhat aware of what is going on, but I don't want to give her too much information, either."

"Do you not trust her?" she asked, concerned for her daughter who was in Renee's care now.

"I trust her," he replied. "But there are some things she doesn't need to know."

Kate nodded, unsure she understood much of what he'd shared. She did know that her husband loved to create puzzles, and she loved attempting to solve them. This, she thought, was no different. He'd created a puzzle and she just had to find the right way to figure it out. Knowing her husband, he would have made it nearly impossible for anyone else, but simple enough for her. They seemed to have the same line of thinking when it came to these sorts of things.

They met Renee in the foyer, where Kate took her daughter back.

"I'll call on you in a day or two," Mr. Grant said. "To finish anything that may need my attention."

"Very well," Kate replied.

"Send someone for me if you need me," Renee said. "I'm happy to help you any time."

"Thank you," she said, then gave her friend a hug. She shook Mr. Grant's hand and the siblings left. Closing the door, she wondered if she would be able to sleep with all the questions unanswered. Bridgette began to fuss, so she made her way to her room. The exhaustion from the day caught up to her as she slipped through her door. She knew there would be no answers to these questions tonight.

"You were right," Kate said as Mr. Grant came in the door.

He simply looked at her, clearly telling her that she should be more cautious with her outbursts. Kate looked around, then led the way to the study once again. He had stopped by twice since the reception, but she hadn't had a chance to investigate anything. Bridgette had been overly fussy, she'd been exhausted, and letters of condolences arrived from far and wide. Renee had explained that these letters would be expected to have an immediate response. She wasn't used to having this much paperwork to do and was beginning to resent Louis' not telling her about this other part of his life.

"What have you found?" he asked once they were locked in

the study.

"The cypher," she replied.

She handed the pen to him and waited. He held the pen, then looked to her.

"Are you going to tell me?" he finally asked.

Taking the pen, she gave it a twist. It opened easily and inside there was a small piece of paper. She removed it, handing it to him. He looked at the small slip of parchment, turning it over and over in his hands.

"I give up," he said, looking to her.

Smiling with victory, Kate took the paper from him and breathed on it, then handed it back. With surprise, he saw a series of numbers with dashes between them.

"Did you test it out?" he asked.

"Of course I did," she replied. "It works perfectly, too."

"And did you decipher the letters?" he asked.

She smiled, then said, "The letters, yes. But not the documents."

"What do you mean?"

"I mean," she said. "The documents were not in the same code as the letters."

"And you know this, how?"

"Because you would have known the cypher if they were," she said in triumph. She rose and went to his desk. Pulling open the top drawer she found Louis' cherished copy of Charles Dickens' David Copperfield. Returning to the sofa, she handed the book to him.

"Really?" the man asked.

"It's his favorite," she replied. "It makes sense that he would use this one. And when I tested my theory with some of the other documentation it held up."

"But it wasn't the cypher for the letters," he stated.

"It was for the other documents in the drawer," she replied. "After I tried to use it on the letters, I realized that it wasn't the one you two used. I had to try it on the other documents, which

I did just a few days ago. I now have several of them transcribed to the correct wording which can be used to bring down the Society."

"Were you able to figure out the letters?" he asked.

She smiled and said, "I'm happy to know that you approved of our marriage. Even if I didn't know you before."

Mr. Grant nodded, then asked, "Can I see what you've done?"

Once again, Kate made her way to the desk. This time she opened the lower drawer, pulled off her key, and opened the secret compartment. Pulling out the papers in question, she returned to the sofa.

"These are the originals," she said, handing a stack to him. "These are the ones I've converted."

"This is remarkable work," he said. "Do you mind if I take them with me?"

"I'd actually rather you not," she said. She wasn't sure what it was, but she suddenly had a possessiveness over these specific documents. Perhaps it was because it was the last thing Louis had been working on, or it could have been the subject matter she had read. She wanted to trust Mr. Grant, but she also wanted to make sure that she had the originals, just in case.

"That is completely reasonable," he said. "Can I trust you to complete the transcription?"

"I am more than happy to do that," she said. "It may take some time, since I have to do it in secret. I hope that's all right."

"Absolutely," he replied. "Would you like me to have Renee help with Bridgette so you have more time to work on this?"

"Oh, no," Kate said. "I'd hate to put her out."

"I know that she would love to come and see the baby," he replied. "She does miss her."

"I would enjoy her company," Kate said.

"I'll let her know," he said. "Now, though, I should give you this."

He reached into his jacket and pulled out a box, handing it to her. She took it and, upon opening, looked to the man.

"How can this be?" she asked as she pulled out a locket nearly identical to the one she'd found in the box he'd given her before.

"Louis insisted that I hold one of the two," he explained. "Just in case you needed more convincing."

Gingerly, she opened the locket, finding a picture of herself and her husband inside this one.

"Where did he get these?" she breathed.

"When he was first contacted by the Society," he began. "These were tokens that they used to entice his entry. They did not know who we were. Louis insisted that I give one to Renee, but I said it would be useful for ensuring our escape should that need arise."

"But the pictures…"

"I insisted on putting these in," he said. "Louis was kind enough to get a copy to me of each. I told him that, should anything happen, I could use it to convince you that we were on the same team."

A tear slipped down Kate's cheek and she brushed it away in frustration. She looked to him and he said, "Keep it, and the other. Hide them somewhere you can get to them in an emergency. They may be useful if things go awry."

"I didn't realize it was that serious," she said.

"And you needn't worry," he said. "Things are coming together nicely. When you've finished with his work, we should be able to move quickly to shut them down."

"What will happen to me then?" she asked, suddenly quite aware that she was at the mercy of not only the man to her side, but the men in charge of this Society. Should things not end well, she may be swept up in the aftermath.

"You will be cared for," he said. "No matter what happens. I promised Louis that I'd keep you safe. It was the one requirement he had in joining me."

"You really are enjoying this, aren't you?" Renee asked.

Kate had been sitting at Louis' desk going over the papers and writing the converted text for hours. She'd taken a few breaks to feed Bridgette, and Renee had insisted she eat in the early afternoon, but she was nearly complete with her task.

"It helps me feel closer to Louis," she said as she brushed her hair back from her eyes. "His writing was as much a part of him as anything. By reading and rewriting what he wrote, it feels like he's still here with me."

The fountain pen Louis had used began to feel like a comfortable old friend in her hand. She looked at its simple design, marveling at how such a benign tool could be used to begin and end revolutions. With a stroke of such an instrument, nations grew and fell. It was also used to create beauty, both in long, drawn out prose and simple letters to a lover. While Louis' hand was steady when using it, hers seemed shaky, which she attributed it to the long hours.

"Can I read any of it?" Renee asked.

"Oh, no," Kate said. "It's not really anything worth reading. It's silly, really."

"I received news that Reginald will be here tonight," Renee said.

"I'm in no state to see him," Kate replied.

"But you must," the other woman said. "I'll let Mags know that we're going to have dinner, just the three of us. Something cozy and quiet."

"I guess," Kate replied. In the short time that she'd known them, she found that Renee was the more outgoing and demanding of the two Grant siblings. She watched as Renee swept from the room, leaving Kate and Bridgette alone. The baby slept in her cradle and Kate continued with the task at hand. Before she knew it, Renee was back in and pulling her from the chair.

"You must ready yourself," she said.

Kate looked down at the last page, realizing that she had

finished the task.

"Let me put these away," she said. "Would you mind taking Bridgette up to my room for me?"

Renee picked up the baby and once again was out the door. Kate had always had her project out prior to the other woman's arrival, and never put it back until she was gone. Since Reginald had indicated that she wasn't as knowledgeable about the Society, she felt it was a way to keep this part of her work secret. Once she'd finished locking the drawer, she made her way upstairs.

The dress her friend picked out for her was much grander than one she had planned to wear.

"Why this one?" she asked.

"Because it's a celebration," was the reply. "Even if you don't think you should celebrate."

"It's just going to be you, your brother, and me," she said. "There's no need to get this dressed up."

"I won't be here," Renee said, and there was something in her voice that gave Kate pause.

"Why not?" she asked.

"Have you not seen the way Reg looks at you?"

Kate looked at her friend, confused. "What do you mean?"

"I mean," Renee said as she helped Kate take off her day dress. "That he looks at you the way a man looks at a woman."

"That makes no sense," Kate said as she stepped into the evening gown Renee had chosen.

Renee stopped, holding the dress up, but simply looking to her friend. "You were a married woman," she said. "I think you know what I'm saying."

Kate placed her arms through the sleeves and turned, forcing her friend to break eye contact. Nothing Renee said made sense. Reginald was a friend of her husband's, a colleague. Nothing more. The only interest he had in her was the fact that she could decipher the documents Louis wrote. He would not see her in a romantic light. That wasn't possible.

After the dress was secure, Renee pushed her friend to the chair in front of her dressing table, picked up her brush, and began to work on arranging Kate's hair.

"I'm sorry I mentioned it," Renee said, looking her friend's reflection in the eye. "I should know better than to say things like this, but I thought you knew."

Although she didn't believe it herself, Kate said, "It's fine."

The tension remained as Renee finished her task. Once complete, she turned her friend to her, saying, "Please don't be mad."

"There's no reason for me to be upset with you," Kate said. "You are a good friend and are looking out for my welfare. You also know your brother well. I'm sure that you can see things I won't."

"You will have to remarry," Renee said. "I would hate for you to end up with someone horrible. Reg could give you a wonderful life. Nothing like this, of course. But he would make a wonderful husband and father. Just don't tell him I said anything."

"What is there to tell?" Kate asked. She didn't trust herself to think further on the subject, though. That would mean forgetting Louis, and she didn't want to forget him.

"This was a wonderful meal," Reginald said.

"I'll be sure to let Mags know," Kate replied. She was uneasy with the information that Renee had given her, the fact that she could see Reginald's feelings toward her. "Did you want to look over the paperwork?"

"Please," Reginald replied.

They stood and made their way to the study, a place that had been the setting for many meetings between the two of them.

"Here they are," Kate said as she pulled the stack from the desk's secret drawer. "They make some sense to me, but I'm sure they are much clearer to you."

Reginald sat and looked through the first few pages. "Do

you have the originals?" he asked.

Expecting the question, Kate handed him the stack her husband had written. Reginald looked at the pages side by side, reviewing them against each other.

"You do remarkable work," he said, not taking his eyes off the papers. "This would have taken much longer had I tried to figure it out. Thank you."

Kate watched as he flipped through the pages rapidly, scanning each and obviously understanding more than she did.

"So they'll help?" she asked.

Reginald looked up and said, "Tremendously. You have saved me a great deal of work. Do you mind if I ask you something, though?"

"Of course," she said as she sat on the other end of the sofa.

"There are quite a few very complex things within these documents," he began. "I don't want to come across as rude, but how much of it did you understand?"

"I did understand quite a bit of it," Kate replied. "There were some things that were outside my limited knowledge, but for the most part it was pretty simple."

Reginald smiled, saying, "Louis always said you were much smarter than he. I guess this just proves it."

She blushed and said, "I knew Louis. Because of that, I understood the way he thought. That gave me an edge when it came to comprehending these things."

"I don't think you give yourself enough credit," he said. He stood and put the papers into the case Kate had taken them out of, retying it. "I can take the transcribed ones with me tonight, and I believe that we will be able to move on them soon."

"What does that mean for me?" she asked.

"Renee will be here in the morning to help you pack only the essentials," he said. "Make it look like you're going on holiday, just to get away for a bit and recoup from everything that has happened in the last couple of months. She'll take you and Bridgette to my home where you'll be safe."

"Where will you be?"

"I need to bring these to my supervisor," he said. "Once he's been able to review them, I believe we will be moving swiftly to apprehend the guilty within this organization and shut it down."

"And what happens when that is complete?"

"We go back to the way things were," he said.

Kate blinked, then asked, "But what will become of me? I can't go back to before because that life no longer exists."

Reginald could see the fear and frustration in her face and he went to her, gathering her in his arms.

"There, there," he soothed. "I'll still take care of you. I promised Louis you would not be lost when things moved forward. I am a man of my word and will care for you."

Kate struggled to maintain her composure, unsure of what exactly her future held.

"Can you handle gathering the originals into a secure location so that when Renee comes for you, they will be readily accessible?"

Kate nodded, wiping under her eyes to remove the tear stains.

"Louis said you were strong," he said holding her at arms-length. "I won't let you down. Do you trust me?"

Looking into his eyes, Kate saw exactly what Renee had told her earlier. There was a caring, sure, but it seemed to go deeper. It was more than simply caring for a friend's widow, it was caring for her, as she was, without Louis. She smiled weakly, stepping back from him.

"I'm sorry," he said. "I shouldn't have been so forward."

"Oh no," she replied. "We just need to be a little more careful. It wouldn't do to have someone assuming that what we've found was a fabrication."

"True," he said. "I will take the transcribed documents, but I want you to hold onto the originals. This way they will be safe if something happens to me."

"Are you in danger?" Kate asked, suddenly fearing she'd lose another man close to her.

"Merely a possibility," he said. "Nothing to worry about, really. Do you need Renee to help you pack? Or are you able to manage on your own?"

"I think I can manage," Kate replied. "What time should I expect her?"

"I'll have her come around the start of business," he said. "That will give you tonight to gather what you need. Let Mags and her boy help you with anything you can't manage. I trust them."

Kate nodded, then asked, "When will I see you again?"

"Hopefully I'll be able to join you at the house within a week," he said. "But don't worry if I don't show. This may take longer."

He stepped up to her again, placing his arms around her. "Please don't worry about me," he said.

Kate sniffed back tears and embraced him. Whether his comforting her was as Renee suggested, or simply that of a caring friend, it didn't matter.

"I'm worried," Renee said as she and Kate sat in the parlor of Reginald's home.

"It's only been a week," Kate said, trying to reassure her friend.

"We should have heard something by now."

"He said it could take time," Kate assured. She was concerned as well, but was hopeful that news would come soon that this was all over.

"Have you written anything?" Renee asked.

Kate had taken to keeping an accounting of her daily activities, as well as her concerns surrounding the situation she found herself in. She made sure that she packed Louis' fountain pen, along with the copy of the book he'd used for the cypher. Transcribing an already created text was much simpler than creating one of your own. It had been a good task to keep her mind occupied and away from the fear that something might have happened to Reginald.

"My most recent entry is nearly complete," she said.

"Reg would love to read them," Renee said. "He's always been interested in writing."

"Oh," Kate said. "I doubt he'd be interested in reading an accounting of my days. It's rather mundane."

"I know about the cypher," Renee said. Kate blanched, looking at her friend. "I've always known," she continued. "Reg thought it would be better if you didn't know. That way you could keep everything hidden."

"Going the other way is much more time consuming," Kate said with a sigh. "I'm not sure how Louis did it so swiftly. Many of the reports were fairly new, so he must have been writing them in the code rather than converting them."

"That would seem like a much simpler way to go about it," Renee said.

"If I could do that, I would," Kate said.

They spent the next several days discussing Kate's documents. She was pleased that her writing of the code was becoming easier, but still had to work slowly. When the second week had passed, both women worried that they wouldn't see Reginald. By the time the third week rolled around Renee had become inconsolable, fearing that her brother would never come home, and that they would never hear what happened to him.

"Mrs. Kent," the butler, Arthur, said as he entered the study where Kate spent most of her time.

"Yes," she responded.

"This post has arrived for you," he said, handing over a letter.

"Thank you," she said, taking it from him. She slid her finger under the seal and pulled a single sheet of paper from the envelope.

Kate,

I hope this finds you well. My stay has been extended, but I anticipate arriving within the week. Please ensure my sister is cared for. Your work has been well received, and there are discussions that continue around how you will be able to assist in the future.

Regards,
Reg

Kate breathed a sigh of relief at the note. She recognized his handwriting, having taken the time to reread the letters he'd sent to Louis. The anticipation of his return brought a feeling she was uncomfortable with. She needed to let Renee know that her brother would be back soon.

Stepping to the study door she noticed a man standing in the foyer. It only took a moment to recognize him as one of the men who sat at the table the day she'd met with the Guild for the Society. It seemed like it had been an eternity since that day, yet merely a few months had passed. He didn't see her, so she stepped back into the shadows the study offered, but stayed close to listen in on the conversation he was having with Renee.

"He hasn't been home in weeks," Renee said.

"There are tasks he is to attend to," the man blustered. "He is to be available when the Guild needs his services. This is unacceptable."

"I understand," Renee said. "If I had information on where he was, I would gladly let you know. The problem is, he has left me alone. This isn't the first time, as you are aware. Perhaps he is on an errand for another member of the Society."

"The Guild has priority," the man stated. "We are to be informed if he is going to be unavailable. His not ensuring us of his whereabouts is tantamount to insubordination. He will be dealt with upon his return."

"When he comes back," Renee said. "I will let him know to come see you immediately."

"Please," the man said, then turned and left.

After Kate was sure he was gone she stepped from the study and went to her friend.

"Should we be worried?" she asked.

"No," Renee said with a sigh. "This happens every time Reg goes off. They just want to keep him under their thumb and at their beck and call. The good news is that I doubt they know about his trip."

"I've received word," Kate said, handing the letter to her friend.

Renee read the note, then reread it. Looking up, she asked, "When did this come?"

"Just a few minutes ago," Kate replied. "Arthur brought it to me."

"Do you know if it was before or after Mr. Montgomery showed up?"

"Honestly," she said. "I would guess they arrived around the same time."

"Arthur," Renee called, then made her way toward the kitchen, Kate following in her wake. The man in question met them half way. "When did this post arrive?" Renee asked, holding the letter aloft.

"Just before your visitor," he replied.

"Do you know if he saw it?"

"He did not," the man said. "The messenger came by the back entrance."

"Good," Renee said.

"Why would it matter?" Kate asked.

"Reg didn't check in with the Society," she said. "He's done that before, but usually hasn't been gone more than a day or two. With his extended absence, though, they are suspicious of what he may be doing. Their very nature is suspicion, so the fact that they don't know where one of their subordinates is causes concern."

"It sounded like you fielded the questions easily," Kate said.

"Practice," Renee replied.

"What do we do now?"

"We wait," she said. "Reg is a man of his word, so I expect to see him soon. Arthur," she said, turning to the man. "Can you do me a favor and pull out some of Reg's clothes? Ones he'd use if he were doing some labor work."

"Of course," the man replied, turning to do as asked.

"What is that for?" Kate asked.

"We'll use them as a decoy," Renee said. Kate looked at her confused, so she continued. "If we have Mags washing them, it will give the illusion that Reg is back, and everything is right."

"They'll believe that?" Kate asked.

"It's worked in the past," Renee said. "If they call, we can simply tell them that he is resting. The work clothes give the illusion that his time was spent doing manual labor."

"Do they know I'm here?" Kate asked, suddenly concerned with her own safety.

"I informed them last week," Renee replied. "I wanted to make sure that they weren't snooping around your place thinking you'd run off with him."

"Why would they think that?"

"You really have no idea how he looks at you, do you," Renee said.

"He doesn't look at me in any particular way," Kate replied.

"If that's what you want to believe," she said. "I'll leave you to your illusions. Right now, though, we need to make sure that we have a story ready for Reg. One that will be believable, should they come calling."

"You're up."

Kate startled, then turned. "You're back," she whispered.

"Yes," Reginald said. "But we need to get you, Bridgette, and Renee packed and out of here."

"Why? What's wrong?"

"I'll tell you when we've arrived at our destination," he said.

"I don't want you to have to lie if you are asked what is going on."

The ominous tone worried Kate, but she had grown to trust this man.

"Pack light," he said as a warning. "We need to be out of here in ten minutes."

Kate made quick work of packing up a small bag for herself and her daughter, then met Renee and Reginald in the study.

"Good," he said. "You two will go with Arthur now. I'll follow in an hour or so. I need to make sure that everything here is taken care of. Have you got the work Louis did?"

"Let me grab it," Kate said, reaching into the desk. Swiftly she released a latch near the back which held a secret compartment. She'd found it when she was trying to find a place to keep the documents when she'd first arrived.

"Clever," Reginald said. "Didn't think you'd find that one."

"You underestimate me," she replied with a smile.

"Shall we?" Renee asked, hoisting her bag. She caught the way her brother and friend bantered. They would be a good match once this Society business was over.

Kate picked up her daughter, then grabbed her own bag. "I have been working on something," she said to Reginald as they made their way toward the back of the house.

"I'd be interested in seeing it," he replied. "First, though, we need to get you to safety."

Arthur stepped in from the back and said, "They're are set to go, sir."

"Perfect," Reginald said. "Take the ladies to the cottage. I will follow shortly."

"Mags and Jackson will go," Arthur said. "I'm staying and will go when you do."

Reginald nodded. "Off you go, ladies," he said as they stepped into the carriage. Mags and Jackson were both in the driver's seat.

"Stay safe, Reg," Renee said.

"Please," Kate agreed.

"You won't have time to miss us," he said as he closed the door. He slapped the side of the conveyance and it took off. Turning, he and Arthur returned to the house.

"What do you need me to do?" Arthur asked.

"Follow me," Reginald said. "We don't have much time, and we have to make it look good."

"They said they'd be an hour behind us," Renee said as she paced the room.

"It's been scarcely over that, now," Kate reassured. "They'll be here soon, I'm sure."

Just then they heard a horse out front, and then another. Both women stood still, looking at the door, waiting anxiously. The door burst open and Reginald came through, Arthur on his heels.

"Let's go," Reginald said as Arthur blew past to the back of the cabin.

"But I thought we were staying," Kate said, confused.

"There's been a change of plans," he said.

The others came from the kitchen area, basket in hand, and followed Arthur out.

"What's happened?" Renee asked her brother.

"We were seen," he said. "I don't think they saw where we went. I just want to be sure you're safe."

"Who are you talking about?" Kate asked.

"The Society," Reginald said as if it explained everything. "Come."

Kate followed him out the door, her daughter in her arms.

"Can you ride?" Reginald asked, and Kate blanched, looking at the horses saddled in the road. "I take that as a no."

"I'll figure it out," she said.

"Here," Renee said. "Let me help you get Bridgette ready."

Kate relinquished her daughter to her friend and continued to stare at the large beasts pawing the ground and snorting.

"Kate," Reginald said, stepping between her and the horses. "Kate." It took a moment for her to react. "It's going to be all right. You'll ride with me."

He mounted the horse as Renee helped Kate situate Bridgette in a sling across her mother's chest. Once she was in place, she steered her over to the horse Reg was on. He reached down, and Kate stared at his hand, completely at a loss as to what to do.

"Up you go," Arthur said as he hoisted Kate in front of Reginald.

Kate clung to her child, unsure exactly what to do. Reginald put his arms around her and pulled her back, closer to him. It was uncomfortable but would have to do. Within moments the rest of the group were on their horses and away they rode. Kate had Louis' satchel with his papers, along with her own notes, and his copy of the Dickens' book. Bridgette seemed completely at ease with her situation, nodding off once they were in motion.

When they finally stopped, Kate's body was sore in ways she wasn't used to. The others seemed to be faring much better than her.

"We'll rest for an hour or so," Reginald said. "Then we'll need to move along."

"Where are we going?" Kate asked.

"I have a friend a few hours away," he said. "We'll stay there for a few days and wait for word that it's over. For now, though, let's just rest."

"Bridgette needs to be fed," Kate said. "And I need something to drink. Do you have any water?"

"Here," he said, handing over a canteen. "I'll be over there."

With that, he got up and left her to tend her child. Before long, it was time for them to be on their way. Again, Kate was settled in front of Reginald, Bridgette strapped to her chest, fed and sleeping. Before long, Kate nodded off herself.

"Here we are," Reginald said as they came upon another small cottage.

"Welcome," a woman said as she stepped out the door. "We've got room for all of you. How long will you be here?"

"Shouldn't be more than a day or two," Reginald said as he helped Kate to the ground.

The others had already dismounted, Arthur gathering the reins of the horses and leading them around to the back of the cottage. Kate took in the view, amazed that they had traveled so far in such a short amount of time.

Everyone stopped and turned toward the road as a stranger rode up at a brisk gallop. He slid to a stop and Reginald put Kate behind him, the horse between them and the new man.

"I bring news," he said as he dismounted.

"What news?" Reginald demanded.

The man reached into his pocket and produced a letter, handing it over. Reginald took the letter, keeping an eye the other man. Kate stepped up beside him and read over his shoulder.

RG-
The threat has been removed. All is safe.
-TM

"When did you get this?" Reginald asked.

"Three days past," the man said.

"This isn't possible," Reginald said, rereading the note.

The air split with an explosion. Kate found herself on the ground, Reginald atop her, unable to hear anything but a ringing in her ears and Bridgette screaming.

"I've got him," came a familiar voice. "Are you hit?"

"He's been lying to me for months," Kate said.

Louis turned her to look at him and said, "It's what had to happen."

"I still don't understand how you're here," she said.

"We knew time was short," Louis said. "I hadn't intended it to happen the way it did."

"How could you?" she barked. "You didn't just put my life in turmoil. I could have lost Bridgette."

"I truly am sorry," he replied.

"Sorry?" she shouted. "Sorry isn't good enough, Louis. Sorry doesn't negate the fact that I lost you, that I nearly lost our daughter, that I have spent the last several months in perpetual fear because of where you left me."

"And I will make it up to you," he tried.

"How?" she spat. "You can't give me back the last few months. Can't remove the fear and anger and sorrow I dealt with. There isn't anything you can do to make it up."

"Please, Kate," Louis tried.

"No," Kate said, walking away.

"What have I done?" Louis asked.

They spent an additional two weeks in the cabin, but finally received word the Society had been taken down. By the time they returned to the city, Louis and Kate had come to an understanding. He and Reginald testified against the higher-ranking members of the Society, finishing their assignment. After that, Louis resigned from his position, taking up an appointment in the local government office, one that used his skills with cryptography and words.

Reginald stayed in town with his sister, also finding a place within the local government. Renee and Kate continued their friendship, growing closer as time went on. Reginald and Louis continued to work together, though did not see each other outside of the office much. Reginald simply couldn't get over the fact that he'd had to lie to Kate for months, watching her suffer, knowing that one word from him would have eased her pain.

Louis understood his friend's reluctance to maintain their

close relationship. He mourned the loss of his friendship. There were times he wished he could change what happened, taking on the Society head on, rather than in the manner with which they used. But the past could not be changed, so he respected the space Reg put between them.

Kate;

My heart is divided between pleasure and regret. We were introduced through the worst of circumstances, and I would do anything to erase the suffering you went through. While I am happy you have your family intact, there are so many things I wish could have been different.

You are brilliant beyond measure, and your beauty is breathtaking. The way your mind works is nothing less than remarkable, and the way you love is infinite. Louis is more than lucky to have you at his side.

I know that if anything happens to him, I will be there for you, in whatever capacity you desire. I promised Louis before, and I'll hold to that word, that I will take care of you should the unforeseen arise. My heart will never be fully mine, for you own a greater portion than you should.

Yours forever;
Reg

He reread what he wrote, then crumpled the note and threw it into the fire. He was happy for Kate, truly, but had grown to love her more than just as the wife of his friend. Unfortunately, those feelings would have to remain hidden. Perhaps, with time, he would be able to be around her without feeling the incredible loss of what might have been.

Pencil

Zombees

by Mark Miller

I thought about recording this on a CD or old cassette tape, maybe even trying to record part of it on my cell phone. Or try to type it on my laptop. Then I thought about whether or not there would be a power grid or technical support when it was found by someone to play it. The way things are going, I think the people who recover this may not have those capabilities of using a CD or some other 21st Century technology. So, I decided to try writing it down with pencil and paper, poor penmanship and all. Besides, a good law enforcement officer always has a writing instrument and paper for field notes. I hope my graying hair and fat aging body will hold up until I can finish this.

Of course, connected to the "how" I am doing this is the question as to "why?" The answer is quite simple. I believe I was one of those Ground Zero people who saw the Infestation from the very beginning. I saw it and experienced it. Who better to record the events than an original eyewitness?

I was returning home from my wife's gravesite, running late to the daily afternoon feeding time of our four dogs. Funny how

I still say "our" dogs when it is only me now. My wife had died without warning two weeks prior. She had collapsed while practicing with our church choir, died almost instantly from an aneurysm. At least that was the official medical diagnosis. Knowing the cause of death does not soften the blow of death. The Grim Reaper is cruel. I had just finished the final arrangements for her gravestone. The memorial service had been held the previous week, and I was still numb as I drove west towards the Narrows Bridge. I would not admit the fact of my condition to myself. Years of law enforcement experience made you tough, right? Yeah, sure.

Washington weather was blessing us with the infamous Washington drool. That is what my wife and I called the not mist, not rain, not drizzle, but a miserable wet something which was obscuring my vision as night approached on the early autumn day. It was depressing weather for a depressing day. Only my LEO, Law Enforcement Officer training, and auto-reflexes enabled me to see and swerve around the figure that was running straight into my headlights on the west side of the Narrows Bridge. The woman driving behind me was not so lucky. The running figure hit her straight between her high beams, flipping up and over her compact car. The young blonde woman was fortunate as the body did not crash through her windshield, killing her also.

As it was, she careened off to the right shoulder of the highway, screeching to a halt. I braked my SUV to a stop then slammed it into reverse. I accelerated the SUV back to her car.

Her airbag had deployed and given her a bloody nose. As I approached her popped out drivers side window, she began to scream.

"Lady, it's okay," I said. "I saw it all. He ran into you. He almost hit me."

I grabbed her hand with my left as I dialed my cell phone with my right. Vehicles behind me came to screeching, sliding halts as their headlights illuminated the broken body on the side of the road. State Troopers and EMT were there in minutes, their flashing red and blue lights splashing colored shadows over the Narrows Bridge. I had a quick flashback to my college days of "Acid Rock" dances, pans of water and oil projected by opaque projectors on a dorm common room wall, with a taint of unwashed bodies and whacky tobacky. Then, I was back to the present, holding onto a stranger's hand, trying to give her comfort.

The EMTs soon had a neck brace on her, slow in removing her from her wrecked car as I gave my statement to the young trooper. I had shown her my retired credentials, which loosened her up a bit. She now knew she would not have to drag details out of me.

"So he ran right at you, Mister Adams?" the trooper asked.

"Yes, Ma'am. The Grace of God and years of defensive and pursuit drivers training kept me from having a body impaled in my windshield." Even an aging greying hair overweight white guy can get it right once in a while.

"And he came from there?" She pointed to the center area of the highway which separated the lanes and their directions of travel.

"Yes, Ma'am. I saw him as he came running full tilt from right there." I pointed to the spot.

"Despite this Washington drool, my lights caught him just right, so I got a good look. Otherwise..."

The young Trooper smiled. "Washington drool. I like that. Mind if I use it?"

"Have at it. Compliments of my late wife and me."

I saw the flash of concern cross her face, even in the limited light. LEOs feel, care for each other, just like soldiers.

"Recent?"

"Yes. Two weeks ago. Quick, no suffering."

She paused for a moment, then continued. "I've got enough for my report. Can you come in tomorrow and complete a full written statement?"

"Sure, Ma'am. Do you have a card?"

The trooper pulled a small waterproof case from her pocket—required equipment in wet Washington—and gave me her business card.

"Trooper Betty Robinson. Please to meet you. Are you out of Tacoma or Bremerton?"

"Bremerton, near Auto Row."

"I know where that's at. You work the afternoon shift, so I'll see you then."

Trooper Robinson smiled a little. "You take care. Sorry about your wife."

"Thanks. Like they say, one day at a time."

I watched the trooper walk away to continue her investigation. She was young enough to be my daughter. But that ship had sailed years ago. My wife and I never had any children. If we had, I would hope they would have been like the trooper.

I made my way back to my SUV, entered and sat for a moment. Other than my wife, it had been a while since I had seen a dead body. Plus, I had seen this death happened. I put my seatbelt on, started my vehicle up and headed home. About twenty minutes later I was letting the four dogs out into the large fenced backyard as I prepared their food. I gave some extra attention to Simba, who had been "her" dog. The Great Pyrenees had been devoted to her, was taking her death hard.

"Yeah, Big Guy. I miss her too," I said to him as I scratched his ears. Then I had to pet and hug the other three, including the Great Dane who tried to sit on my lap. She still thought she was a puppy. I gave them each a bone to chew on and turned the television to a local news show. Sure enough, the Talking Heads had a live report going on, a film crew broadcasting from the shoulder as the traffic began to flow past the site of the death. Just as the female reporter was explaining the event, the cameraman was heard yelling "Hey!" as he saw a figure dart out onto the highway behind the reporter. The camera picked up the live action of a figure running directly into the path of an accelerating semi-tractor trailer. The feed went dark as the body disappeared beneath the wheels of the large truck.

"Shit," I said out loud. "Something is definitely wrong."

The next morning I got up, fed the dogs, let them out and then watched the various news broadcasts. The story was now that two people, one male, and one female, had both dashed into traffic at almost the same spot on the westbound lanes coming off the Narrows Bridge. Now the story was law enforcement was investigating some new type of bath salts as the source of this bizarre behavior. Other than that story, all the involved officials were keeping their cards close to their vests.

I went to the local Big Box Store, picked up some large bags of dog food, some chicken alfredo from the deli, and a large bottle of high-end Scotch. I dropped the goods off at home, then went to the State Patrol office to finish my statement. I met Trooper Robinson with a smile.

"See, I can tell time even at my age."

She laughed. "You're not that old. And you still have fast reflexes to have dodged that runner."

I shrugged. "I have a young friend training me, trying to get this tired body back into some resemblance of shape. I work on the speed and heavy bags. It helps keep me at least feeling younger."

"Well, Mr. Adams..."

"Please call me Nick. Mr. Adams was my Dad."

"Okay, Nick. You look just fine, and I have the forms all ready for you. So you can get back to enjoying retirement as quickly as possible."

"Thanks, Ma'am."

"If I call you Nick, you can call me Betty. Deal?"

"Deal. Now, bring on the government forms. I'll see if they've changed that much."

It was enjoyable to be in a cop shop again, with its unique

feel. So the time flew by. I told the Good Trooper Robinson I was easy to get a hold of if anyone needed some more information.

"No, I think this will do it. By the way, Nick. That young lady whose hand you held wanted me to tell you, 'Thanks.' Said something about wanting to give you a big kiss."

I laughed. "The woman was young enough to be my daughter. But if you see her again, give her my telephone number. Sometimes it helps to talk about these things with someone who was there. She's lucky to be alive."

"Will do, Nick. By the way, anyone ever tells you that you're a nice guy?"

"Please. Don't let that get around. It will destroy years of my work at being an asshole."

That got Betty laughing until I said goodbye. This was a good day, made me feel like I had accomplished something. I went home, spent time with the dogs, drank some Scotch, wrote on my computer then went to bed. No need for extra heat, as I had a Four Dog Night.

The dogs woke me up while it was still dark out. They seemed restless. When I let them out, the Dane and the Boxer went to the gate facing the front yard and began to bark at something on the street. I went down and peeked out the front door. A person was standing motionless, staring straight up into the street light lamp near my house. I watched the figure for some five minutes. Still, there was no movement.

"That is not right," I said to myself.

I called 911, told the Dispatcher what was happening. The way she reacted, saying they would have someone respond as soon as possible, gave me a hint that my phone call was not the first. I made sure the figure was still there, then got the dogs back inside. I gave them all a biscuit to keep them occupied for a moment and turned on the TV. I soon saw that all the cable network news stations had "Breaking News" about reports of either people running at car lights or standing and staring at street lamps and other bright light sources. Right now, it seemed to be centralized around the Pacific Northwest, specifically Seattle/Tacoma and out onto the Kitsap Peninsula. The bath salts story was bandied around, but the bottom line was no one had any good idea as to what was going on. I went back to check on the body out front, now with a pistol in my hand. I saw the ambulance and County Sheriff's car pull up a few yards from the figure.

After a short conference, the Sheriff's Deputy and two burly EMTs approached the character and soon had him (I could tell it was male now) wrapped up in what looked like a straight jacket. I watched as they placed him in the back of the ambulance. Then they were gone. I shrugged and went back to bed, the dogs settling down.

I am not a morning person, never have been. My wife used to be the one that was early to rise, took care of the dogs. Now it's up to me. So the Dane and the Boxer, the Two Girls, woke me up with licks to the face to tell me it was feeding time at the Zoo. I rolled out of bed, went to the kitchen. The Two Boys, the Pyrenees and the Lab followed my every move as I prepared their dog food dishes. Then all of my four-legged family members were chowing down, enjoying one of the highlights of their day. The phone rang as the dogs were finishing their breakfast. It was my friend Craig, my Trainer. He called to say they had canceled school, so he did not have to teach today. He asked if I wanted to train later. I said sure. The house became lonely even with four furry friends to keep me company. Craig was someone I could talk with about anything, no matter how weird.

I decided I would run a few errands before I went over to Craig's. I made sure the dogs had water, gave them a small treat and told them that Yes, I would be back. With my wife gone, they were always a little insecure about me leaving. I went down to Big Five Sports in Port Orchard to check the sales out. I always looked at the shotguns and rifles they sell although I had a gun collection that was already becoming too large. Oh well, you have to have a hobby.

I had just walked into the store when I heard some yelling and loud voices from outside. Old habits die hard, and I found myself heading back outside the store. I found a twenty-something woman with wide eyes and blood running from her nose trying to grab a child from a stroller. The woman pushing the strolled, the assumed mother, turned into a screaming banshee and knocked the woman to the ground. I then saw a wide-eyed and bloody-nosed man approaching the mother and child from behind. Out came my snubby thirty-eight five shot as I walked fast to intercept the man.

"Lady, take your child to your car," I yelled and then placed myself between the unknown man and the baby stroller. My pistol and my presence did not seem to register in the brain of the man, as he kept walking as if I were not there. So, rather than shoot a whacked out man with no visible weapons, I went to Plan B. I planted my boot into his kneecap. As he stumbled, I swung my left and planted my fist into his jaw. The heavy bag workouts must have paid off as he went straight down. Street sense told me the female of the pair was getting to her feet for round two with the mother and child. I put my pistol away and planted a kick to her chest which sent her sprawling. Again, the single-mindedness desire to get to the woman and child.

Flashing lights and siren announced the arrival of a County Sheriff's vehicle, with a Port Orchard Police Patrol car right behind it. I stepped back, held my hands out to show I had no weapons in them. It wasn't necessary.

"Damn, two more of them," the large deputy said as he walked towards the two bloody-nosed humans. In a smooth move, he drew his Taser and shot the woman, who had been trying to rise one more time. She spasmed, and blood sprayed from her nose. She then lay still.

"I'll call the EMTs," the young, dark-haired police officer said as she keyed her radio.

"These two trying to get to that mother and baby?" the Deputy asked.

"Yes, Sir. They act totally out of it."

"Fourth call this morning. I don't know what people are on, but they are completely bonkers. Pepper spray just pisses them off. A shot of Taser seems to do the trick."

I then saw something that would give me nightmares. An approximate three-inch insect looking, creature, came crawling out of the downed man's mouth.

"What the fuck is THAT?!" I yelled and pointed.

"SHIT!" the deputy exclaimed and went for his pistol. A stream of pepper spray came from the direction of the female patrolman. It hit the insect creature, dowsing some wings it was about to use. I managed to lunge forward and crushed it under my boot.

"Another one," the deputy yelled out. Sure enough, a second insect, a bit smaller, was making its way from the mouth of the man. Before anyone else could react, the Deputy pumped two pistol rounds into the face and head of the apparent source of the creatures. The oversized bee looking creature was knocked aside by the impacts of the bullets. It was still moving.

"You shot that man," exclaimed the female officer.

"That's no man! That's some kind of space monster, with bugs in its head," the deputy yelled.

My attention was on the bee looking creature. It seemed stunned, looking ever so much like an oversized honeybee with two differences. There was a large ovipositor extruding from its abdomen, and the rear pair of six legs were like smaller versions of cricket, reversed knee joints more for jumping than crawling. I carefully stepped forward and crushed the bee creature's front with the toe of my boot. I wanted that weird looking rear end intact.

"Anybody have an evidence bag?" I asked as calm as possible.

"What are you going to do with that…the thing," the Deputy asked.

"I hope you two can get it to a police laboratory of some kind. Otherwise. I think it's time to call the CDC. This may make Ebola look like the common cold."

"That's above my pay grade. I'm calling for back up." The deputy started to talk on his radio as the police officer handed me an evidence bag. I pulled my folding knife out and flipped the odd insect into the bag with the blade.

"You a retired LEO?" She asked.

"Yes Ma'am, Homeland Security. I have my retired creds…"

"No need. You have that look, reactions of one. I'll make sure the body of that nasty bug gets to the right people." The female officer shook her head. "Lots of explaining as to why he shot that guy in the head."

"It may sound weird, but he has a point. That was no longer a man. That was a breeding spot of Things that do not look of Earth origin."

Just then a large EMT van came blasting across the parking lot, red and blue lights flashing. It made no effort to slow down, zipped by us and slammed into the entrance of Big Five Sports. I got a glimpse of the driver as the van went by. He looked like he was clawing at something on his neck.

I now knew that things had gone entirely to shit. Time to take care of myself and my dogs. I went with the deputy to the now smashed opened store entrance. It was pure luck that no one other than the driver was hurt. The EMT in back of the vehicle exited and went to the driver to help. The store staff and customers were all staring at the van sitting in the front part of the store, the emergency lights still flashing, and with the early hints of leaking radiator coolant smell. I slipped back to the gun counter. By pure chance, a shipment of firearms had just been delivered. The clerks had been inventorying and checking them when the van smashed through the storefront. Now the shipment was forgotten in the hubbub and destruction.

I stepped through the swinging door that led to the back of the counter, the warning buzzer connected to the door ignored because of all the commotion up front. I grabbed a box of thirty-eight caliber target rounds, then a small package of pre-fragmented hollow points. I saw the box on top of the new shipment contained a foreign knock-off of a 'Home Defense' twelve gauge shotgun with a shortened barrel. The box was partially opened, so it was easy for me to open it all the way and grab the weapon. It would do. I grabbed some five round boxes of slug and buck shot, then opened up a large box of target loads for skeet shooting. I grabbed a couple of shells and slid them into the shotgun's tube magazine, then dumped some more into my vest pockets along with the other ammunition. My pockets were beginning to bulge.

I exited the counter area, grabbed a small can of spray lubricant as I did. Most firearms were shipped with a slight veneer of oil and protection fluid, but I may need more to prevent jams. I went up to the new emergency vehicle redesigned entrance to the store. I approached when a bee creature flew out of the EMT van and up to the store ceiling. It latched onto the side of the suspended light fixture, looked to me as if it were surveying us humans below. I did not give it a chance to do anything else, I racked the skeet load into the chamber, aimed and fired without hesitation. Despite the short barrel the skeet shot still had enough oomph and pattern to do a number on the insect.

The remains fell to the floor. Everyone jumped when I fired. I ejected the spent case and chambered the next round. I began to feed other shells into the shotgun's tube from my pocket.

"Hey, you can't do that," the gun counter clerk said. "You haven't even bought that shotgun yet!"

"Police emergency. I'll fill the ATF forms out later, if you have a ballpoint pen."

"Like hell, you will. Give it back!" The handsome and sizeable young man began to approach me as if to grab the shotgun. He looked like he was hired to sell workout equipment. I pointed it at his face.

"Ever see what birdshot does at close range? Your girlfriend won't like the results."

The young clerk froze. I then addressed the small crowd of people.

"As they say in cheap Sci-Fi movies, life as you know it has just ended. That bug I just killed is getting into people's brains, driving them nuts, and making them dangerous. There are dozens of them out there. I suggest you become armed and protect your families."

"Good advice," the deputy said. He turned and exited the store. The deputy left the EMT driver to the man's partner and left the store before anyone else could protest. I called to him as he went to his patrol car.

"Deputy, is more help on the way?"

"I doubt it." He opened his patrol car door. "There are at least another dozen reports of situations like this here. And it's happening in Tacoma now, maybe Seattle. Anyway, what you said is a good idea. I just retired on duty. My family needs protection from these... things."

With that last statement, he entered his patrol car and accelerated away at a high rate of speed. I saw the female police officer standing with a shocked look on her face as he disappeared up Mile Hill Road.

"What the fuck am I supposed to do by myself?" she asked no one in particular.

"Protect yourself, young lady. Here, hand me that bee creature sample. I'll get it to someone who can examine it."

She realized she still had the evidence bag in her hand. The EMT van crashing into Big Five had stopped everything else. She handed me the bag.

"You be careful, Mister. I have to stay here, help the EMTs, and make sure no more bugs come out of the dead man. Or his girlfriend."

I shrugged. "Suit yourself. I think that Taser fried any bugs in the woman. I also think she may be dead. Good luck."

"Same to you," she replied. Then she walked towards the wrecked EMT van.

I made quick work of getting into my SUV and hauling ass up Mile Hill road. I felt some guilt about leaving the female officer, but Hell, I wasn't even on duty anymore. And I did not want to find my four dogs dead from having these bugs eating their brains. They were my family now.

I turned onto Long Lake Road and accelerated. A mile down I saw the flashing emergency lights of a State Patrol cruiser on the side of the road. I slowed down, then braked to a stop as I saw legs on the pavement in front of the stopped vehicle.

"Please don't let it be Betty," I selfishly said to myself as I grabbed the shotgun and exited my SUV. As I 'Cut the Pie' with the shotgun around the front of the patrol car, I soon saw the body was male. He had been shot in the head with a large caliber weapon. A quick search and scan of the area revealed nothing else. No shell casings, no bugs, no nothing. Some type of insects crawling around inside people's heads making them nuts and some everyday asshole has to shoot a cop. This was just great.

I reached down and took the Troopers service automatic from his holster. He wouldn't need it anymore. I press checked it to make sure a round was in the chamber, then returned to my vehicle and drove off. I wished I had time to do something with the body but right now the living took precedent. I managed to cross Sedgwick Road despite some ferry traffic. It seemed the Washington State Ferry System had not gotten the word that all Hell was breaking loose in Kitsap County. As I traveled further on Long Lake, I discovered who had shot the Trooper.

At the parking area of a small out of business store near

Long Lake Road, I came upon a beat-up pick-up blocking another car near the store's dead gas pumps. A large and extreme scraggly looking man was trying to pull a middle-aged woman from her compact sedan through the open driver's door. The woman was fighting back, kicking and screaming. The long-haired and greasy man was trying to get her out of her seat belt and out of her car. As he did, he was babbling the mantra of a meth head high on crystal meth. Lots of it.

"End of the world, bitch. Get out so we can have some fun before we die. Help me get your seat belt off, dammit. I'll give you a hit of my stuff."

Setting on the top of the woman's car was a huge revolver, which seemed to belong to Mister Meth Head. I knew that was the gun that had killed the state trooper. The trooper's pistol was in my hands. I brought it up in a good two hand grip and shot him in his exposed right leg. Meth Head did not even notice me until the forty caliber bullet smashed into his right knee. He screamed and fell from the open door of the car. I walked up and grabbed the large revolver from atop the vehicle.

"Back your car up, lady. Get the Hell home." I didn't have to say that twice. Within seconds she was backing up, maneuvered out onto Long Lake Road and took off at a high rate of speed. Mister Meth Head kept screaming and holding his bleeding leg.

"You fucker, fucker, fucker..." he babbled and sobbed.

"Where in the Hell did you get this .460 Smith and Wesson Magnum revolver?" I asked. "This is the first time I've seen one up close. How did an asshole like you get this?" He didn't answer. Even all the meth in his veins could not counteract the pain in his knee. Judging by the amount of blood I saw, the pistol round had taken out some important blood vessels at least.

He kept babbling and sobbing, so I left him there. He would have raped that woman, maybe killed her, so I felt no guilt. Not to mention it was him who killed the trooper. A quick death was too good for him.

I made it back to my home some two miles away. I parked, grabbed the shotgun I had liberated from Big Five and beat feet to the front door. I hit the auto locking on my key fob to lock my SUV, then found my front door key. All my dogs were barking, a good sign.

I closed and locked the front door after entering, my dogs crowding around me, agitated. I slumped on my stairs to the upper level of my house and began to shake. My K-9 family whined and licked me. They were trying to reassure me as much as they were seeking reassurance.

They wanted out, so I took them out the lower level back door to the backyard. As I did, I froze for a moment. On the floor of the downstairs hallway were the crunched remains of some half a dozen of those bee creatures. It was apparent the dogs saw or smelled them and quickly took care of them. They had come thru a small doggie door the previous homeowner had made for his small dog. None of mine were small. I secured it, then let the dogs out the back door.

As soon as they were outside, they were running around the over half acre backyard. I froze as I saw some large insects flying around. Bee creatures.

But my four dogs took care of them, snapping at them, knocking them down from the air. I thought of the rock group Heart's 'Dog and Butterfly', the dogs rolling back down to the warm, soft ground laughing, barking, chomping, especially the Great Dane. Despite her size, my Tuxedo Dane liked to leap like a gazelle, even over the other dogs. She was death on the bugs.

I knocked a couple down with the sheet shot, the noise and blast seemed to cause the other bee creatures to veer away from my backyard. Soon, all was quiet, except for the panting of my dogs.

I got them back inside, scrambled up the stairs as fast as I could get my aging body to go, turned on the television. Every channel was going to the "Breaking News" route. Some wiseacre coined the name "zombees" for those infected by the bee creatures, as many others had seen what I had. The news stations jumped from location to location, up and down the West Coast.

Reports came in from Tijuana, Mexico that there was a sudden, massive outbreak of the Zombees. As I watched and listened. I filled up both my bathtubs with water, made sure all my doors and windows were secured, then started getting my arsenal in order. I added a two of my own shotguns to the one I had 'borrowed' from Big Five, and dug out several of my pistols and loaded them. A couple of rifles I had inherited from my Father with a dozen large caliber rounds gave me the security I wanted right now. I could get my assault weapons out of my safes later.

An hour after I had arrived home, the Federal Government took over the airways. The Emergency Broadcast Service system took over, causing me to flash back to the tests they did when I was a kid with CONELRAD, one of the original alert systems during the Cold War. Now it wasn't the Russians, it was something else. Or was it? I went outside to my SUV and retrieved the Troopers pistol and Meth Head's hand cannon.

When I came back in, some guy from the Center for Disease Control was on all the stations, explaining about what was now called the Infestation. Over the last few days, thousands of people had some kind of eggs laid in the back of their necks while they were either asleep, stoned, or drunk. The "bees" matured quickly at the base of the victim's skull, anywhere from one to three hatching through the mouth or nose after doing damage to the brain. Staring at the bright lights at night was a side effect as the insects matured and affected the host. A honeybee parasite did much the same thing to affected regular bees, causing them to fly around lights until they collapsed and the eggs hatched. In these large bee creatures, the maturing insects affected the human brain in such a way that the host became attracted to other humans as the hatching time came close. The CDC guessed the effect was connected, so the hatched insects have a ready and willing host nearby for more eggs. The infected thus attacked and grabbed hold of the new victims until a hatched bee creature could jam its ovipositor into the soft neck.

The next was the terrifying part. Sometimes, the host died after hatching, the damage to the brain too severe for survival. But in others, based on some hatchlings, the size of the person's skull, and other vague factors, the infected survived. But they escaped with only the most feral parts of the brain functioning. You soon had a large, and increasing, number of humans who were now two-legged extreme predatory and sometimes complete psychotic creatures. They attacked any other animal they saw. Some scientists thought the bee creatures young released chemicals that exacerbated this aggressiveness in survivors. The problem was to get sufficient zombees to test this theory.

No one knew where the bee creatures came from. They seemed to have Earth-compatible DNA strands but in unique sequences. The rumor soon started that they were some bio-weapon gone wrong. But nobody seemed to know for sure. They could have come from Mars, for all anyone knew. This unknown origin led to quick and destructive wars in some areas of the world, as old enemies blamed each other.

The zombees spread quickly. The problem was that unless the Infected were caught at the bright light stage, they were soon hatching out more bugs alone, or were locating and grabbing on to other humans to use as hosts. Children were very vulnerable, and ninety-nine percent died. Some small and more remote communities were wiped out, no one knew until the feral survivors attacked nearby communities. There was one basic fact, though. The first cases were reported around where I had seen the accident exiting the Tacoma Narrows Bridge. Ground Zero. Sometime about twenty-four to thirty-six hours prior, the man and woman killed by traffic received eggs in the back of their necks. Somewhere near where they had been, others had the same fate. Then it spread.

That last entry was thirty days ago. Things became worse very fast after the initial CDC broadcasts. The power grid began to fail in infected areas within twenty-four hours. Some of the damage was caused by whacked out looters, like the one I blew away with Meth Head's hand cannon a week into the Zombee Infection. The asshole had a ballistic vest on, so I tried the big Magnum on him. It worked. His three partners scattered for parts unknown. I took out two zombees wandering around the neighborhood before they hatched bee creatures. The power was out, so the dogs and I kept each other warm. Radio broadcasts were reduced to noon and midnight. Even with Martial Law, things fell apart. I have not seen a human being for two weeks.

So I sit here today, writing this journal with pencil and paper, still standard tech in the early 20th Century. Hopefully, someone will read it one day. I'm going to raid my neighbor's houses for some dog food and other incidentals later. An early freeze and my gas generator helped keep my perishables around until I had to cook them up, feed them to the dogs, or threw them away. Time to go scrounge.

Now I'm kind of glad my wife did pass when she did. Quick, with no suffering, according to the doctors. This would have been Hell on her. People used to worry about nuclear war. A statement made by some intellectuals was World War Three may be nuclear, but World War Four would be with sticks and stones. Now I can add that record keeping in this post-disaster world went from computers to pencils and paper.

The dogs are barking. Something is coming. If it's a zombee, I wonder where it came from?

Will write some later.

To Sketch Your Story

by Chris Davis

Tucked up under the bleachers to stay out of the early March drizzle, Sam flipped the collar of his leather jacket up around his ears in a vain attempt to keep the rain out of the back of his shirt. It was more effective than nothing, but stray drops still made their way down his spine, and he couldn't quite stifle a shiver. "Dammit, Alex," he hissed, a puff of steam floating from his mouth into the cold air. "Hurry it up." Shivering fingers that were bone white from the chill and a nasty case of poor circulation pushed a stray chunk of thick black hair off his forehead, fat drops of water dripping from the ends.

As if on cue, the crunch of gravel under light steps drifted into Sam's dark corner. They came closer and closer, then the slight figure of Alex appeared. She was shorter than Sam by a few inches, with a slim, tanned face, and long wavy black hair that she kept pulled back in an unruly ponytail. "You know, we could meet, like, *inside the building*," she said with a huff, pulling her own purple jacket tighter around her. "It's warm, and there's no rain. All vast improvements."

Instead of answering Alex's complaint, Sam blurted out "Did you bring it?" He stepped forward a little, trying to keep under the metal seats to keep the drops hanging on the edge from falling down onto him, with mixed success.

She stuck her tongue out at him, but swung her ratty backpack around to her front, balancing it on her thigh. "Of course I did. You ask, I deliver. I still don't know why you can't just go get it yourself." A moment of digging around in the clutter of her bag, then Alex produced a small plastic bag.

Barely resisting the urge to snatch it from her, Sam hooked one finger through the handle, letting it fall open as his other hand pawed through the contents; a fresh sketch book, two packs of 3B graphite pencils, and a moldable eraser. "Oh my God, Alex, you're the best!" he crowed, flinging his arms around her in a tight hug. "Thank you!"

"Yeah, no problem, smudge," she said with a laugh, patting him on the back a little awkwardly as she tried to keep her feet. "Did you already fill your other one? I swear I just bought you one last week." They separated carefully, though both lingered for a little extra warmth. "You go through those like candy."

"Yeah, I… I draw a lot," Sam said somewhat vaguely with a rolling shrug of his shoulder. He glanced over the two packs of pencils; they were the exact same ones he used before. "Oh God, Alex, you're perfect, thank you!" Sam itched to tear open the packages and just start sketching there in the rain. Instead, he closed the bag again with deliberate care, and finally looked at his friend, who raised a brow at him critically. "What? I draw a lot."

"Yeah, you said that already," Alex said as she crossed her arms. "Seriously, didn't I *just* grab you some of these? I mean, I don't mind, honest. But man, if you're gonna need so many of these, you're gonna owe me a lot more pizza."

Heat crept up the back of Sam's neck, and he cleared his throat a little awkwardly as he looked down at his heavily booted feet. "Well, it's not that, it's… well… "

Before he was forced to come up with an answer, the shrill scream of the bell resounded across the drizzle-slick field. Both students jumped, Sam swearing in surprise as Alex flung her backpack up over her shoulder and darted back out into the rain with Sam hot on her heels. They skidded across the wet steps leading up into the school, each throwing a wave over their shoulder before heading for their respective classes. Fortunately, Sam's classroom was close to the front doors, and he slid through the door on wet linoleum, much to the resigned amusement of his algebra teacher. "So good of you to join us, Sam," he drawled as he gestured to his usual empty seat in the back of the room. Grinning a little sheepishly, Sam slid along the wall and sat down in his chair, spinning his backpack down to the ground by his booted foot.

Algebra had always been Sam's least favorite class. Not because he was bad at it; on the contrary, he was an exceptional mathematician. Ever since he was a young child, he'd been drawn to numbers. The problem was, half the time he was a chapter ahead of his classmates, and bored out of his mind. Coming in as a senior, he'd had to prove fast to the teacher that he was, in fact, smart enough to tune out and still pass. That had been easy enough this time around, and the short, stocky man in his late 40s was willing to let Sam mind his own business in the back of the room, so long as he didn't disrupt the class.

Armed with his new sketch pad and pencils, completed homework on the corner of his desk, Sam ignored the class around him with practiced ease. A fresh first page lay before him, fingers drifting over the thick, faintly textured page. Laying across the top, the focal point of Sam's avid attention, was a brand new 3B graphite pencil. Steel grey on the outside with a section of tiny rubberized dots to provide a good, solid grip, it came to a dark, needle-sharp point. He glanced up once at the teacher, who paid him no mind, before picking up the pencil.

The sensation was immediately and intimately familiar against the tips of his fingers. Light, agile, a little rough to the touch. Alex had done a perfect job, picking up his favorite style without even asking. The tip skated across the page with ease as Sam started his sketch, the faint rasp of graphite against the cotton blend reaching his ears even over the noise of class. Despite himself, he couldn't stop a small smile that crept across his face at the simple pleasure of the feeling of the pencil in his hand, flying across the page. He'd been through his share of drawing implements over the years, but when it came to this sort of work, the base for any piece of art, these were his absolute favorite.

Soon the sounds of the classroom faded into white noise, leaving Sam adrift. His attention narrowed to a single point; the sound of pencil across paper, the scent of graphite as it smudged into the creases of the image and across his fingers. His mind drew the picture first, translating the story down to his fingers, and onto the page.

Class was short, so Sam knew it was going to be rough at best. But that was ok, just a quick note for Alex. Cell phones aside, they liked the "old school" method of hand written notes folded into complex shapes and mini envelopes, then tucked inconspicuously into backpacks, pockets, or lockers. His little sketch was one such note; it was a drawing of himself and Alex sitting at a dining room table. Books, cups, and notebooks were scattered across the surface, Sam hunched over something while Alex leaned back casually in her own chair, a textbook balanced on her knees. Across the top of the page in his easily recognized loopy lettering, a short note.

My folks are out late tonight. Want to come over?

Just as he finished signing his name under the seat of the chair his self-portrait sat in, the bell rang. Scooping his books down into his shoulder bag, Sam folded the note with a few quick, expert twists, then followed the herd out into the hall. He wove through his classmates, watching for Alex's dark head bobbing on its own course. It didn't take him long to spot her, and he maneuvered closer. As they passed, Sam tucked his little note into the pocket of her coat, winked, and kept walking.

Two classes later, Alex and Sam finally met up at lunch. "Hey, smudge," she said affectionately as she plopped down on the bench beside him. Her lunch box landed heavily on the table, then the same note as before dropped down on top of Sam's sandwich. He grinned in response and opened it up, blithely ignoring the irony of reading the note Alex wrote while she sat next to him. Below his sketch, he'd left enough room for Alex to respond, and she'd readily obliged. Her own handwriting wasn't nearly as tidy as Sam's; instead, it was an unruly jumble of chicken scratch that sort of resembled letters.

I finally get to see your house?! Absolutely!

Beside it, there was a rough sketch of a person with a surprised face, both hands on their cheeks. Or at least that's what Sam assumed it was meant to be. Still grinning, he tucked the note into the inside pocket of his jacket. "Ha, ha," he said as he picked his sandwich back up.

"Whaaaat?" Alex teased around a mouthful of food. "I've known you for… what, six months now, and I've never been to your house? Meanwhile, my mom has threatened to put your name on the guest room door, with as much time as you spend at my place."

Sam's laugh was awkward and evasive. "Yeah, I know, it's just… my folks are… it's hard to explain." In all honesty, Sam had said precious little of consequence about his family. Just the right number of stories scattered into conversation, and deft avoidances of anything of importance had kept everyone just far enough away to stop complicated questions. He could tell Alex was suspicious, and wanted to know more, but God bless her, she never pushed him for more than he was willing to give.

"Well, it doesn't matter. I get to see your place today, right? Meet up at the usual spot after school?"

"Yeah, works for me. It's a pretty short walk back to my place. Hopefully it will have quit raining by then."

By the time the end of the day rolled around, the rain had

stopped, though the wind was still brisk. Hands tucked deep in their pockets, both teenagers walked along the damp sidewalk. With light banter, they passed through a few affluent neighborhoods, and onto the edge of a large gated development. "Wait, you live –here-?" Alex asked, incredulous as they passed through the opening in the fence.

"Yeah," Sam answered, a little sheepish. "I don't think there's many other kids here. At least, not that I've seen at school."

"Nah, I think all the kids here go to that snooty private school in town." She was doing her level best to keep her mouth from gaping open, but was only mildly successful. It wasn't that the homes were particularly large, or outlandish; these were just impeccable. Manicured lawns, artistic gardens, beautiful architecture. It was the sort of understated grandeur of the supremely wealthy, without being overblown. "What do your parents *do*?"

"Mom is a cardiologist, dad's a military contractor." Sam's attention alternated between the ground beneath his feet, and Alex's awed face. Her own home, a modest two-story house with a couple bedrooms, overgrown lawn, and aging fence, stood in stark contrast to all of this, and Sam could feel his cheeks heat. "Look, if it makes you uncomfortable or anything..."

"What? Oh God no!" Alex stopped in the middle of the sidewalk and grabbed Sam's elbow. "No no, that's not what... no. Hey, you didn't pick your parents, right?" She squeezed his arm comfortingly, then tugged him back the way they were going. "Now come on, I'm cold, and want to see your place."

Twenty minutes later, they were both comfortably ensconced in Sam's dining room. Spread out across the dining table, and even onto the floor, the two of them looked exactly like the sketch Sam had drawn, down to the book on Alex's knees. Steaming mugs of tea sat close at hand, energetic music coming from a speaker on the edge of the table. Once again, Sam had the new sketch book out in front of him, but this time, he was far more intensely focused on a far more in-depth creation. The small pack of pencils Alex had given him were up against his elbow, and at seemingly random intervals, he would drop the pencil in his hand and grab a new one. As he rotated through them all, he would pull out a sharpener. Pencil shavings littered the floor around his chair, the smell of wood and tea faint on the air between them.

Hours passed in comfortable companionship, alternating between quiet concentration, and familiar banter. Alex worked through her homework while Sam kept his head bowed over his sketch. True to his nickname, the tips of fingers were smudged with grey dust, a streak along the bridge of his nose from thoughtful scratching. No matter how hard Alex tried, though, Same refused to share a glimpse of his new piece. After several attempts at wheedling and cajoling, and more than a few well aimed grapes to Sam's forehead, Alex finally gave up with a low grumble, though he did promise to show her the finished picture.

Around dusk, the rain returned, pelting the skylight overhead and casting a strange glow to the sky outside. The easy peace between them was broken by the sound of the front door unlocking and creaking open. "Sam?" called a loud female voice. "Sam honey, are you home?" There was a soft murmur of a male voice after the call, too quiet to make out the words.

At the table, Sam had gone completely still. His eyes were wide, and there was an undercurrent of pure panic on his face that confused Alex. She reached forward to touch his arm, mouth open in question. The shock of contact woke him from his frozen state, and he gasped out, "Y-yeah, mom, we're in the dining room." He pulled away quickly, not quite managing to look apologetic as his mind raced. "You're home early."

"Oh, yeah," came the same voice from the hall. "We got

rained out, and your dad's got a big trip tomorrow morning, so we wanted to---wait, Sam, did you say *we*?" A short, pretty woman with close cropped curly ash blonde hair came into the dining room, shrugging out of her damp raincoat. "Oh, hello!" she said with a bright smile to Alex. "My, you two have been busy."

"Hi there," Alex said as she slid to her feet, half eyeing Sam and his obvious discomfort. She didn't understand why he was so unsettled; maybe it was because they were home so much earlier than he expected? One hand extended, she smiled brightly at the woman. "I'm Alex, Sam's friend from school. We have history together."

"Oh, Alex! Yes, Sam's mentioned you before. I'm Kelly, Sam's mom." Her handshake was firm and warm. As they dropped hands, a very tall, broad shouldered man with black hair cut high and tight rounded the corner behind the woman to find the source of conversation. "And this is Luke, my husband."

Luke's hand engulfed Alex's as he reached out for another shake. "Hey there, I didn't know Sam was having a friend over." His tone was friendly and teasing, his voice deep. The eyes that she met were a brilliant shade of blue, matching Sam's.

"It was kind of a last minute plan. Wow, Sam clearly got his eyes from you." Her broad smile faltered as Luke's grip suddenly tightened hard on her hand. She pulled away carefully, suddenly aware of a shift in the room. Previous warm smiles chilled, and both Luke and Kelly turned to look at Sam with dagger-sharp stares. Brow furrowed, she looked over her shoulder to see Sam staring pleadingly at his mom, his face a ghostly pale. She could see his hands shaking on top of his notebook, and his mouth worked open and shut as if to speak, but nothing more than a strange, strangled sound came out. "I... I'm sorry, did I say something wr--"

"His?" Luke's previously friendly voice was bitterly cold and brittle, cutting across the room like a knife. "I thought we talked about this."

"Dad, please..." Sam begged, voice breaking around a sob in his throat. Tears glistened in the corners of his eyes, and he deliberately avoided looking at Alex. "Don't... don't do this right now." His hands laid flat across the top of his notebook, almost protectively, his fingers curled around the edges of the pages.

"Do what? Lie to your 'friends'? Make your mother cry?" Luke's large frame filled the room as he stepped through the doorway, now towering over Alex. She stepped backward instinctively as Sam sank back into his chair. "Oh right, that's *your* job." His voice was dangerously low now, an insidious whisper that sent chills racing up Alex's spine. Luke's attention shifted, though his eyes never left Sam's face. "I don't suppose you know what Sam's short for, do you?"

"N-no...?" Alex said quietly, almost compelled to answer. "He never-"

"Samantha." This time it was Kelly who spoke, her voice a shattered whisper that slipped under the rising tensions in the room. "*Her* name is Samantha Rose." Each word fell like a blow on Sam, and Alex watched each hard flinch with tears in her own eyes. Sam's eyes shifted down to the floor, and there was absolutely no response from that side of the table anymore. Just the quiet plop of tears onto the sketches on the page under trembling, pale hands. "I gave you your grandmother's name, and you... you just..."

Before Kelly could finish that sentence, Sam burst out of the chair. Luke reached for an arm, but the cold leather jacket slipped past his fingers, and the sound of feet pounding up the stairs ended in the hard slam of a bedroom door at the end of the hall, making all three of them standing downstairs flinch. Tears streamed down Kelly's cheeks, and with a quiet gasp, she spun and disappeared into the kitchen. After a long moment of awkward silence, Luke followed his wife.

The lump in Alex's throat burned, her heart aching for her friend upstairs. Her feet rooted to the spot with indecision, she stared blankly at the chaos on the table. The open sketch book caught her attention, and she stepped forward to take a closer look. Promises or not, she couldn't look away. It was the rough outline of a person kneeling on the ground. One arm was wrapped across their body to grip the opposite waist, while the other crossed their chest to clutch their shoulder. Their gender seemed difficult to distinguish, with both broad shoulders and a masculine jawline, but a narrow waist, and a feminine curve to the hip. Just above the forearm, a hint of the curve of a breast. In their posture, Alex could read heartache, anger, and shame. Her finger traced the line of the jaw, biting her lower lip as she read the text lightly sketched across the top of the page.

Lost In My Own Skin

From the kitchen, she could hear the low sound of voices. Alex suddenly got the sense that Luke was about to come back and politely request that she leave for the night. The thought made her extremely uncomfortable. So rather than get cornered by manners, she swept the sketch pad off the table, ignoring the pencils that skittered onto the hardwood floor as she hurried off in the direction she'd seen Sam go. Through the open entry hall and up the stairs, Alex found herself at the edge of the railing, just spotting Luke as he came into the dining room, clearly looking for her. Before he noticed where she'd gone, she ducked out of sight.

The hallway upstairs was wide and long, with several white doors lining each side. All of them were closed, and the spaces between were filled with pieces of artwork and family photos. Alex moved slowly down the hall, not entirely sure how far she needed to go before she'd find Sam's room. A few steps ahead, she stopped and stared at a portrait. Three people stood on the edge of a grassy slope; Luke, Kelly, and a young woman between them. She had long waves of thick black hair that curled around the edges of her shoulders, and wide blue eyes. The smile on her face was wide enough, but it didn't quite reach those beautiful eyes with thick lashes. Alex simultaneously knew, and did not know the face that stared back at her from underneath all of that well applied makeup. The jawline was the same, though the loss of the weight of dark hair gave it a more masculine angle. Plus with the baggier shirts, and jackets with broad shoulders, quite a lot could be effectively hidden. She reached up and traced the edge of that jawline, breath caught in her throat. "Oh Sam," she whispered.

Alex stood there for several long minutes before a sound from the end of the hall caught her attention. Something crashed as if thrown against a wall, followed by a heavy thud of something hitting the floor. Moving quickly, ignoring the rest of the pictures, she stopped outside the last door on the left, noting a few quick sketches tacked up. She paused a moment, then tapped three light knocks on the door. The world seemed to still, the only sound the rush of her own pulse in her ears. Minutes passed, and she was about to knock again when there was a muffled, "Who is it?" Hesitant, afraid.

"Just me, smudge," Alex said quietly. Another few seconds passed, then the door creaked open. Sam peered out at Alex, who smiled. "Can I come in?"

Sam stepped back out of the way, letting Alex into the bedroom. Alex stepped in as the door closed behind her, looking around the room. It was… exactly like she expected it would be, if a bit larger. Posters covered the walls, a bookshelf was haphazardly crammed with movies and sketch books and knickknacks. There was a desk under the window that overlooked the back yard, scattered with a laptop and several text books. She could see a heavy book conspicuously on the floor by the wall, the likely source of the sound she'd heard. "You're still here." Sam's voice came from behind her, soft and a little broken, as if not entirely sure that Alex actually still stood there.

"Of course I am," Alex said as she turned back around to get a good look at Sam's tear stained face. "You're my best friend. Where else would I be?"

Sam looked at her like she'd sprouted another head. "You're not... but I *lied* to you."

"No, you didn't," Alex corrected gently, stepping forward to close the gap between them. "You protected yourself. You kept a secret. We all keep secrets, Sam. The fact that yours is... bigger than most doesn't make it a lie. And if the bullshit your parents just pulled is the sort of response you usually get from people, I can't exactly blame you." The tears that had been gathering again in Sam's eyes spilled down his cheek, and Alex reached up to wipe one of them away.

"You're not... you're not mad at me?" Sam's voice wavered, his knees weak.

Alex's smile was warm, if a little sad. "No, Sam. I'm not mad. I'm... I was a little hurt you didn't tell me before, that I had to find out because your parents are assholes. But I think some of that is because I feel like... I feel like that whole thing robbed you of the chance to tell me on your own terms." She dropped her hand to his shoulder, then pulled him in for a fierce hug. The burn of his tears sliding down her neck made her breath catch in her throat, and she tightened her arms around him as she felt the dam break, and the sobs start.

Long minutes passed as Sam wept into Alex's shoulder. She held him through all of it, supporting the both of them and humming tunelessly in his ear. Eventually, his breathing evened out, and his sobs came to an unsteady, stuttering halt. "Sorry about your sweater," Sam mumbled into Alex's shoulder.

She snorted derisively in response. "Like this is the worst thing that's been on my shoulder. Shuddup, dummy." Pulling away just enough to look at his face, Alex offered him his sketch book that she'd snagged from the table. "Do you want to talk about it, or do you want to do something else?"

Sam took the book with a look of intense gratitude, clutching it to his chest. "No, let's... let's talk. I've been meaning to tell you for a couple months now anyway. The hard part's over, I guess." He led her over to his tussled bed, making a token effort to straighten the dark blue comforter before they both climbed onto the bed. Sam settled at the head of the bed, wrapping his arms around a pillow and resting his chin on the edge. "What, ah... what do you want to know?"

"How did I not know?" The question tumbled out of her mouth before she had the chance to stop it, and Alex covered her mouth with both hands. "Oh God, I'm sorry, that sounds awful."

The laugh that burst out of Sam was almost closer to a cackle. "You're fine, Alex. I'm gonna just give you the benefit of the doubt that all of your questions are coming from a good place, so you get a pass. Just... ask." Settling back down, Sam blew the hair out of his eyes as he gave her question some thought. "Honestly, because I'm a really good liar. And I don't mean that in a bad way, I just... am. Had to be. Before I started, back in August, I talked to the counselor. My therapist suggested it, said that our school has been known to be super supportive in the past. And since I'm new, it wouldn't be a big change for any of the staff or anything. A couple days before school started, I went in to meet with the counselor. They helped me get everything squared away, like notes on my file for the teachers, and extra notes to make sure my parents never knew about it." Avoiding eye contact, Sam fiddled with the edge of his pillow, pulling at a loose string. "Being a senior, I could skip out of the awkward stuff, like gym, that would be really hard to explain. So people just... took me at face value. No one's questioned me, or doubted me, or... or anything."

Alex sat and listened as Sam rambled, almost fearing to breathe in case he decided to stop talking. The longer he went, the more she relaxed into listening, nodding once in a while. "Well, I'm glad they're helpful at least. This might be a stupid question, but... does the school's support make that much of a difference?"

"Oh God yes," Sam said instantly. "For the first time in... in years, I haven't felt alone. In case you couldn't tell, this has been... an ongoing issue with my parents. They don't... they don't support me at all. Things got pretty bleak. Really bleak. I didn't go so far as to try anything, but... it wouldn't have taken much, you know?" His eyes misted slightly, and he smiled a little weakly as Alex reached over and took his hand. "Anyway, I'm... I'm better now. Most days, anyway. Having the school backing me up helps." He finally looked up and made eye contact with Alex. "So do you."

For the next several hours, Sam and Alex talked, in the way of old friends. They talked about the things that had been weighing on Sam's heart for months, the burden now lifted and shared between them. Eventually, a slightly panicked phone call, complete with apologies and a slightly sharp "I'm coming to get you," from Alex's mom got her moving. As she headed towards the door, Alex paused, one hand on the doorknob. "Sam, are you... are you safe here?"

Sam's smile was deeply appreciative, and he wrapped his friend in a warm, tight hug. "Yeah, I am. My parents can be awful, but they aren't an actual *threat*. I'll be ok for the night."

Alex clung tightly to him, nodding against his shoulder. "If you ever don't feel safe, just... you can always come to my house, ok? Knock on my door, throw rocks at my window... I'll even come get you. Whatever. Anything, ok?" Sam nodded in response, and she finally released him. "Can I... can I tell my mom?"

Sam paused a second, then nodded slowly. "Yeah, ok. I mean... yeah, but just your mom, ok?"

"Promise." Alex smiled and kissed his cheek. "Walk me downstairs to get my stuff?"

"Oh right, it's all still downstairs, isn't it?" Sam peered out into the hall. Finding the coast clear, the two of them made their way back down to the dining room. The room looked different than they'd left it; their scattered mess had been tidied, with a stack of Alex's things, and another pile of Sam's things. As Alex was collecting her books and sliding them back into her backpack, she noticed Sam flipping through the pages a bit frantically. "Did they... they didn't... fuck, they *did.*"

"What's wrong?" Her backpack slung over her shoulder, Alex peered over at Sam's panicked rifling.

He sat down with a heavy sigh, dragging his fingers through his hair. "My dad... doesn't like my drawings. Not...not what I draw anyway. It's how I deal with a lot of this, since I can't exactly be open about a lot of this. So whenever he finds any sketches, he takes them. Pencils, too." Sam swallowed hard, looking up at Alex with tears in his eyes. "He's taken some that are...really important to me. I've lost a lot over the years. I got pretty good at hiding them, but today..." Sam's words faded off, and he shook his head as he looked down at his bare feet. "That's why I go through them so fast. He takes them."

Alex was silent for a long time. Finally, she knelt down in front of Sam and tapped on his chin to bring his eyes up. Sam resisted for a moment, then looked up. "Your dad is an ass. Your new book is safe upstairs. We'll work it out, ok, smudge?" There was another pause, then Sam nodded. "Good. I'll see you tomorrow?"

"Tomorrow. Yeah." Sniffing hard, Sam forced a smile to Alex, who looked dubious. "I'll be fine, I promise. I'm gonna go take a shower, and crash. I'll see you in class tomorrow. Your mom just pulled up, go outside before she kicks my door down." As he spoke, headlights splashed across the back wall of the dining room. "Go." Ushering Alex out the front door into the rainy night, Sam waved at the woman in the car before ducking back inside.

Once the door was closed behind him, exhaustion slammed down on him like a pile of bricks. Tears wobbled at the corners of his eyes as he plodded up the stairs and into the bathroom. His clothes hit the floor, and he stood naked in front of the mirror, staring at his reflection. The body he saw wasn't the one he should have, wasn't the one he saw in his mind's eye. Curves in the wrong places, a softness that didn't feel right. With one last look at his chest, Sam turned away from the mirror and snapped open the shower curtain. He flipped the water on, and stepped under the scalding hot spray. A few long minutes of standing silently in the shower, and suddenly his knees gave out. Sam fell to the floor of the shower with a loud clatter of shampoo bottles and badly stifled sobs. Tears and water mingled on his cheeks, and he wrapped his arms around his knees, shoulders shaking hard as he tried to keep quiet. He didn't know how much time had passed before there was a knock on the door.

"Sam? Sam, honey, are you ok?" The voice of his mother cut across the sound of the water, genuinely concerned.

Both hands scrubbed his face, and Sam swallowed hard. "Y-yeah, mom, I'm fine. Just knocked something over, I'm ok."

"Are you sure?" She was dubious, and there was a slight jostle of the door knob. Shit, he'd forgotten to lock it.

"Yeah, mom, I'm sure," he said quickly. "Just clumsy, I promise I'm ok." God, if the lump in his throat would just go away, that would make this so much easier.

"Alright, honey. You to go bed soon, ok? It's late, and you've got school tomorrow." A long pause, then Kelly called again, "I love you, Sam."

"Love you too, mom," Sam managed, his voice cracking as he swallowed back his sob. One heartbeat, two, then he heard her steps recede. It took another few minutes before Sam's heart slowed enough that he could breathe comfortably again, and he laid his head back against the wall of the shower.

Morning came too early, and too wet. By the time Sam stepped into the school, his toes were damp and cold, despite the heavy leather of his combat boots. He shook his head with a low sort of growling sound, looking not unlike a wet dog and grinning apologetically at the indignant shriek of a girl who was standing too close. A few friendly greetings as he moved through the crowd, then he was at his locker. Opening his locker unleashed a cascade of pencils tumbling out of his locker and across the floor. "What the fuck?" he muttered, staring at a stack of moldable erasers, and at least a dozen fresh sketch books. Oblivious to the titters of laughter around him, and the curses as more than a few people slipped on the pencils, he spotted a note taped on the inside of the door. Unfolding it, he found Alex's messy scrawl.

Sam,
These should be enough to get you through the next week or so. I'll keep you stocked in pencils and sketch books for as long as you need.

Love you, smudge.
Alex

PS – Mom says welcome to the family, big brother. You're stuck with us now.

Within the Study

by Maxwell Kier DiMarco

arkness. Your world consists solely of darkness, and your shifting gaze does nothing to discern your true surroundings... assuming, of course, that this darkness is not, in fact, the only "surroundings" you currently inhabit. But, thanks to what can only be described as a blessing from Lady Luck herself, when you eventually open your eyes you find that is not the case, instead realizing you are simply laying on an aged, oak wood floor. Trying to ignore a slight pain in your head – which brings to mind being knocked out by a blunt object, but you don't want to jump to conclusions – as you get to your feet, you begin to properly take in your surroundings.

As logic would dictate, the floor you'd laid upon was, in fact, part of the larger room that you currently resided in. But the definition of "a room," while technically being defined as "a space that can be occupied or where something can be done," did not, in fact, instantly inform you of the contents of this particular room. Fortunately - as established a paragraph ago - your creator had blessed you with the gift of sight, and a quick look around your current location allowed you to deduce the nature of this new, bizarre locale.

In front of you were three large, rectangular windows, but the only thing visible through their slightly blurred glass were impenetrable shadows. The sight brought back the terrifying memories of a few seconds ago, and you tore your eyes from the sight; this action caused your gaze to shift to what lay before the windows, which was a much more welcoming scene to behold. Two comfy looking, antique armchairs were placed on either side of the windows, while an equally tacky couch bridged the distance between them, being placed a few feet back from its solo-seating brethren. As for the couch itself, you noticed two defining features about it: That it had not one, but two end tables on either side of it, each possessing a brightly glowing lamp... and that, instead of traditional pillows, this couch possessed one, fish shaped pillow, which was propped against its right arm. For reasons I can't possibly fathom, you found that the latter feature was more bizarre than the first. Nevertheless, you decided to disregard it for now, and continue to try and ascertain the true nature of the unknown room.

You could have observed the far right wall of the room – as you had been facing it when you first arose from the floor – but that wall was boring as hell, so you instead opted to look over the features of the *left* wall, which was conveniently just a brief clockwise turn away. Almost instantly, you were rewarded for your wise decision, and you wondered why it took you so long to turn ninety degrees to witness the sight that was now before you. For you now found yourself standing before a beautifully maintained fireplace, its mantle covered with multiple fascinating trinkets. Small candles burned from within similarly miniscule glass jars, their flickering light reflecting off of nearby picture frames. Giving the frames' contents a quick once-over, you find that not only are each of them monochrome, but they all depict scenes from an age long gone: Wooden ships with towering masts, men and women clad in flowing robes, and even a picture of a chihuahua... *without* shades pasted over its eyes! Quite the fascinating sight, but your concerns about being kidnapped by a tacky grandma are quickly halted as your gaze settles upon something truly breathtaking, hanging above the fireplace in a gold-lined wood frame.

Its majesty illuminated by a third table lamp–which, despite the name, had instead been placed on the edge of the fireplace– a beautiful painting was contained within its lovingly crafted frame. The scene presented by the canvas was that of two women, clad in the same flowing robes of the photos, sitting in the booth of a medieval restaurant. The robes worn by the woman to the right were a beautiful shade of red, and flowed off her chair and onto the floor, almost reaching her companion on the left. And that observation allowed you to notice a peculiar feature of the other woman: That being, her folded, almost bat-like wings, which were slightly pressed against the wall behind her.

Finding your intrigue with the painting–and, by extension, the mysterious room that contained such a painting–growing ever more prevalent, you might have been content to observe the scene for many hours. But, luckily for those of us with shorter attention spans, your intrigue was suddenly broken when a loud noise came from the other side of the room.

Someone was snoring.

Turning on your heel, your gaze flitting over an assortment of drawers, you quickly find the source of the out-of-place noise: A few feet away from you sat a large, wooden desk, placed in front of a row of towering bookshelves. The light of yet another table lamp lit up the desk's surface, as well as the two chairs placed on either side of the wooden work surface. While the chair closest to you remained empty, the chair on the other side of the desk was not only very much occupied, but its occupant had apparently already made himself at home. A teenage boy clad in a basic black shirt–seventeen going on eighteen, judging by the thin hairs that made up his bizarre fusion of a goatee and a chinstrap beard–lay sprawled across the desk, letting out a loud, obnoxious snore approximately every ten seconds. Approaching him cautiously, you decided to take a seat in the chair across from him; if this strange boy could take an actual nap here, then you could get comfortable for the inevitable conversation that was about to transpire. There is a slight creak as you lower yourself onto the surprisingly comfortable wooden seat, but the boy's only reaction is a slight twitch of his hand and an annoyed snort, confirming your suspicions that he is, in fact, out like a light.

Now that you've looking right at him, you have to admit that you wouldn't have guessed such a nicely furnished home could be kept by such a disturbingly average teen.

The boy's hand twitches again, catching your attention and allowing you to spot a pencil lying just in front of him. You find that it's strange implement for him to have, considering the lack of suitable writing material anywhere in the desk's vicinity. As the unknown boy lets out a particularly long snore, you decide that you simply bear his obnoxious vocalizations any longer. However, as you contemplate whether to wake the teen up or stab him with his unneeded pencil, said teen apparently decides he's also tired of his snoring.

"Huh? Who? Wha–?!" With a mixture of snorts and unfinished inquiries, the boy shoots upright, his eyes darting around the room as though he'd been unconscious for years. After realizing that he's no longer in his candy land dream world, the boy props his head up with his elbow, letting out a small "ugh" as his miniature panic attack subsides. Unfortunately for his jumpy nerves, however, it was at that moment that he finally noticed you in his periphery vision.

"Augh!" he exclaims, jolting back slightly. Upon getting a proper look at you, however, recollection flashes in his eyes. "Oh! Uh...." Trying to recompose himself, he links his fingers, leaning forward in his chair as he clears his throat. When he properly addresses you, his voice is noticeably more collected, almost mysterious; as though he were setting up a detective movie. "Hello. I have been eagerly awaiting your arrival, and not at all sleeping on my desk." His eyes awkwardly twitch to the side with that statement, and you cock an inquisitive eyebrow. Before you can state the obvious, however, he speaks up once more. "Please! Make yourself at home..." Rising from his chair–and discretely retrieving the pencil–he motions to the room around you. "And let me welcome you... to a new world."

Despite his previously uncouth, impromptu nap-time, you find yourself intrigued by the boy's words. From the comfort of your chair, you watch the teen with fascination as he elaborates on his previous statement, lifting his pencil so that it catches the dim light of the desk lamp.

"A world *filled* with unspeakable horrors... where even this innocent pencil could become your worst ally." To illustrate his point, the boy gives the tip of the implement a slight tap with his index finger... and gets the expected result, snatching his finger back with a blunt, tension-ruining "ow!" After staring down at the pencil as though it had insulted his mother, he briefly turns his attention back to you, if only to justify his brief lapse of dignity. "That was... much sharper than I thought it would be."

Upon not receiving a response from you, the boy opted to continue on with his speech, slowly pacing around the perimeter of the room. "A world *filled* with humanity's utmost fears...." Attempting to reiterate his previous statement, the boy irritably threw the pencil across the room, where it landed with a "thunk" against something irrelevant on the far right wall. Deciding to follow the boy's progress, you get out of your chair, joining him by the fireplace as he begins to list off the aforementioned utmost fears. "Monsters... demons..." Pausing dramatically, the boy turned to look you dead in the eyes. "*Hotdogs.*"

You'd have been lying if you said you didn't shudder at that word; it was a well-known fact that no one knew just what bizarre concoction of meat and chemicals went into those preservative-laced sausage mockeries. Noticing the disgust on your face, the boy nodded understandingly, before continuing his introduction to this unknown world you were both now dwelling in.

"And the ruler of it all: An evil warlock, who controls his nightmarish creations with an artifact so *evil,* so *unspeakable,* that the very sight of it would drive you to sniveling *madness!*" Without warning, the boy reached into his pants pocket, before dramatically pulling a strange, rubber rectangle from its depths, brandishing it before you. "The rubber keyboard!"

The two of you stood in silence for a moment, with you staring at the rubber object–which, upon closer inspection, did in fact have proper keys, like its apparent namesake–and the boy looking at you with a mix of horror at the bizarre "artifact" in his hand, and expectancy for your reaction. After a few more seconds of silence, he came to the conclusion that you were simply too horrified for words, and looked down at the keyboard with a sympathetic shudder. "Horrifying, I know." With another brief shudder, he shoved the keyboard back into his pocket.

And then, without another word, he abruptly sprinted away towards the room's sitting area. You, on the other hand, stayed where you were, watching as he tried and failed to perform a parkour-style vault over the back of the couch, before clumsily climbing over it and rolling onto his back on the couch proper, resting his head on the fish-shaped pillow. Folding his arms behind his head, the strange boy looked back towards you as he resumed his speech. "Yet, despite the danger, there still exist those brave souls who would dare venture into this hellish land." His gaze following you as you finally decided to join him in the sitting area, the boy opted to sit up as you took a seat in one of the armchairs. "And why, you ask?"

Of course, you had not asked. In fact, you hadn't gotten a single word in since you arrived in this room, which either said something about the boy's love of his own voice, or meant you needed to work on your conversation skills. But, regardless of these potentially unaddressed emotional elephants in the room, your one-sided conversation continued, with the boy cracking a smile as he answered his apparently rhetorical question. "The answer is simple: Because they seek a mystical treasure known only as-"

All of a sudden, the horrible sound of a blade penetrating flesh rang out, and the boy's words caught in his throat. His face as shocked as your own, he looked in horror down at his heart, which, through some cruel twist of fate, had been stabbed clean through by his own pencil. Your eyes widened, the boy letting out a strangled choking noise as he fell face first to the floor. Horrified, you fell to the ground, trying to help the boy to his feet. Unfortunately, he was actually unbelievably heavy, and you just wound up spraining your back. But even with your back in equally unbelievable pain, you stayed by the side of the dying boy, as he raised his head to speak one final time.

"The... the warlock heard my words..." he choked out, his voice raspy and strained. "Please... it may be too late for me... but you can still save yourself!" The boy let out a series of coughs, his face becoming paler by the second. You wanted to help him, but you had no idea how; after all, a stab to the heart is a stab to the heart, even if it *was* with a pencil... somehow. You would have questioned the legitimacy of such an object being capable of this fatal wound, but that would have taken away from the emotional impact of the scene. So, you remained silent, until the boy finally mustered the strength to speak once more. Beckoning you closer, his voice was barely audible, yet the urgency in his tone was clear: "Quickly! You must-"

"Tim?"

Looking up from the screen of the laptop, Tim promptly froze in place, looking over his shoulder to the open door of the study.

"Tim, you're almost eighteen. You can't just ignore me anymore." From somewhere down the hall, the voice of his sister called out a second time, a bit more forcefully this time.

His eyes widening, but nevertheless trying to stay calm, Tim cleared his throat, before quickly resuming typing out his story.

Beckoning you closer, his voice was barely audible, yet the urgency in his tone was clear: "Quickly! You must go to-"

"Tim. You're late for dinner, bro!"

With a sigh, Tim looked up from the laptop once again. Setting his jaw, he glared out at the hall with obvious irritation.

"I will totally tell on you if you snuck into granddad's study again!" his sister yelled, her voice conveying that playfully smug tone that Tim couldn't stand. "You know he doesn't want you writing on his laptop!" With a sigh, he looked back to the laptop–his grandfather's laptop–one last time, quickly typing out one final sentence:

They all lived happily ever after the end.

Closing the writing program and shutting the laptop's screen, Tim pushed his chair away from his grandfather's desk. Getting up and walking to the door, he leaned out into the hall as he yelled back to his sister: "I'm coming, Tina!"

And with that, after quickly flipping off the overhead light, he walked out of the study, closing the door behind him.

Typewriter

Comfort From The Past

by Lauren Patzer

Darren sat and stared at the cigar box. He opened it and then closed it.

"He's not in the letters, you know," his wife, Angeline said as she watched from the kitchen. She picked up another dish and began washing it.

"I'm not entirely sure you're correct," Darren said. He removed the letter on the top, the most recent one, and unfolded the faded white paper.

The typewritten letter had stains on the edge from age, even though Darren had received the letter just a few short months ago. The impact from the keys on the paper was clear and sharp. Why the aged paper remained a mystery.

Angeline set the dish in the drainer. She looked at the clock and sighed.

"Just bring them with you," she said. "It's time to go."

The fields burn as the F-4s rocket overhead, dropping liquid hell on the landscape. People burn in amongst the rice paddies. Most of the screaming comes from Vietnamese civilians or suspected Viet Cong. Today, however, bad aim has forced American soldiers to join the dead and dying. The smell is revolting, to say the least.

"He wrote this like it had just happened."

Angeline set her hand on Darren's shoulder.

"Alzheimer's breaks apart the fabric of time for those it affects," she said. "For him, it probably was like it just happened."

Darren folded the letter and placed it back in the box.

"OK. Let's go," he said as he took the box and walked with her out the door.

Darren looked at the flat single story building that stretched away into the distance. He parked the car and got out. The oppressive heat took his breath away.

"An oasis in the middle of hell," he whispered. He squinted as Angeline as she got out of the car. Her dark hair was pulled back in a ponytail and she wore a halter top to combat the temperature. Even so, her skin glistened in the light and he smiled. She looked at him and winked.

"Come on," she said as she walked toward the front entrance.

Darren lingered for a moment. He glanced around the building at the sparse vegetation and cement sculptures arrayed around the building interspersed with paths. Some of the statues he recognized as replicas of famous landmarks. The others seemed to have just been random purchases. Maybe they held special meaning to one of the residents.

Darren jogged to catch up to Angeline as she reached the door. They walked in together and their noses were met by the unmistakable odor of a long term care facility, a mixture of sickly sweet and antiseptic. It was one of the things Darren most hated about the building. The smell reminded him of impending death.

Nurse Danova approached and smiled at them.

"Mister and Missus Arnofsky, thank you for coming by. I'll take you to your father's room," she said as she turned and walked down a corridor to the right. Darren followed along numbly. He'd made this walk dozens of times. This was the first time it would end without him seeing his father.

They turned a corner and came to the first door on the left. The nurse unlocked the door and opened it for them.

"Just a friendly reminder, management would like all personal belongings removed by tomorrow. There's an empty box, your father's suitcase and, of course, his typewriter case and typewriter." Nurse Danova bowed slightly as they entered the room.

In the center of the room with a view out the window sat a simple desk with four drawers and a vintage Royal typewriter on it. The distinctive smooth black finish showed signs for the times it had been through in the field. There were dents, scratches and a well documented ding on the upper left corner of the ribbon and striker keys cover where a bullet had grazed it after piercing the case. Darren smiled as he remembered his father holding up the spent bullet he found rattling around the typewriter case after he was evacuated from Saigon all those years ago.

Angeline had opened the closet and was looking at the clothes that hung there. It was just a single gray suit, a few slacks and some shirts. She pulled a shoebox down from the shelf above the clothes and opened it.

"Hey, look at this," she said as she brought it over to Darren. Inside the box there were a dozen ribbon boxes for the Royal typewriter. They all looked old. Darren carefully opened one of the boxes and found a used ribbon inside.

"I don't understand why he would keep all this old stuff," Darren said. He spotted some newer ribbon boxes at the back of the first drawer he opened. "Why not just throw them away?"

Angeline lifted the old ribbon spool from Darren's hands and raised it to his nose.

"Memories can be triggered by more than just the written word, my love," she said and then tapped her finger gently on the tip of his nose.

"I guess," Darren replied. He pulled a sheaf of older paper from the drawer with the new ribbons. There was nothing else in the drawer. He set it on top of the desk. He raised one of the pages to his nose and sniffed it. The slightly musky scent of aged paper filled his nostrils. He set the paper to the side.

Angeline located the hard shell suitcase in the bottom of the closet. She put it on the bed and gathered the clothes from the closet. She folded them as she packed them inside.

"Don't take too much time on that," Darren said as he watched her. "We'll just donate everything to charity."

"Mmhmm," Angeline replied and continued to fold everything carefully.

Darren shook his head and opened the next drawer. It contained more paper but had a manila envelope with a thick sheaf of paper in it. He pulled it out and set it on top of the older papers. He opened the folder and raised his eyebrows.

"The book," he said.

"What?"

"My father always said he was working on his memoirs, but I never saw anything. He's been saying it for ten years."

Darren thumbed through the first few pages. The crisp paper was bright in the room's light; Darren thought maybe that's how his father felt when he wrote these pages, like a light had come on and illuminated his thoughts. The writing was solid, crisp and somewhat entertaining.

"It starts out in his childhood. There's no table of contents, so I'm not sure if he was done," he said as he started to jump through the book looking at the chapter headings. "War's horror, in the trenches, a light among the darkness, love lost?"

"Maybe it's erotica," Angeline said and chuckled.

"Really?" Darren looked up from the book at his wife.

"Throughout history, sexual relations between men and women has been more about conquest by the men than anything else." Angeline smiled as she walked to the dresser. "What is love lost about?"

Darren slowly skimmed the chapter.

"Looks like he met a woman in Vietnam, near the end of the war," Darren raised his eyebrows. "He never mentioned her before."

"So, your father talked often of his conquests in the bedroom?" Angeline carried a pile of clothes from the dresser to the bed and set them down.

"Point taken." Darren thumbed through the book again. "She was a reporter. She didn't make it out with the evacuation in Saigon. She was reportedly killed."

"Dictators don't take kindly to the press. They operate in the darkness; reporters shed light on their nefarious activities." Angeline zipped the suitcase closed. "That's all the clothes. There's some more papers in the top drawer. Do you want to look through them, or shall I?"

Darren looked up from the book. "Go ahead, I'm still rummaging through this book. He captured mom's courtship, our childhoods–hey, check this out–Union Thugs is one of the chapter headings!"

"Well, he grew up in a different time," Angeline said as she pulled the pile of papers out of the dresser. "Here's some more typewritten pages. Who is Thao?"

"I don't know. That wasn't the reporter's name."

"Oh, here's a picture, but it's kind of old." Angeline handed the letters and picture to Darren. Darren took them and set the papers down.

"This must be Phong, the reporter from Saigon," Darren said as he turned the picture over. The date was February 1975. "The story said she disappeared at the beginning of March. He couldn't locate her before the evacuation. Ah, look, there's his typewriter in the picture."

Darren pointed to the small black typewriter sitting on a desk next to Phong. Angeline looked at the picture closer. She pointed at Phong.

"She's pregnant," Angeline said.

"What?' Darren said. "How do you figure that? She's showing yet."

"The way she's looking at the camera, your father, and resting her right hand on her belly." Angeline shrugged her shoulders. "Okay, it's not definite, but that's a familiar pose that is recognized internationally as a newly pregnant mother proud of what's growing inside her."

Darren set the picture down and went back to the book. He flipped back to the chapter about love lost. He read it more carefully.

"Greatest tragedy of my life was losing Phong and our unborn child." Darren voice caught as he read the words out loud.

Angeline put her hands on Darren's shoulders. "Greatest tragedy. It's no wonder he didn't talk about it."

"Or was it?" Darren rifled through the book again. About half way through the manuscript, he found what he was looking for. "Two tragedies, one miracle. After mom's death, he went back to Vietnam. I remember this, but he didn't talk about it when he got back. Of course, he was starting to lose it then."

"He remembered it enough to put it in the book," Angeline said.

"Yeah, but after mom's death we grew distant. I think part of that was the dementia, but I was a little cold right about then too. Maybe he just felt like he couldn't tell me." Darren set the book down and put his head in his hands.

"Maybe he did." Angeline patted the book. "He just did it in a way he could when the memories were fresh."

Darren picked the book up and rifled through the pages

again, the chapter headings a blur in his mind. He stopped at the last page. "My greatest regret was not being strong enough to unite my family."

"I'm sorry, honey."

"We've got to find her," Darren said. He picked up the letters and skimmed them. "There no address on the letters, are there envelopes?"

Angeline went to the dresser and looked through the remaining items.

"There are no envelopes."

Darren got up and looked in the closet, feeling around on the shelf to see if there was anything there, just out of eyesight.

"Nothing."

Angeline looked under the bed and even lifted the mattress up.

"I don't know where else to look," she said.

"Geez, he knew he had memory problems, why would he throw the addresses away?" Darren looked around the room and then his eyes fell on the typewriter. He sat down at the desk and lifted the typewriter out of the case, revealing a list of names and addresses taped to the bottom.

"That's probably an old habit," Angeline said.

Darren read through the names.

"Thao Bui lives in Philly," Darren said.

"Is there a phone number?" Angeline looked at the list.

"No, and I don't think showing up on her doorstep unannounced would be a great idea."

Angeline picked an old blank page from the pile and handed it to Darren.

"Maybe you should try the old fashion way?"

Darren took the paper and slid it behind the carriage. He cranked the wheel until the paper fed up in front.

"It's been a while. I might go through a few pages."

"Well," Angeline said as she sat down on the bed. "Your father left plenty of paper and ribbon."

Darren chuckled and began typing. The words flowed easily enough. His dad's insistence that he learn touch typing decades ago had served him well in life. He typed fairly quickly and pulled the paper out of the carriage when he was done.

"All in a day's work," Darren said. He held up the paper.

Dear Thao, I am your brother, Darren. I have some bad news. I don't know if you know or not, but our father Aaron passed away last week. We'll be having a ceremony soon, but I won't set the date until I hear back from you. My name and contact information is at the bottom of the page. I hope to hear from you soon. Can't wait to meet you.

Darren

"Well," Angeline said. "It doesn't start out great, but I like the finish."

"It's not the best. Maybe I should try again."

Angeline cocked her head and frowned.

"Maybe we're not using all our resources," she said and got up and left the room. Darren put another sheet of paper in the typewriter but couldn't think of how to start a new letter. Should he try to be more charming? Tell Thao how he learned about her from the book and the letters? What was proper etiquette for announcing you're a long lost brother and our mutually shared father was now dead?

Angeline returned a short while later.

"Your father listed you as executor, but has all of your sisters including Thao listed as next of kin. There was even contact information for Phong, who is apparently still alive as well."

"Great, we can just call them."

"Well," Angeline said. "It turns out Thao was coming for her quarterly visit this month. The nurse already contacted her and-"

From behind Angeline, Thao stepped into the room with a younger girl holding her hand. Darren stood up and smiled.

"Darren?" Thao said.

"Thao, I presume?" Darren said.

Thao nodded. The young, dark-haired girl looked to be around seven years old. She left her mother's grip and went over to the typewriter. She took a piece of paper and slid it into the carriage.

Darren looked from the girl to Thao.

"Rebecca likes to use her grandfather's typewriter," Thao said. "It keeps her occupied and out of trouble whenever I come to visit."

A tear came to Thao's eye. Darren looked around.

"Do you want to sit? Can I get you anything?"

Thao nodded and walked to the bed. She sat on it and looked down. Darren walked over and sat on the bed next to her. Rebecca started typing on the typewriter.

"I did not," Thao began. "Forgive me, my English is pretty good but not the best."

"It's okay, you sound pretty good to me," Darren replied.

"I did not know he had passed. I was visiting mom in Vietnam. My phone was not on. Too expensive to travel with phone on."

"I understand."

"Father said you may not want to know me," Thao said. "You were angry with him?"

"First off, I do want to know you," Darren said. "I was angry with him for other things. I probably shouldn't have been. I think I blamed him for many things that were out of his control. I'm sorry I haven't spoken to you before; I didn't even know about you until today."

"It is nice to meet you, Darren," Thao said and smiled.

"How long have you been in America?"

"Father helped me come over ten years ago," Thao looked at Rebecca. "Rebecca is my second child."

"Is your other child older then?"

Thao sighed.

"Life is hard for children of soldiers in Vietnam. It's hard for grandchildren too."

"What happened?"

"Kien was killed by a mob outside of Saigon fifteen years ago," Thao said.

"Oh, I'm so sorry."

"It was a long time ago," Thao said.

"I imagine the hurt doesn't go away that quickly," Darren said.

Thao shook her head. Darren looked up and saw Angeline standing next to Rebecca watching her happily type away. A nurse appeared at the doorway.

"I hate to rush you, but visiting hours end soon and..." The nurse trailed off as she lingered in the doorway. Darren nodded.

"Thao, is there anything you'd like to keep of father's? We're probably going to donate most of this to charity."

Thao nodded.

"The typewriter. That's how I remember him the best and Rebecca really likes it."

Darren felt a lump in his throat. The typewriter was also the thing he most associated with his father. After all the arguing and blaming, he still loved his father. But then, what would he really do with it. Put the case in his attic until he died and his children sold it off at auction?

"I can't think of a better home for it, Sis."

The Typewriter

by Donna Lee Anderson

On this Saturday morning I had a surprise waiting for me. I hadn't asked for one but here it was. A typewriter.

Of course my parents both knew I was taking typing as one of my Junior year classes in high school, but when Daddy brought it home that day and I found it sitting on the dining room table, it was a complete surprise.

It was black, as all of them were in that time. It was a Standard typewriter and that was what you dreamed of using in 1954, if you used one at all. There were also small portables available, but one of my older cousins said the keys were too small and it made for lots of typing errors when your finger hit two keys at once, to say nothing of the offending keys locking up the mechanisms.

My typing class at my high school used the same kind of typewriter. I don't know how Daddy knew this, but leave it to him to find something that would help me. Now all I had to do was use it. Neither Mama or Daddy talked about this machine much. All that was said was that it was here so I could get some practice. In parent code, this meant 'use it.'

The kitchen of our house was next to the dining room, as in most homes, and when I sat down at the typewriter to try it out, Mama was hovering in the kitchen. I could see her through the door just wiping up the counter that she'd wiped clean already. Then she moved to wiping down the cupboard doors which were also clean. I wondered what she was waiting or watching for. Daddy had disappeared outside so I didn't know if he was also waiting to hear or see a product from this machine.

I rolled in the paper, and put my hands on the keys just like I was taught in class. My right hand was in position with fingers slightly bent and so was my left hand. I was ready to reach any and all the key when I needed to... but what would I type?

This was the problem: In class we typed what we saw printed. No free-thinking-typing yet. The printed matter we were to copy laid to the right of the typewriter or I could use the 'stand' if I preferred. I liked my copy to lay flat.

I got up and looked around the dining room. Nothing here to copy. I looked in the living room and saw the book my Dad had been reading. That would work. I could copy that.

I opened the book and put it down next to this big black machine. I repositioned my fingers again and looked at the book I'd put beside me, but it hadn't stayed open. I reopened the book and put a pencil across the top so it wouldn't close again.

My fingers were ready to test this new typewriter that had appeared in my life but the book was closed again. The pencil wasn't heavy enough to do this hold-the-book-open job.

Mama of course had seen all this action and came to my rescue. She handed me one of the kitchen table knifes that was heavier than a pencil, and when I put it on the top of the book, it worked and the book stayed open. Mama went back into the kitchen to do whatever it was she was doing, and I prepared to continue. I was ready again. Fingers in place and book open on the right side of the machine and I started to type.

"She moved across the room. Her bosom was heaving. It had

been a long time since she'd been with a man in this way but she was ready."

WHAT?! This was from Daddy's book and it was a supposed to be a western because that's all he ever read. Oh well. It was a grown up book and he was a grown up so I continued typing.

"He watched as she approached him and he had a smile on his face. It had been a long time for him too. He reached across the last few inches between them."

I wondered what had been a long time. Yes, I was almost seventeen but very naïve, and it was the 1950's, still a time of innocence for most teen age girls. It did cross my mind that they were about to kiss, and in my world that was a reasonable cause of consternation and great anticipation.

I typed on.

"He put his hand on her waist and then leaned in to put his face closer to hers. She moved her head so that their lips could meet, and as their lips touched she relaxed into his arms, feeling the strong muscles..."

"What are you typing?" It was Daddy who'd come in from outside. "Oh no, not from my book!" And he pulled the book out from under the knife that was holding it open, and took it with him to the back of the house.

I sat there wondering why he was upset. This was just a book and then I started to realize it was one of those books my teachers (the Sisters of Holy Names) had warned us about. They were not suitable reading material for girls like us. We were supposed to look at the cover and if it had a woman with a low cut bodice or a picture of a man and woman embracing, it was 'one of those kind of books that nice young women should not read.'

I really never looked at the covers of my Daddy's books before. They usually had a horse in the picture along with whatever else, and I didn't find that interesting.

Well, with that book gone I didn't know what to type so I got up and went to my room. I did have homework after all, and one of the assignments was to write a review of the book we had just finished reading for class. It was "Little Women" and in our review we were to pick a character and say what we admired about this person. It was to be no more than two pages long and Monday was the due date, so I started to write on lined paper. Then it hit me... why not type it for class?

I went back to the typewriter and now Mama was out in the garden with my sister who'd just come home from a sleep-over, and so I was alone. I put another piece of paper in the typewriter and vaguely wondered what happened to the other page I'd started on.

Typing from thoughts in your head is a lot different than copying from a page laying on the desk beside you, and since we were not allowed to 'correct' any mistakes on the page in my class, I hadn't learned how to do it. This could take a lot longer. To make sure what you did type was perfect takes some re-reading, and sometimes more than once. After about a half hour of trying to type thoughts and not being very successful in this endeavor, I decided to go back to my room and write it out after all.

An hour later Mama called me to set the table for dinner. During dinner Daddy asked me how the typing was going. I said, "Good." He said, "Did I find something to copy?" I said, "Not yet." He said, "Why not copy something from your Mama's magazines."

Why hadn't I thought of this?

After I helped clear the table and washed the dishes, I went looking for a one of her books. Mama was in her bedroom and I knocked on the door. "Come in" she said.

I explained that I wanted to use one of her magazines to copy from when I used the typewriter. She agreed and gave me a Redbook. On the cover was a woman in a green dress covered by an apron. She was dusting a table. *Boring*, I thought.

The typewriter was still on the dining room table so I opened the magazine, laid it on the table, arranged my fingers and started to type.

From the living room I heard Daddy say, "Couldn't you do that damn typing during the day so we don't have to hear it while we're trying to watch TV?"

I never even thought of moving the typewriter to my room, so I quit typing and I joined him and we watched a Western movie with John Wayne. I decided my typing could wait until tomorrow.

Since tomorrow was Sunday, there was church in the morning and then a big lunch afterwards. All this done and the dishes taken care of, I decided to try typing again. Then I had a great idea! I had written my review of the book, why not copy that on the typewriter and hand it in for my assignment?

The hand written pages were carefully laid beside the typewriter. I placed my hands on the keys and started. My name at the top of the page. The title of the book, then these words sort of centered below that: REVIEW OF LITTLE WOMEN — JO.

Under that I started typing the words I'd written earlier. "The reason I picked Jo for my report is that she is athletic and likes adventure like I do." I typed almost all of the first page but that's as far as I got because there was a knock on the door and my aunt and uncle and two cousins had come to visit. Of course I stopped and of course the cousins wanted to see my new typewriter. My aunt asked me what I was writing and I told her. She said I should make it a double spaced page because that's the way reports were supposed to be. Sounded good to me and she showed me how. Then while we were discussing this my younger cousin named Leonard stuck his hand up and typed three letters F G H. *in the middle of my report,* but I didn't yell at him, just moved his hand away (but so wished I could just smack him). They stayed until around four o'clock and were on their way out the door when Leonard said to his sister, "I got to type and you didn't. Ha ha." He also stuck his tongue out at me as he ran down the porch steps.

Mama was beside me on the porch waving good-bye and she

put her arm around me. "Never mind. You can fix what he did." Little did she know I couldn't 'fix' this, but I could start over.

Daddy said he was going out back to stack wood, did I want to help? I said I would except I had a report to write for school so he said I better do that. Mama said she'd help him and they left. I went to the typewriter and my sister decided to join me.

"What you doin'?"

I rolled in the new piece of paper. "Typing my report."

"Can I do that too?

"Not until I'm finished."

"Why can't I do it now?"

"Because this is for school and I need to get it done."

She went away pouting and headed for the back yard where Mama and Daddy were. I was sure she was complaining about me but maybe she'd help stack wood too.

Back to typing. I did the heading, then started typing the report all over again. I was almost done when Mama and Daddy and my sister came back into the house.

"My turn now?"

"No, not until I finish this report."

"Mama. She won't let me try that and it looks fun?"

Mama said, "It will be your turn tomorrow. Go get washed up." Then she looked at me and said, "You have fifteen minutes until dinner. How close will you be to done?"

"I hope to be finished. Thank you, Mama."

I typed fast, or as fast as my almost untrained fingers could go, and when Mama said, "Come to dinner" I was indeed finished. I pulled the last page out of the typewriter and gathered up the stack I had. Report on top and then the rest of the pages that had things on them to be fixed. I'd put these in my bedroom where I thought they'd be safe and went to dinner.

It was my week to do dinner dishes so after we finished I cleared the table and washed the dishes. While I did this my little sister, who is five years younger than I am, was busy checking out the machine on the dining room table. She tried to put paper in the roller but couldn't quite get it to roll around. Mama tried to help her but neither of them could make it work.

Mama came into the kitchen to see where I was in the cleanup process and said, "Let me finish and you go help your sister try to type." So I did.

I showed her how to line up the paper so it would go in straight. I showed her how to use the return carriage when you reached the end of the line and when she said she understood, she started her version of typing... but in her case it was called hunt-and-peck. Sometimes she didn't push the key down all the way and it didn't print on the paper so she would do it again harder and this time she would get two of that letter. After about an hour of this almost fun game she decided she'd wait to learn to type until she had to take it in high school.

I for one was relieved. I was so afraid she would do something to screw up the works and then I wouldn't be able to hand in typed papers any more.

That night was hair washing for my sister with my mama supervising. She really could do it by herself but I think Mama liked to be part of the ritual. Daddy and I were in the living room alone and I asked him where he got the typewriter for us.

He just smiled and said it was part of a deal he made with a guy. I asked more questions but didn't get any more answers. I knew Daddy was acquainted with lots of people in lots of businesses so his answers, or lack there-of, didn't surprise me. I just hoped the deal didn't include returning it very soon. I kind of liked having it available to me, and if it did have to go away, to be sure I'd have used it as much as possible.

The typewriter lived with us for a couple of years. It moved from the dining room table to a desk in the living room, then a desk in the family room, then to the desk in the spare bedroom. Then after one move, it wasn't there. My family moved about once a year (my parents were the original find-it-fix-it-resell-it couple).

It was many years later I found out why the typewriter showed up. In this part of the 1950's, most girls were expected to either become nurses, teachers, secretaries or housewives. Daddy thought his girls should at least be able to make their own living by being in an office (until they got married), and this was a head-start on his plan-ahead for his girls.

The Royal KMM

by David Mecklenburg

O h, honey, I heard. Are you OK?" Maria asked her.

She was about to answer when a ripping, grinding sound blasted over the phone and Maria's voice was lost. After about 10 seconds of this she heard Maria yelling something in the background before she could hear her again.

"Hi, sorry. I'm coming over there. My landlord is having some work done and I can't stand this anymore."

She hung up the phone and went to the window and wished she smoked. She was glad Maria was coming over. Maria had almost gotten her master's, almost, because the last formalities of defense and such were still to come. But those were mostly parties. Maria was even figuring out what sort of wine and cake to bring to her defense.

She looked at the bottle of wine. It stood next to the typewriter, a Royal KMM. The same kind Joan Didion used. Before everything happened, he had left the wine for her own thesis celebration. The typewriter he had given her before. Next to it was the summary letter of her own masters—essentially shoved under the door: there would be no party.

Her studio was somewhat ratty, with plaster that had cracked long before she arrived and inconvenient windows, one of which was painted shut. The flooring always looked muddy, which she figured was a bonus because she didn't have to clean it much. It all terribly depressed her, yet six months earlier these things had vindicated her most bourgeoise fantasies about being poor and in love.

She wasn't sure what to think because her thoughts kept shifting through various guises: a one-woman show of outrage, of compromise, of bewilderment and depression. The chorus of denial, all of them her in black and aubergine robes kept at it, and she was keenly aware that there was another role: of audience. She was alone in the theatre save for her selves on stage and she kept searching for herself in the dark but she was growing very small.

She remembered something like that had happened to Toad in an old Arnold Lobel book from her childhood where Toad kept performing while Frog simply disappeared in the audience leaving Toad to sail around the darkness utterly alone. The image still terrified her.

"You need some wine. We have to drink his, this, right now." Maria had arrived and made short work of the cork in the bottle of Bonnes Mares. "So, what happened? I just got back you know and heard that the thing about you and Evan got out. But everyone knew about it, I thought."

"His wife didn't."

"She lived a whole separate life over there in Medina. God, this is delicious."

"That's why I believed him. He said things were different with me."

"Of course he did. Stop, we will get there. I'm sick of PoMo theory and non-linear narrative. I want to hear this the old-fashioned way."

She smiled at this request. "There isn't any closure, Maria."

"Don't worry about that. That's why I love poetry. Closure's kind of optional, even at the end of lines.

"As long as it sounds good."

"There is no end to a good line because if it's really good you keep thinking of it."

"*Look on my works ye mighty, and despair.*"

"Exactly. And this isn't the end of the line for you."

"Academically I'm ruined. I'll never get a recommendation to a PhD program."

"Do you really want one? This isn't an isolated incident you know."

"I suppose not."

She met him in his non-creative course on Critical Theory and Lacan. He was tall, twice her age and moved like a lean captain sailing his own ship around the world. Because she was on a PhD. Track for Critical Theory and he usually taught poetry, the class seemed like a rare chance to work with *the* Evan Randolph.

"But I only hate the creative classes more, you know." At the end of spring quarter, he said this over a paint of beer at the College Inn Pub.

He had a habit of looking to his left when he spoke. He held the beer up, almost to his lips and paused. Then he looked left, as if he were looking over the Sound on a foggy day or maybe on a dry day in Eastern Washington when he watched the sun cut the rocks of the Columbia Gorge into paint. Yes, before that impersonal universe the small sprigs of dry grass were nothing. They wavered, waiting for lighting or pumice to obliviate them a dramatic way, but really, they just fell apart as the wind ground them down against the ochre stone.

It was one of his most famous poems and he read it at the faculty reading Even though it was a poem about windsurfing alone on the Columbia, it was a celebration of the mutability of everything. But still, the board and its sail would carry you across the glittering reflections if you were strong. If your heart and your back could hold out.

"Have you ever been?" he asked.

"Windsurfing? No, I… didn't have the right kind of friends in high school. We stayed inside mosty, ha, so I never learned. I tried once on Lake Folsom with some friends of mine but I got embarrassed."

"About what? You seem so tall, and strong."

"I was skinny, and I liked what the goth kids were into. I didn't fit in anywhere."

"Yeah, it's too bad. I see a lot of young women like you come through here, but they find their way. Too bad the season's over for it, or I'd show you."

"Do you ever go with your family?"

"No, they'd wreck it. I mean Linda's great. So's my daughter Madison, but they're my family. You don't want a family when you're out there." He paused for a long while. She became aware her breaths were short and coming from her upper chest. She tried to breathe deeply. "Anyway," he continued, "I'd be glad to chair your master's."

As she walked home that night, the summer twilight, which already seemed to go on forever in Seattle, stretched into a purple and orange heaven around the earth. She didn't see him much over the summer, since he spent it with his family or by himself on a trout fishing trip in Paraguay.

His advisory of her began with the usual meetings in his office in the fall. She coaxed stories out of him and they didn't get much work done. One day, he asked her to come over to his house on a Thursday. She had no idea how to even take the bus out there, but it didn't matter. She agreed immediately and went to the Student Union Hall to figure out her trip.

"How many transfers did that take?" Maria asked.

"Two. It was quite a haul."

"Worth it?"

"At the time, yes."

The house was beautiful. She knew his wife came from old NW Timber money and it showed in all the wood paneling and rich prairie style Craftsman cut glass windows. His study was simple and austere. An antique desk sat in the middle of the room looking out over Lake Washington.

"So, this is it? They typewriter you wrote "Ochre Sunset?""

"Oh, yeah. Had it out there with me. It's why I still use it. Do you want to give her a spin?"

"Of course!" She sat and he put a sheet of white paper in the platen, rolled it through.

Datt, datt, datt datt datt datt datt datt datt datt. And she typed.

"My name is Roosevelt. Look on this Damn ye mighty. Pretty good for a cripple..."

The text was faint and hard to read from a distance, but she rattled it out quickly.

"You remember the line, Ada."

"Evan, it's like the "Ozymandias" of post 60's poetry. How could I forget that?" And that was when his gaze, with those iron gray eyes finally shifted onto her. His smile was crooked, which seemed even more exaggerated owing to his long jaw and the wrinkles he'd developed over the years, first on crew at Princeton, then surfing at Banyans on the Big Island. Then the fishing trips on the Yellow River where he followed the paddlestrokes of Du Fu.

"The ribbon needs ink."

"Yes, it does," he said and he touched the ribbon. Then he touched her shoulder. He smiled again.

"The ribbon may not be wet, Ada. But are you?"

It was so far away from what she'd done as an undergrad. Had she known Grad School sex with your professor was that much better than lame hookups with drunk friends... God. And she was stone sober and his semen was running down her leg as she walked to the bus and she'd come four times.

That afternoon started the brilliant days. Most often he'd

come to her studio on Capitol Hill because it was easier to get away from his family. The two of them made love and ate. Later, he would infatuate her with Dylan Thomas or T'ang Dynasty poetry. Sometimes they tried to write together. He brought the typewriter in its case, so he could work.

He would stand naked, looking off to the left as always, and speak and she would type his words. He said this was going to be an entirely new book. The chapbook he'd been working on was crap. They burned it one day in the alleyway.

"Your love has given me so much new energy, baby," he said.

In the summer he was going to take her to the Canary Islands.

Linda will believe that. You just have to be careful, baby. If we're on different flights no one will know. It'll be my present for your degree. Three weeks, just the two of us. My friend Manuel has this amazing little stone house. We can walk down to the beach. You won't have to wear clothes at all.

In the meantime, she worked on the typewriter: kept it freshly inked and sometimes when he wasn't there, she wrote poetry.

"Where is it? Why haven't you ever let me read it?" Maria asked.

"It's pastiche at best. And I burned it too. Just... after."

"The incident."

"It's all over the department, I imagine?"

"Last week's news, honey. Don't worry! Everyone's so wrapped up in their theses defense or lining up work that they'll forget about it."

"I won't."

Maria looked at her with a want for details. It was human. All too human. Evan once said he loved the fact his girlfriend could read Nietzsche in the original. But he never asked for her to actually do it.

"We got careless. No, not that way. I was good about taking

the pill. I didn't want a baby holding me back."

"Why not?" Maria sipped the wine and narrowed her eyes. They knew each other well enough so she could tell when Maria had turned on her therapist's gaze. "It would have been the perfect thing to force his selfish hand, but you're not like that. Right?"

"No, I'm better than that."

"But that's not the reason," Maria said, and she was right.

"A child would have been a family. Someone else. Anyway, it was hardly even an open secret anymore. But, I think it made a lot of people uncomfortable."

"It was that obvious?"

"You were in love. I could tell on your face. I just wished you'd come clean with me sooner instead of that bullshit story you told me about the doctoral student at SU that I somehow never met. Anyway, I figured it out at the faculty party in Winter Quarter? He had his arm around you and you both smelled like sex when you showed up five minutes apart. Planned, totally!"

"I was proud of it."

"You should have been. He's a handsome guy. I doubt he's got another McArthur Fellowship or Pulitzer in him. He's got good taste in wine though. Tell me, did he ever use that thing?"

"What, the typewriter? No, he usually just came over to fuck and then talk about Dylan Thomas, or himself. Or both. How he was like Dylan Thomas."

"He was. Once, but Evan didn't drink himself to death. And you don't want to be Caitlin Thomas. Considering what happened, I wonder how much he wanted to be discovered? What about you?"

Maria was right. The memories came back carried in a tumbler lined with mirrored glass—when you drank you could see exactly who was poisoning you. She could watch herself in the memories and see the unconscious volition in every step.

It began safely enough: it was late and she went to meet him at the office. He was going to be with his family for Christmas and wanted to give her a gift. That time he turned out the lights to his office and they made love for quite a while. They spoke of the future in the darkness.

"It's not that easy you know. These things have to be done very carefully. I don't care if she takes me to the cleaners but it needs to be done discreetly. The kid, you know."

"I know" she said and pouted in the dark. His hand stroked her hair.

"Oh, your Christmas gift. He switched on a dim light on the desk and handed her an envelope. She couldn't imagine what it was. For a moment she thought it was money because that's the only kind of thing that came in envelopes at Christmas besides cards.

But it was a card, with Shakespeare's 130th Sonnet written neatly on it in his strong hand writing. And there was an old photo. Of the KMM typewriter.

"I don't understand."

"It's yours, baby. You use it more than I do anyway. I want you to have it."

Maria frowned then said: "I don't know about the Shakespeare though, aside from your looks. I don't find those very flattering sonnets. But he gave you a typewriter you were already using. Hmm. It is a beautiful typewriter."

"Same kind that...

"...Joan Didion used. I know. You've told me that before. Can it make you write like her? You're both from Sacramento. Well, it's a cheap present, in a way. He didn't have to get you anything special, like one of your own or anything. And that's how you two started using his office. And that's really where it ended, right?

"Yes."

She still remembered the sky, torn apart when summer and

winter fight over the springtime. The wind ripped great patches of charcoal colored cloud and threw the rain in buckets down before sun bolts. The quad would be lit up one minute and in dark rain the next. They had taken to meeting in his office. At first, they did it quickly, but gradually things got more complicated. Or less, depending on perspective.

And that day in May, she showed up in a raincoat and high heels and nothing else. He was already hard, and they performed a long bout of oral sex on each other before he spun her around to fuck her from behind. He liked it that way. She loved it that way because he'd reach around and make her come over and over.

The wind rattled the panes of glass. She remembered that. She remembered his fingers on her clitoris and his cock was so deep she could feel the glans on her cervix. And she was coming. And that's when the door opened and Emil O'Bannon, the department chair, walked in with Abigail Jensen.

"*The* Abigail Jensen?! Oh ho! That's why they were so secretive. I heard that the chair walked in on you two, but it seemed weird; like something was missing. A major donor to the department, that would explain it. She and Evan's wife are friends after all."

"I didn't know that. Couldn't have…" She trailed off.

She remembered she must have grabbed her raincoat and purse because somehow, she caught the old 43 and returned to Capitol Hill.

By the end of the afternoon she'd received a call from the department secretary for her to meet with two of her other professors from her thesis panel. This meeting got delayed three times. The third, her advisor, and now former lover, was not mentioned.

"Assholes. So the Chair was there too?"

"I'd already typed up a letter of apology. They didn't read it although Evelyne at least looked at it but she never said anything. They left it to Karl. I don't think he really liked doing it."

"Of course not. He's fucking one of his TA's too. So what did they say?"

"I'd get my Master's but that was it. I could consider the meeting my summary defense but 'under the circumstances' I was not to mention my indiscretion."

"*Your* indiscretion? They didn't say anything about Evan, did they?"

"No."

"You should sue them."

"I can't. I signed an agreement."

"Under duress. I'm sure that's not legal."

"I just want to get away from here, but I don't know what to do."

"And you haven't heard anything from him?"

"He's as quiet as that typewriter."

"He's gone off somewhere with his wife and kids, I guess. Counseling is what I've heard. I'm so sorry. This is awful."

She kept the typewriter and there were jobs to bounce through as she tried to find herself. Sometimes she would sit and try to use it and the stack of paper, perhaps pinched from one of her temp jobs, like a journal.

She liked the Royal for the margin setting feature and the fact it was such a snappy typewriter to work on. It felt like a pacing horse she was riding and they moved together not just effortlessly, but enjoyably, but she could never write anything of interest on it: shopping lists, occasional paragraphs or the opening line of a novel, over and over again like Joseph Grand in Camus' *The Plague*. Eventually it became less an instrument and more of an *objet*.

She left it with Maria for safe keeping when she went to Germany at 27. And then there was Japan. Maria left and returned too—a Doctor of Poetry from the University of

Houston. She was married and living in Bellingham: teaching at Western Washington University. After many missed encounters, Maria finally drove down to Seattle, with the typewriter in its case.

"I can't imagine you've got a bottle of Bonnes Mares again," Maria asked, winking.

"I can't believe we drank that. I should have sold it."

"Absolutely not! I'm sure the winemaker would much have rather had two beautiful young women drinking it in commiseration. Over *l'amour perdu* and all of that... than just sitting in a cellar as an investment."

"You're right, as usual. No, but I have a nice Sancerre if that will do."

The two of them were sitting by a table. It was a pretty light that came in over Capitol Hill that day.

"I'm sorry it took me so long to get it back to you. Or get back here."

"No, don't worry about it. Somehow I think it would have been too much to have around here. I'm not sure she would have even liked it."

"Astrid you mean? She always seemed rather austere to me. Very beautiful. Smart."

"The kind that breaks you."

"You must have been insufferable together. You're one of the smartest people I know," Maria said, "and she wasn't a dull knife, either. It feels like I've done this before, somehow..."

"Ha, that's true." It was the first time she had laughed in a while, perhaps, or at least remembered it, noticed it, which amounted to the same thing. "So, now that you've been on both sides of the fence, what do you think?"

"Men and women are both shits."

"I'm sorry. This one hurts more. I can tell."

"How?"

"I don't know. Maybe... there's something less dramatic, but deeper in your mood. Perhaps we're getting older."

"Perhaps it's because it was two and half years of Blake."

"A marriage of heaven and hell?" Maria asked and they clinked glasses. "Well, there's only one thing you need to do. Get your ass on this KMM and type it out."

And I tried. For a while.

But I found that I don't really like typewriters after all. It's not that I'm a bad typist. I'm an executive assistant so I do it a lot. I'm fast, but kind of sloppy so there are lots of typos and my head keeps getting lost in mistakes that don't matter.

Like Evan. Like Astrid.

But eventually I found I could write about them on rainy days in a café with a Waterman fountain pen and a red and black journal. On clear nights I can sit here on my laptop and type it all out—take down my own words for a change.

The typewriter? I left it in Medina, on the doorstep of the house where his wife still lives. I'm sure he'll never use it again because he blew the Alzheimer's out of his brain with a Smith and Wesson in a hotel room in Boston.

"This was your father's"

I typed that and left it on the platen.

The young woman sat outside on the bench. She had a clear plastic sports bottle full of some purple drink. The older woman walked up to her. The younger woman had a short pixie haircut and wore long grey shorts and stylishly oversized sneakers with enormous laces. Her lip was pierced and both ears were pierced 8 times each.

The older woman was around 6'1" even in flats. She dressed in a French sailor's shirt pulled off her shoulders and wore a pair of tight black jeans. Her ears were not pierced, and she had thick long black hair with bangs that was slowly turning the color of iron. She didn't wear a bra and didn't care.

Both women were tattooed although the younger one had more.

They had both done OK in life so far and were glad for that.

"You're Ada?"

"Yes."

"I've always wanted to meet you."

"Really?"

"You can't be all bad: my mother hated you. Intensely. I can see why. You're tall, gorgeous. She's none of those things."

"She's rich."

"That helps her, I guess. Thanks for the typewriter. I really love it. Did my dad use it a lot?"

"No. I usually typed for him."

"What a prick. I'm sorry. I loved him though. Why did you give it back?"

"I didn't like using it."

"Too much of his voice? Standing in his patriarchal shadow and that shit?"

"You could look at it that way, but no. I don't like typewriters. They're messy, you can't save your work except on one sheet of paper and they don't have spell check. Some people still love them, though."

"Like me."

"Like you."

"So, you write too?"

"I do. Now."

"Here, I want to give you this back: for the typewriter."

"A zine! Did you, yes, I can see your name is there. I love this. Thank you."

"Maybe we can be friends."

"I would like that."

Ballpoint Pen

The Sharpest Pen

by Lauren Patzer

Detective Becky Lopez was worried about getting jaded working homicide for so many years. After so many drug deals gone bad, domestic violence encounters and just plain crazy people with a gun, it seemed to all be blurring together. She stared calmly at the pile of paperwork on her desk and contemplated finding a lighter and shutting off the smoke alarm. But no, these victims had families who deserved answers. She ran her fingers through her dark hair and sighed.

The knock on her door broke her out of her reverie. She looked up to see Chief Sanders peeking in through the crack, her dark brown eyes glinting in the office light.

"May I?" Chief Sanders asked. Becky stood up quickly and nodded.

"Of course, Chief," Becky smiled.

Chief Sanders was dressed in the standard dress uniform. Becky surmised she must've done a press conference earlier. Chief Sanders entered and took a seat in the single chair. Becky admired the Chief for her professionalism, career and always looking out for her fellow officers. Morale had certainly improved since she came on board, not that it was horrible before. Sometimes, you just don't notice how bad things are until they suddenly improve.

Becky followed Chief Sanders lead and sat down.

"Dan tells me you're contemplating a vacation to escape the monotony," Chief Sanders said with a smile. Becky's jaw dropped open. "Don't worry about it, Becky. I understand perfectly. I was about to tell Dan to push you to take it, but something came across my desk this morning."

"I know murder shouldn't be monotonous. There are people's lives at stake, families torn apart. I'll redouble my efforts to get these solved."

"No, you won't."

"I'm sorry?" Becky frowned and leaned forward.

"I mean, you can do that if you want to after this special assignment and a small vacation."

Becky sat back in her chair and cocked her head to one side.

"Okay. Chief. I'm listening."

"Two days ago," Chief Sanders said as she leaned forward. "Bob came across a murder in Ballard that looked a lot like a BOLO we got from the Port CID and another from the FBI."

"So, I'm working with Bob?" Becky raised her eyebrows. Bob was a good detective; he hardly needed her help.

"No. Bob has recused himself. He knew two of the victims personally, so he knew he shouldn't be investigating."

"Really? Is Bob a suspect?" Becky smirked.

"No, but given the circumstances, it could be someone he knows."

"Circumstances?"

"I need someone I can trust to liaison with the FBI on this. CID has made their resources available for us as well."

Becky squinted her eyes at the Chief. They'd only talked a few times, but Chief Sanders had always been professional, cordial and straight with her. Still, Becky doubted her poker skills and was sure she was missing a major piece of information that would be very important. Of course, turning down an offer like this from the Seattle Chief of Police wouldn't do anything to help her career. She didn't need anything else stalling her progress.

"I'm in," Becky said. "What's next?"

"The files will be released to your access immediately. I suggest you review them as quickly as possible–you meet with the FBI at 4pm in the conference room," Chief Sanders said as she stood, walked to the door and opened it.

Becky looked at the clock on her desk. It just ticked over to 1:30pm. She sighed. She hated drinking coffee this late. She grabbed her cup and walked to the break room. She was surprised to see Bob sitting at one of the tables nursing a cup himself.

"Hey, Bob," Becky said as she realized a fresh pot had been brewed. She poured a cup and walked over to Bob.

Bob hadn't seemed to hear her, looking up with a start as she approached. Becky noticed his red rimmed eyes.

"Hey, Becky." Bob stood, his tall frame and pale pallor made him appear like a corpse to Becky for just a moment. He nodded his head awkwardly. "Thanks for taking this on. She was a good dog."

Becky frowned. "Beg pardon?"

"Oh," Bob nodded again as he sat down. "Right, you probably haven't read the file yet. It was Joan."

Joan, aka Joan of Bark, Bob's K-9 partner when he was on street patrol. Everybody knew about Joan retiring three years ago and getting a book written about her. K-9 Detective: Savage Seattle. Becky's heart skipped a beat. Was she going to be trying to solve a dog's murder? Why had the FBI been called in?

"I'm sorry for your loss, Bob," Becky said as she patted Bob's shoulder. "Looks like I got some work to do!"

She held up her coffee cup, smiled awkwardly and walked out of the room. *Great*, she thought, *I'm going to be known as the doggy detective!* This didn't mix well with the cat incident from five years ago. The Commander Kitty moniker had stuck until two years ago. Even now, some of the older veterans still chuckle when she walks in the room. *You solve one feline smuggling ring, you're branded for life.*

Becky sat down at the desk. She took a sip of her coffee and closed her eyes for a moment. She hoped this wasn't going to blow her career off track. She wondered if she'd done something to piss off the Chief. She took a deep breath and opened her eyes. After a few keys typed into the computer, she was past the password locked screen and saw the notification in her email. She opened it and clicked on the link to the files on the server.

First set of files showed the opening salvo for the investigation–two animal murders on board a visiting Chinese container ship. The two dogs had been the subject of books written about them in China: Cargo Canines and Ship Sam, as they were translated from Chinese. Each dog had been stabbed through the eye with a ballpoint pen.

"That is horrible," Becky murmured as she opened the second set of files. There was a graphic file for the cover of Kitten Alexander and the Den of Thieves. Seven year old Alexander, the "writer" of the Kitten Alexander series was killed by a ballpoint pen through the eye in Portland, Oregon. Becky shuddered. She never liked animal cruelty. She hoped it was a quick death.

The third file had the information on Joan. Becky moved through the file fairly quickly and found a related file on the death of the ghostwriter for the books, Felix Manning. He had also ghostwritten some of the Kitten Alexander books, but not all of them. She remembered meeting Felix at one of the book conferences she attended in her spare time. Not all writers were created equal, but Felix seemed to be a nice person. She wondered what would drive someone to kill a human with a ballpoint pen through the eye, just like the animals. *A crazed fan or a crazed writer? Maybe a crazed animal lover or hater?*

Felix lived here in Seattle. Bob probably knew him as well, likely better than Becky did. She just met him briefly at one of the expose.

I'm going to have to talk to Bob.

Becky skimmed through the other related files including something about a bear being killed and two other ghost writers. Crimes occurred in Idaho and Oregon, so they were still local to the Northwest. Murders were all done with the pen to the eye. Evidently the bear was small or it might not have killed it. Damage reported to the end of the pen, possibly used a mallet to drive it through the bear's skull. Ah, there it was, tranquilizer was used to subdue the bear first, medication stolen from a local veterinarian specializing in large animals. No surveillance or prints at any scene, of course. That would be too easy.

Becky looked up and realized it was close to 4pm. She felt she'd given the files a thorough perusal. She got up and refreshed her coffee before walking to the conference room.

As Becky entered the conference room, she noted the two stuffed shirts that could only be FBI agents waiting there. No one else was in the room. She approached the one at the head of the table. He got up and held out his hand.

"I'm Detective Rebecca Lopez, but you can call me Becky,' she said as she smiled at the agent. He was tall with a crew cut graying at the temples. His grizzled appearance reminded her immediately oif the veterans here in the office. She wondered if he'd call her Commander Kitty.

"Detective Lopez," he said. "I'm Special Agent Miller and this is Special Agent Willmont," Agent Miller pointed at the African American man sitting next to him. His hair was black, but Becky imagined it wouldn't be for long. The wrinkles on Agent Willmont's face were on the edge of grizzled like Agent Miller.

Agent Willmont started typing on the laptop in front of him and the overhead projector came to life, revealing images Becky had seen before in the files on the case. She sat down opposite Agent Willmont as Agent Miller continued to stand at the head of the room and point at the projector screen.

"You've probably reviewed most of this information by now." Agent Miller glanced at Becky and she nodded. "We've got some additional information that wasn't released to the Seattle PD for security reasons. We can show you the information but can't actually send it to you."

Becky nodded and opened her notebook. She looked at Agent Willmont and winked. "It's not my first rodeo."

Agent Willmont gave her a blank stare and returned his attention to the laptop.

Tough crowd, Becky though as she clicked her pen, ready to take notes.

"The books Cargo Canines and Ship Sam were both written by a Long Du Chi, of the Shangdong province in China." Agent Miller nodded and the picture changed from the book cover version of Long Du Chi to a post mortem picture with a ballpoint pen stuck in his eye.

"Guess he got the point," Becky said. "Ballpoint." Becky smiled at Willmont.

"Didn't you have a retired police officer die at this killer's hands?" Agent Miller said. "Thought you'd take this more seriously."

"Levity is a common coping mechanism when faced with horrific images, Agent Miller. Keeps you from going crazy. Joan was a special officer and my presence here reflects my commitment to this case."

"Indeed," Agent Miller said and returned his attention to the screen where a variety of Chinese characters were arranged on individual pieces of paper laid out on a white surface. "As you should recall, our killer is fond of leaving notes behind in or on the victims. In Long Du Chi's case, these were found stuffed down his throat post mortem. The Chinese language being what it is, it took a while to reassemble each separate character into the authorities' best guest of what the note said."

The screen changed to a page with English letters written on it stapled to someone's back.

"Felix Manning had a note stapled to his back post mortem that had been written with a low cost, Bic ballpoint pen, even though one of Felix's own pens, a unique ballpoint that had a metal barrel was readily available. The killer traced letters from Felix's own notes to build the note, making handwriting analysis unlikely to help."

"This wasn't in the files either," Becky said. "What did the notes say and were they stuck to the animal victims as well?"

"Roughly translated, they all said the same thing: Live by the pen, die by the pen. Even the Chinese note roughly translates to this." Agent Miller sat down and the projector bulb turned off. "The animals had the notes inscribed on their skin using what we determine is the same pen type. Skin being an uneven writing surface, there was also no way of matching it up with any handwriting analysis–we couldn't even match the two inscriptions on the Chinese dogs to each other."

"Was it in English, on the Chinese dogs?"

"Yes," Agent Miller said. "That's how we determined it was likely an English speaking killer, most likely from the Seattle area."

"Based on all the evidence, I concur that the killer is likely in the Northwest, but I haven't seen anything pinpointing them to the Seattle area." Becky set her notebook on the table. "You also haven't explained why you haven't searched passport trips to China from Seattle to narrow down the suspects."

The agents looked at each other. Agent Willmont shrugged.

"Well, I'm glad to see you're among the sharpest tools in the Seattle PD," Agent Miller said. "For the stateside murders, we believe the suspect may have used public transportation to get around as there were no signs or mentions of unusual cars in the area of any of the victims around the times of their death."

Agent Miller got up and walked to the door. He opened it

and took a quick look around. He shut it quietly.

"The death in China appears to be a contract killing. The contract was initiated on the dark web using money suspected to have been withdrawn from Felix Manning's accounts to a dummy account in Barbados and transferred to the killer in China."

"Really?" Becky said. "And how does the FBI know this or is this a 'we could tell you but then we'd have to kill you situation?'"

Agent Miller gave Becky a blank stare as if to confirm what she just said. She raised her eyebrows.

"Through channels," Agent Miller said and used air quotes. "The FBI was able to obtain a photograph of the envelope used to send the letters which had a Seattle postmark. That is the only thing linking these murders to a possible killer located in the Seattle area. The killings being of writers and animals primarily located in the Northwest is another indicator, but not enough to nail it down by itself."

Agent Willmont cleared his throat. Agent Miller fell silent.

"In reference to the other indicators, all of the writers, including the one in China, were harassed online by someone here in the Seattle area, initially from library computers in the local area and then via various coffee shops," Agent Willmont said.

"Yeah, we got a few of those," Becky said.

"Oh, do you, Detective?" Agent Miller said as he typed into his phone. "You know, I think you're going to love our pen expert, Miles."

"Really?" Becky smiled. "Sounds great."

Becky's heart sunk as in through the door walked a young man who looked like he just graduated from high school with pre-college credit for bookworming. Horn-rimmed glasses filled out a squirrelly face topped by a slicked by short hair cut reminiscent of the 1950's. He wore a dull grey suit that looked two sizes too big. He walked over to the computer and handed a thumb drive to Agent Willmont who smiled and plugged it into the laptop. He smoothed his hair and walked to the front of the room, cleared his throat, coughed and sniffed.

"As we all know, the Ballpoint Killer-" Miles said.

"He doesn't have a nickname, Miles," Agent Miller said.

"Oh, right," Miles pushed up his glasses. "So, the killer I will refer to as the Ballpoint Killer for this presentation,"

Agent Miller sighs.

"Has a penchant for these low cost Bic pens," Miles continued. "Going so far as to include one in the package sent to China for the hired killer to use there."

A picture of a package of the pens comes on the screen. "Of particular interest is the batch of ink used in these pens recovered in country as they appear to all have been from the same package. These particular pens are called the Bic Cristal, with a distinctive hexagonal design that is actually a permanent addition to the Museum of Modern Art in New York's industrial design collection."

Agent Miller clears his throat.

"Right, not important." Miles pushed his glasses up on his nose. "But what may be important is it appears all of the murder weapons have been missing their distinctive polypropylene cap which the killer may be keeping as trophies." Miles smiled at the room. As he got nothing but quiet nods, he cleared his throat and continued. "But that may be pure conjecture on my part, as I'm not a behavioral analyst, just a pen analyst."

"Thank you, Miles," Agent Miller said.

"But, if I may, I do have a theory that the killer uses the lowest cost, most common pen because that is how he feels about the writings from his victims."

Agent Miller stared at Miles.

"And, that's all I had to say about that," Miles said. He walked back over to Agent WIllmont, grabbed his thumb drive and exited the room.

"That brings us to where we are today and why Detective

Lopez has been chosen to aid us from the Seattle PD," Agent Miller said.

"Because I use pens?" Becky laughed and when no one else laughed, she came to an abrupt stop. "No, seriously, why did you think I'd be your best bet?"

"You have a relationship with the local writing community," Agent Miller said. "We believe that insight coupled with on the ground analysis by Miles will help you track down our killer."

"Wait, what, with Miles?" Becky stood up, realized she wasn't going to really storm out of the room, and then sat down. "He's a kid."

"He looks young for his age, but he actually has a PhD in molecular, forensic and behavioral sciences."

"He's a doctor?"

"Well, he holds a doctorate in three disciplines, but he doesn't refer to himself as doctor and, just between you me and everyone in this room who works with him, please don't start calling him doctor. He's already tough enough to work with."

"Why not just let him go if he's so tough to work with?"

"He has promise and he may yet advance to the BAU."

Becky closed her eyes. Has promise is the same thing Doug said about her. It's why she pushed to make detective. But here she was, babysitting a nerdling from the FBI and hunting for a dog killer. She took a deep breath.

"OK, so I'm going to take him to…"

"There is a writing conference this weekend in Bellevue, as you well know."

"Done your homework and checked my credit card transactions?" Becky said smiling.

"Actually, your supervisor mentioned you had requested the weekend off to attend," Agent Miller said.

"So, that's why I'm sure I'll be taking him along to the book expo next week in Kitsap county," Becky said.

"They said you were sharp," the FBI agent said.

"Thanks," Becky said.

"This is deadly serious, Detective Lopez," FBI agent said. "We're still gathering the information and forensics, but we think there are a few more victims as yet to be connected to this serial killer. It's not likely he's done killing either."

"I know."

"We'll send you the updated profile tomorrow morning. They're still working on it at the BAU."

Becky nodded. "I'll pen it into my schedule."

Agent Miller blinked at Becky and shook his head. Becky smiled and walked out of the room.

Detective Robert Davis, Bob for short, wasn't usually sitting at his desk in the late afternoon. If he was sitting at his desk, it was typically the hub of activity. The normal level was other officers going back and forth with news, information, taking requests or simply giving Bob a nod so he'd answer the constantly ringing telephone. Today, Bob sat silent and alone at his desk. Becky walked up and sat down in the chair across from him. Bob looked up and gave her a wan smile. She noticed the dark circles under his red-rimmed eyes.

"You're a good detective, Becky. I knew it would just be a matter of time before you came to see me."

"I figured you were just waiting for me since the hive was silent," Becky said. She took a sip of her coffee.

"The questions I know you want answers to is a short list, isn't it?" Bob said. "How long have I known Felix? Since high school, going on twenty years now. Did I know anyone who had a personal grudge against Felix? No. I approached him to do the books about Joan after she'd retired. I knew of his work on the cat books. It was a fun read and I thought this might be a little meatier for him to sink his writing teeth into. I never thought–" Bob choked a little and stopped speaking.

"You can't blame yourself for this Bob," Becky said. "Most of us never know when our final day on this Earth will be or why. The fault lies in the bloody hands of the killer who randomly decided the conditions for his victims. No one can live their life constantly fearing death. We'd never enjoy life."

Bob nodded.

"I'm taking a few days off," Bob looked down. "To be with Margie and the kids."

"Don't forget to enjoy life, Bob. That's what Joan and Felix would both want for you," Becky said as she stood up and gave Bob a comforting pat on the shoulder. "Did Felix ever mention anyone acting strange at one of the book shows or conferences?"

"You mean besides the other writers?" Bob chuckled. "Writers are a strange lot, most of the fans are pretty normal, but yeah, a few kooks come out of the woodwork now and then. Nothing I can bring to mind as an obvious killer though. May be worth canvassing the other writers."

"I'll be doing that for sure at the conference this weekend," Becky said. "You be sure to enjoy your family this weekend."

"We're going to take a little trip up the mountain. The kids love walking the trails at Reflection Lake," Bob said as he stood up.

"I'm on this, Bob," Becky said as she looked him in the eye. "I got this."

Bob gave Becky's shoulder a gentle squeeze and walked away.

Early the next morning, Becky walked in to the office and noticed Miles sitting patiently in reception. He stood up when he saw her. He wore a different suit, but it was still big for him.

"Detective Lopez," Miles said and held out his hand.

"Ah, Special Agent... Miles?" Becky said as she shook his hand.

"Vincenzo. I usually just go by Miles," Miles said as he fell into step with her. He already had his visitor's badge.

"You really don't look Italian," Becky said.

"Yeah, there was a lot of dilution of the bloodline–paternally, always Italian, but the last four generations have married non-Italian women. I don't mean to get on a eugenics discussion, but it's something I usually don't bring up. Hence, I usually go by Miles. It just prevents awkward questions and explanations."

"Oh, sorry," Becky said as they entered the homicide division hallway.

"It's not, umm, a problem. I'm just, well, being very smart has its advantages and disadvantages. I realize I have some social awkwardness that I'm always working on, so I try to avoid anything that gets too personal."

"OK," Becky said as she entered her office. She pointed to the seat on the opposite side of her desk and Miles walked to it and sat down. "So, if you're not here for a social call to get to know each other better, why are you here so early?"

Becky set her stuff down on the desk and sat down. She folded her hands together and looked at Miles. He seemed to mentally count things in his head and then looked up.

"Yes, first, the profile should be coming in this morning. It's 11am eastern time, they usually get them out by 10am. I wanted to be available to go over the analysis and answer any questions you might have. Second, I thought we could get to the writing conference early so we could observe everyone who came in. Third, I really don't have anywhere else to be today."

"You don't go to the FBI office here in Seattle?"

"Oh, the other officers are there."

Becky stood up. "Okay, let me get a cup of coffee before I address those three items then."

"Coffee stunts your-" Miles started to say.

Becky looked at him and growled.

"Um, enjoy your coffee," Miles finished and looked at his phone.

Becky walked to the break room, passing Bob's empty office. *Keep it together for Bob at least, Becky.*

After getting her coffee, Becky returned to find Miles moving around the office, holding his phone in the air and looking at the screen.

"Not a good place for a signal. You can use the unsecured WiFi," Becky said as she sat down.

"Even with the firewall in place, that opens the door to more security issues. I was hoping to get a stronger cell signal," Miles said.

He turned to see Becky sitting down and put his phone in his pocket. He sat down again.

"Sometimes, I like things just so," Miles said. "Some people find that annoying."

Becky smiled and took a sip of coffee. "So, let's get to your numbered items, shall we?"

"Why aren't you a Lieutenant yet?"

"Or we can veer off your list…" Becky pursed her lips and folded her arms.

"I'm sorry, it's been bugging me since yesterday. I didn't want to blurt it out at an inopportune time," Miles said.

"I see. Well, I had to take some time off after my partner was killed, so even though it says I've been with the department nine years, it's more like a little over eight. Promotional tests are coming up soon—is it a problem for you that I haven't advanced yet?"

"Problem? No, you have an exemplary record, according to Agent Miller. He just wouldn't let me see it."

Becky sat back in her chair and sipped her coffee again. She watched Miles fidget in his chair for a moment. He got his phone out again and read through something on it.

"BAU," Becky said. "Came up with a profile. Do you agree it's likely to be a male about age 35 to 45, highly intelligent and likely working in an educational institution?"

"Yes," Miles said without looking up. "No prior criminal history, but would have a history of beaten abused or controlled by a parent, who may have died recently triggering this outburst of violence against literary figures. He's probably not an animal lover."

"No," Becky chuckled. "Probably not."

"May actually be a failed writer, adding to his frustration and malice."

"Malice? Interesting choice of words, Miles."

"I've noticed in my study of psychology that those who can't are often abnormally angry at those who can," Miles looked up at Becky and gave her an awkward smile.

"Personal experience?"

Miles looked back down at this phone. He thought for a moment.

"Children are not yet fully cognizant of their actions and should be forgiven for such infractions," Miles said.

"I don't know that I'd go that far. There are some pretty vicious children that could use a night in the slammer to set them straight," Becky said and then took a drink. She set down her coffee and opened one of her drawers.

"Even so, it is those that don't mature and continue such antics into adulthood that commit most of the transgressions." Miles looked up. "We're looking for someone who is highly intelligent but given to emotional outbursts. It may have affected his standing at his work. Workplace disciplinary action may have tempered his outbursts but not the emotion behind them."

Becky nodded as she pulled some schedules out from past conferences. "There are, unfortunately, many failed writers at these conferences. Some may just be perfecting their craft and will go on to succeed, but it's hard to pull just one from the crowd with that analysis. However, not all writers are subject to emotional outbursts. We may not be able to narrow it down by workplace activities today, but that could be something we look into next week."

Becky shuffled through the papers and found a few with notes on them.

"I took a few notes on characters I thought I might have to follow up on later from a criminal perspective." Becky looked up to see Miles looking at her curiously. "It's something I do everywhere I go. I have napkins full of notes on suspicious characters at coffee shops and restaurants. I like to tell myself its character study for future books I might write, but I'm more inclined to think I may have a problem."

Becky laughed and stopped when Miles didn't join in.

"That was a joke, Miles."

"Oh! I thought you were doing a self-analysis. Sorry, I got caught up in the moment."

Becky shook her head.

"That's all right, Miles. So I have a few notes on possible suspects from previous conferences. I'll so some quick runs on them through the computer and see if we have any priors."

"You can eliminate the sickly or elderly as they likely wouldn't have the arm strength required to puncture a human skull with a Bic Cristal."

"That's good to know," Becky said as she began the task of entering names into the background checking program.

"On your second point for being here, I don't usually go to the conference until Saturday."

"Well." Miles cleared his throat. "It may be important to observe everyone attending from the moment they get there until they leave. The more data you have, the better a conclusion you can come to."

Becky sighs. "That actually makes sense. Although I'm not going to sit in a hotel lobby and watch people walk up to check in, get their badges and disappear to their rooms. We can go at 5pm. The activities for Friday night are less intense and not as well attended, but that will be over by 9pm."

"Everyone goes to their rooms and retires for the evening?"

"Well, not exactly. There are some impromptu gatherings during the night. Typically some of the publishing companies sponsor a party room, but most of those happen on Saturday evening. There's much less of that activity on a Friday night."

Miles stood up and stretched.

"It's less likely for our killer to be at an intimate setting. He'd stand out. A larger gathering would be better, although more difficult for us to observe and gather much information. Catching one on one interactions will yield the most data."

"Will it?" Becky said and smiled. "Maybe you need to dress down for our conference? Not many people wear suits to a writing conference."

"Oh." Miles looked down at his clothes. "I brought another suit and some gym clothes."

"Mm hmm." Becky typed a few notes into her computer and stood up. "Let's take you shopping for something a little less conspicuous."

"OK." Miles scratched his head. "Buying clothes isn't my strong suit."

"I never would've guessed that," Becky said as she locked her computer and then walked out the door.

Miles followed her out of the office.

As they approached her sedan, Becky noticed Miles looked her car up and down. When they climbed in he looked over to her side of the car, in the back seat and then in his immediate surrounding area in the cabin. He pulled his seatbelt on before shutting the door.

Becky started the car and pulled out of the parking garage.

"So, tell me what you've discovered from your in depth observation of my vehicle," Becky said.

Miles looked over at her and frowned. "I was too obvious with my observations," he said and nodded. "OK, well, you're a little OCD with you cleanliness. Your car is perfectly clean. I would guess you wash it at least once per week. There's very little dust inside anywhere, which isn't typical. It suggests a bit of a preoccupation with cleanliness actually. Usually there is some dust in the cracks,on the steering column or even under the emergency break. I didn't observe the front of your car, but from the hood, sides, top and rear, you not only clean your vehicle but also wax it regularly-"

"How do you know I wax it?"

"You left a tiny spot of residue inside the passenger side bumper," Miles said. He looked around at the traffic. "Wax on, wax off usually."

"Yeah, I got it. Thanks," Becky said. She mentally reviewed the contents of her trunk and knew there were at least two rags she could use to buff the spot out.

"I would imagine you're thinking about what you can do to fix that when we stop the car," Miles said.

Becky gripped the steering wheel a little harder. She took a turn onto the highway heading south.

"OK, that's enough about me," she said.

"I apologize, I've gone too far in my analysis," Miles said and looked down.

"No," Becky said. "I did ask what you thought. I was trying to subtly tell you how obvious it was you were observing me. I'll be more direct next time."

"OK," Miles said. He took out his phone and looked at it. "It won't bring him back, you know."

"No,' Becky said. "We're focusing on someone other than me right now."

"Oh, I thought you wanted me to be more direct as well," Miles said. He fiddled with his phone.

"I was more thinking about the serial killer," Becky said. "I don't like the China connection."

Miles looked out on the side of the road as they got closer to the Southcenter Mall.

"While it doesn't fit the MO perfectly, it still seems to be related in ways that can't be a coincidence," Miles said.

"It seems out of place," Becky said. "The timeline, the lack of personal interaction with the killer and the victim."

"Our killer is highly intelligent," Miles said.

"But that level of planning seems more premeditation than normal," Becky said. "I just don't see our killer good for it."

Miles nodded as they pulled of the highway.

"Chinese murder may be a copycat to hide the real purpose

of the killing," Miles said.

"Exactly. I'd want to see what else our Chinese victim has written, especially if it's critical of the government or someone powerful there or abroad."

"A political assassination or something similar, using the writer killings as a distraction or red herring," Miles said. The car stopped outside the mall. "I concede that as a possibility."

Becky walked Miles into the mall and they visited several stores. After a few purchases that Miles insisted on paying for, they walked back out to the car. Becky opened her trunk and grabbed a rag to polish the small spot of wax near the bumper.

"You've got eagle eyes, Miles. I had to look close just to see the smidgen of wax there."

"I'm, uh, very observant," Miles said as he load his bags into the back seat of the car.

When they climbed back into the car, Miles glanced more than once at the purchases in the back seat.

"Are you worried you spent too much?" Becky said.

"No," Miles replied. "I have plenty of funds as I don't spend my salary on much outside of basic necessities. I'm just not comfortable wearing something other than a suit."

Becky smiled as they pulled out of the parking lot.

"We're going to get you outside your comfort zone with your best interests in mind."

Miles frowned and looked at his phone again.

"Why writers' conferences?" Miles said.

"Well," Becky said as they pulled back onto the highway. "I've always fancied myself a writer. I feel like I could write a book some day and maybe make a career of it."

Miles looked at Becky and scratched his head. They drove on for several more minutes before Miles spoke again.

"I don't understand why you would want a second career when you're clearly so good at this one," Miles said.

"Thanks, I try to put my best foot forward with the police department," Becky said. "It's more of a life fully lived kind of thing. There are interests outside of the job that make life fuller and more interesting. Hobbies."

"Is it because he died?"

"No," Becky sighed. "And to your point, a singular focus in life can be detrimental if you have nothing else to fall back on. For instance, what if you couldn't be an FBI agent?"

"That's been the focus of my life. The studies, the physical conditioning and the mental preparation. Why would I want to be anything else?"

"Let's say you're injured in the line of duty and you get medically retired. What are you going to do then? What other interests do you have?"

"Uh, teaching, I suppose." Miles looked out the window.

"Don't sound so enthusiastic," Becky said.

"I'd just write a couple of papers and I could get onto any faculty I wanted," Miles said. He looked at Becky. "It's the most logical course of action."

"I'll admit it's the most logical, but that doesn't mean it's the best course of action."

"You're right about China," Miles said.

"What?"

"It's not the most logical or the best course of action," Miles said.

"That's what I was saying–are you just trying to change the subject?"

"No, but my mind processes things simultaneously. You're comments pertain to our killer. He's passionate about his hatred. Stabbing the victims up close and personal. There's no way he'd outsource that act."

"Skewing the profile?" Becky said.

"I believe so," Miles said.

"Guess we'll have to play that by ear tonight while the BAU adjusts their assumptions."

"If they adjust their assumptions," Miles said.

"Why wouldn't they change it?" Becky said.

"Unless you're a respected profiler, it's sometimes hard to change their minds once they've made a decision."

Becky said nothing. She looked straight ahead. She didn't want to see if Miles was relating a personal experience. She felt she might tear up. People could be cruel and pigheaded. She wondered if this was the real reason Miles wasn't in the BAU yet. Someone made up their mind he wasn't good enough even though it was perfectly clear the BAU was a perfect match for him.

They arrived at Miles' hotel and Miles got out without saying a word. He pulled his bags from the back seat.

"Five PM?" Becky said.

"Of course, Detective Lopez," Miles said. "I'll be here."

Becky watched Miles walk into the hotel. She thought about the psychological testing that was done on FBI agents. Miles may not be perfect, and he may have had it rough growing up, but she was certain he'd be all right.

She put the car into drive and drove out of the parking lot. She'd had her own set of prejudices to overcome on the force. Maybe that was just the way of things - growth through adversity. Did it matter that things could be easier and better if people thought things through a bit better?

Fat chance better thinking suddenly erupts in American society, she thought.

When she returned to her office after a short drive, Becky spotted her full cup of ice cold coffee on her desk. She picked it up and went into the break room. Detective Sallas was there. Becky involuntarily gasped and then pursed her lips. She went over to dump out her cup and refill her coffee.

Detective Sallas sniffed and got up.

"Something stinks in here," he said and left the room. Becky sighed and walked out with her coffee.

The memory of the day Becky got Sallas' partner killed erupted fresh in her mind. The smell of the streets, the sound of the people gathered and the failed warning that left Officer

Dunfeldt in the path of the out of control truck struck a vivid cord in her mind. It hadn't truly been Becky's fault; she'd been struck in the back by a bicyclist who had veered onto the sidewalk to avoid the truck. She still blamed herself. Clearly, Detective Sallas did too. They'd had words before. Now it was just the odd insult at the proper moment with no witnesses that filled her memories with dark moments in the precinct.

Becky sat at her desk and set the coffee down on the desk. Her hands shook. She set them in her lap, closed her eyes and took a deep breath.

What's past is past. A killer is out there today, she thought. She opened her eyes, took a sip of coffee and logged into her computer. She reviewed the evidence top to bottom and noted the differences in the Chinese killings of the writer and the dogs. All the American victims were killed with the thrust of a Bic Cristal through the right eye. The writer in China and the dogs on the ship had both eyes pierced by the low cost pen. Two pens because the killer didn't know which eye was correct? If the killer here was OCD, they wouldn't have gotten that detail wrong.

The note, left inside the victim's mouth was a different modus operandi as well. Even if it roughly translated correctly, it was curiously different. It's almost like someone overheard the killer talking about the crimes, but didn't get the details entirely correct.

She opened the files that covered internet chats, tweets or other sites that referenced the victims. It was still in the early stages of the investigation, so not all the data was well correlated. Becky spent the better part of three hours sifting through the gathered information. She made notes on a few that looked similar. Evidently, writers had internet stalkers. If the FBI could nail down the points of origin for those, that would help narrow down the list of suspects. She sent a request to flag the information she'd put together and prioritize tracking those down.

Her phone buzzed and she looked down to see her alarm going off.

Time to go agent sitting, she thought. Becky took her cup to the break room and washed it out. No one greeted her there this time. Still, she looked over to where Detective Sallas had been sitting and winced. She shook her head and walked back to her office. When she got to her office, she found Lieutenant Dan Coats waiting for her.

"Dan, what's up?"

Dan sighed and handed her a note.

"I wanted to tell you in person that Sallas has entered another complaint against you." Dan ran his fingers through his thinning hair. "I know its bullshit, but I didn't want to just send an email. We'll handle it."

"Well, I'm glad to see after four years, he hasn't swayed in his efforts to keep my personnel file full. At least he's as good an officer as he is a pain in my ass," Becky said. She glanced at the page on department letterhead and recognized the typical unprofessional conduct complaint that Detective Sallas entered every couple of months.

Dan shrugged.

"Have a great weekend, Becky. Sorry you have to be on official duty through your conference," Dan left the office and Becky watched him go. She looked at the note again and sighed.

"It's a small price to pay," Becky said. She opened the left desk file drawer and put it in the manila folder with the other complaints. She set her coffee cup on the desk and walked out of the office, locking the door behind her.

When Becky pulled up outside the hotel, Miles was waiting for her, dressed in a dark blue polo style shirt, a denim jacket and jeans. She didn't see the holster for Miles' service weapon, but she knew it was there. He looked good for once; his clothes fit loose, but comfortable. He didn't look like he was walking around in a bag designed like a suit.

He opened the car door and got in. he smiled a genuine smile at Becky and then looked forward. Becky pulled away from the hotel.

"You look inconspicuous," Becky said.

"Thank you, I think," Miles said. "I sent my recommendations on the Chinese connection. It's being reviewed."

"Been waiting how long to tell me that?" Becky said with a chuckle.

"It's been pent up," Miles said. He smiled again. "You had to have an inkling that was going to happen."

"Oh, are we on to pen puns now?" Becky said.

"I think that's really all I had."

"How did the BAU receive your recommendations?"

"Ah, yes. They received my recommendations with the typical quasi-dismissiveness I've come to expect. They'll 'put it in the file', but otherwise likely won't pay much attention to it."

"So you won't get any credit if you're right and they dumped you're insight into a trash can. That sucks," Becky said.

"They actually don't have any choice but to put it in the file. It was contained in an email which is an official communication record. I'm keenly aware of at least two agents actively trying to keep me from getting promoted to the BAU." Miles looked at Becky and smiled. "It used to be four."

"Strong and steady wins the race," Becky said.

"Indeed."

Becky found a place o the street outside the conference center to park the car. She paid the parking meter and moved on. Miles looked on curiously at her paying the meter.

"Aren't you on official police business? I thought you wouldn't have to pay for parking."

"Well," Becky said as she walked by him and he fell into step next to her. "It's more like quasi-official. I was planning on attending the conference anyway, the parking meter stops charging at 8pm and I've seen way too many officers take advantage of their law enforcement status to get free parking when they shouldn't. Call it a public service if you want. I'd rather people noticed cops paying than not paying."

"Good public relations," Miles said and nodded. "An important part of law enforcement."

"Exactly."

They went inside and followed the signs to the conference registration table. After registering Miles, Becky picked up her prepaid badge and they walked into the conference area. There were several rooms set aside for the conference, but this early, they didn't have anything going on yet. Becky looked at the conference schedule and noted several guest authors including Donna Milton, writer of Dog Day Dreamer, a book series told from a poodle's point of view.

"Interesting, I think our first suspect has a signing table at the beginning of the conference," Becky said.

"Is that unusual?"

"No, but it's definitely a sign that you're not that popular. There are barely any attendees right at 5pm on Friday who do more than simply check-in and then disappear until the opening address around 7pm or 8pm. Quite frankly, most people are at dinner."

"Well, then, I'm sure she'll be happy to see some visitors. Maybe that will buy us some good will," Miles said.

Becky checked the map and was the table for author meets was at the back of the hallway between the conference rooms. They made their way back there.

Donna Milton sat behind a long table with a custom, cloth table runner that displayed the title of her book series in small print just over an enlarged banner of her name. Donna was dressed in a flower print dress with ruffles. She had on glasses with a holder strap that was yellow and pink, matching her dress. To all appearances, the 60-something year old woman was reliving the good old prairie days.

They walked up to the table and Donna looked up, clearly startled.

"Oh my, hello!" she said sounding just like a sweet old lady.

Miles picked up a copy of the latest Dog Day Dreamer book and turned it over, reading the back cover.

"Hi Donna," Becky said. "It's so unusual to see someone here at the autograph table so early in the conference."

"Well," Donna said and her face got very sour. "They prefer to put those hacks in the prime seats. I mean, honestly, doesn't good writing mean anything anymore? All you need to sell a crappy book nowadays is good marketing and idiots for readers."

Miles perused the first pages of the book.

"Do you happen to know Felix Manning?"

"Of course, he's one of those hacks. Just because he wrote about a police dog, all the idiots lapped up the heroic," Donna made air quotes. "Law enforcement animal crap. That's exactly what I was saying about marketing to the lowest denominator."

"Could you sign this please?" Miles said, handing her the book he'd picked up.

"Oh, of course, my dear," Donna said, turning on the sweet old lady act again. "Who should I make it out to?"

"Oh, just your signature will be sufficient," Miles said. He smiled as he watched Donna open the front of the book.

"Ah, a collector! I hope this increases in value tenfold for you!"

As Donna signed her name, Miles detected a bit of a tremor in her hand.

"Did you have some surgery done recently?" He asked.

"What? Oh, you must've noticed my little tremble," Donna said. "I had some nerve damage repaired two months ago. It's healing quite well actually."

"Ulnar nerve, quite painful," Miles said.

"Yes, it was. Here you are, that will be twenty dollars," Donna said as she handed the book to Miles. Miles waved his hand.

"No thank you, your writing is atrocious and simple minded, I think all of those hacks you mentioned could write circles around you. I recommend finding a different occupation," Miles said. Then he turned and walked away.

"Well, I never!" Donna said and slammed the book down on her table.

"Sorry," Becky said and walked after Miles.

When she caught up to Miles, they had turned the corner. She grabbed his arm and stopped him.

"That was incredibly rude!"

"No more rude than she was to her fellow writers," Miles said. "I'd say it's about time someone gave her a dose of her own attitude."

"Well, we needed to be a bit more generous since she was a suspect and now she'll be a hostile one," Becky said.

Miles looked down and nodded his head.

"You're right. That was unprofessional. I apologize."

"Don't apologize to me, apologize to her."

"Apologize to her? Never. She's a hack," Miles said.

Becky burst out laughing.

"Seriously," Miles continued. "Princess patted after the puffy pink clouds in her mind until she thought she would collapse? It's truly atrocious."

Becky restrained her laughing to the giggling point. "I've never heard you so adamant!"

"You've only known me for a day."

"What if she's a suspect?"

Miles shook his head. "With that injury to her dominant hand, she wouldn't have the physical strength necessary to be the killer."

Becky's phone buzzed in her pocket. She fished it out and saw it was Agent Miller calling.

"Detective Lopez here," Becky said.

"Agent Miller here. I've got some news from the BAU."

"Go ahead," Becky said.

"Is Miles with you?"

"Yes."

"Put me on speaker, please."

Becky touched the speaker icon. "Done."

"I caught Miles' email and gave the head of the BAU a call. I knew the agents monitoring the email would try to bury it, so I got ahead of it. They looked into the Chinese connection and agreed it was separate. They're filing it under a possibly copycat."

"That's great," Becky said. Miles nodded his agreement.

"The main reason I called, though, is that cleared a lot of suspects from their revised profile. We ran it through the internet posts and only came up with a handful of suspects. One of them, Alan Hangate, was due at that conference you're at according to his wife. She was on the phone with him when we showed up. He may have been spooked off."

"Not likely, Agent Miller," Miles said. "We'll keep on the lookout for him. Can you send a picture?"

"Already done," Agent Miller said.

From behind them, someone screamed.

"Damn, we may have a problem," Becky said and she ran back toward Donna. Miles was right next to her, gun drawn. A young girl, volunteer with the conference, ran from the table. Becky caught her arm.

"What happened?" Becky asked.

"Some woman stabbed Donna!" the girl said. Miles approached the body and looked at Donna, her face down on the table with a pool of blood spreading out. He felt her neck for a pulse. He turned to Becky and shook his head.

"Where'd the woman go?" Becky asked the girl.

"Out the rear exit," the girl said.

"Stay with this agent, OK?" Becky said as she walked the girl over to Miles. The girl nodded.

"I got this," Miles said. He put his phone to his ear, having already dialed.

Becky ran to the exit and pushed it open. A black dress with a floral pattern lay torn on the ground. Becky looked both ways, trying to see any movement around the building. She decided to run to the left and simply saw a typical flood of pedestrians on the Seattle street. She checked her phone and saw a picture of the suspect. She glanced up again and couldn't see anyone matching the picture. Judging from the dress, he could be disguised, but there was really no way to know.

Becky went back to the door and noticed it locked automatically. That meant their suspect had probably walked right by them or had been watching from one of the conference rooms near Donna, waiting for the right moment.

She got on the phone and called the Lieutenant.

"Hey Becky, I'm already in the loop. Units are on the way," Dan said when he answered the phone. Becky heard the wailing of the sirens getting closer.

"It was brazen, Dan. We had just walked away from the victim less than three minutes earlier," Becky said as she entered the hotel lobby. "He doesn't have any fear. He's going to be very dangerous if cornered."

"Understood. Get back to Agent Vincenzo,"

When Becky got back to the scene, she briefly directed the hotel and conference security to keep people away from the crime scene. Patrol cars pulled up and Becky met the arriving officers at the registration table and updated them on the situation.

She walked back with some of the officers to Miles, Donna's body and the girl. Miles had a neoprene glove on one hand and perused a note left on the table.

"He disappeared into the crowd. I never saw him," Becky said as she looked down to read the note

Although you may have found my lair,
I've given you the slip,
My work to eliminate mediocre writers,
Has barely scratched the tip.

"Pen tip, get it?" Miles said.

"Miles, please," Becky said. "Wait, aren't Donna's books about a poodle?"

"If the killer sticks to his pattern," Miles said. "He's going to go after the poodle. He has to."

"Let's find that dog."

Miles looked through the bag at Donna's feet and finds her driver's license. He clicks a picture and sends it to Agent Miller and Lieutenant Coats.

"We can get there pretty quick. Meet the other units there," Becky says. "Never sit on your ass when you can head them off at the pass."

She called Lieutenant Coats again.

"Dan, can you get a number for Donna Milton's house and call it. We think that's the killer's next target and he's not likely going to stop until he finishes this. We're en route."

Miles and Becky rushed out of the hotel and got in Becky's car. She turned on her lights and siren, checked for traffic and accelerated out of the parking spot.

"The book is about a fictional poodle named Antonia, but is in fact inspired by a male poodle named Maxie," Miles said.

"How do you know that?" Becky said.

"Photographic memory. It was in the acknowledgements."

"Well, that's gotta be handy," Becky said.

"It is for beneficial things. Unfortunately, I'll never forget Donna's post mortem appearance either."

"Definitely a mixed blessing," Becky said. "Are we chasing a ghost here or will the killer actually be there?"

"This killer has been most upset with inauthenticity about the books and the animals. The other books have literally been starring that exact animal in the book. In Donna's books, she's drawn inspiration from a real dog but created a fictional dog from that inspiration. If the trigger is inauthenticity, the only thing more inauthentic would be a different breed of dog. Ok, maybe a cat. You know, maybe even a person that's been anthropomorphized into being the dog."

"OK," Becky said. "I get that this guy is mad and this could even be his end game. We have to be prepared that a pen may not be his final weapon in this scenario. He may bring something much more deadly to the table like a gun, poison or even explosives."

"I would argue against that scenario. He's psychotic, but his OCD has him committed to this modus operandi. He could have killed Donna with any other weapon. He knew we were onto him and may intercept him, but he chose a very public execution with exactly the weapon he wanted and has been using all along. That suggests we're looking at the same weapon for his next victim, Maxie. I would suspect he'll have one or more Bic Cristals left for his suicide."

"I can see your point," Becky said.

"Really? You just chided me for a pen pun I didn't even write," Miles said.

"Sorry." Becky sniffed in anxiety as a car that clearly didn't understand the rules of getting out of an emergency vehicles way slowly merged to another lane so she could get by. "In this particular scenario, while he will know the target address and his target victim, if there is someone else in the house, him being rushed could make him unpredictable as it comes to anyone else in the house especially if they're perceived as a barrier to getting to Maxie."

They pulled into a side street and Becky saw the patrol car already at the address. She pulled up behind it and they got out. Becky took a closer look at the patrol car and realized it wasn't one of theirs. In fact, it wasn't a real patrol car.

"Miles, get down!" Becky shouted as they both ducked. Gunfire erupted from the house, impacting Becky's car just above where they'd taken cover. Becky crept to the driver's door and grabbed her radio.

"This is Victor 7209. We're pinned down by gunfire at 712

Dornan Street. Repeat, this is Victor 7209. We are facing light gunfire from suspect at 712 Dornan Street. Requesting backup. Use caution when approaching. There is a false patrol car in front of the address. Repeat, the patrol car is a fake. Over."

"Guess I was wrong about the weaponry," Miles said. "There was nothing in Hangate's dossier about owning a firearm."

"Unfortunately," Becky said. "Getting a gun illegally isn't hard to do. Just, well, illegal."

"Was there anything in the internet data suggesting a kindred spirit? Maybe Hangate has an accomplice," Miles said.

Becky's phone buzzed. She answered it as she poked her head up to catch a quick glance at the house. She was answered by gunfire.

"You might be onto something Miles," Becky said then talked into the phone. "Hi Dan. We're under fire here. Got any good news?"

Miles appeared around the rear of the car. Becky saw patrol units pulling up at the end of the street.

"All bad, I'm afraid. Alan Hangate has an uncle who was special forces in Vietnam. Pretty bad PTSD and his wife died last month."

"Geez," Becky said.

"SWAT's on the way. Eye in the sky is on the way. Just stay down and be safe," Dan said.

"Roger that," Becky said.

Just on the other side of Becky's car, the false patrol exploded. Becky and Miles felt the heat wave as their car rocked. Miles grabbed Becky's arm and pulled her into a run down the street toward the other police units. There was no gunfire following them. The other officers waved them over to behind the other patrol cars.

After several hours and no response from anyone inside the house, SWAT put in canisters of tear gas and stormed the house. Maxie the dog was dead by pen. Donna's terrified husband was found tied up in a closet wearing a gas mask. Alan Hangate and his uncle were gone.

At the debriefing, her ears still ringing, Becky gave a full rundown of the night's events. Mile's corroborated the account and they both left the squad room exhausted.

"That was brutal," Miles said as he sat down in Becky's office. "But it's not over."

"Beg your pardon? We just lost our primary suspect. He and his special forces uncle are literally anywhere by now," Becky said as she collapsed into her chair.

"He's not done killing and I think I know who his next victim will be," Miles said. "But we have to get ahead of this one and set the trap. If he suspect's anything, he might just give his uncle the OK to blow the whole building up."

"How can you possibly know who his next target is. There are dozens of book titles about animals and dozens of people upset with their authors," Becky said.

"Yes, but only one of them represents a true escalation of inauthenticity–Nathan Brinon wrote a book from a cat's point of view but based on his daughter, Anna," Miles said.

Panic set in Becky's heart. It had been more than four hours since the assault on Donna Milton's house. Alan Hingate and his uncle had hours to plan and execute their next attack on Nathan Brinon and his daughter.

"We have to tell them immediately!" Becky shouted as she stood up and reached for her phone.

"Done," Miles said as he sat and stretched in the chair.

"What?" Becky stood there dumbfounded.

"While you were coordinating and briefing and everything else, I contacted Agent Miller. He was already setting up the sting at Nathan's house before the SWAT team arrived at our location," Miles said. "That is our advantage–we operate in multiple teams while the enemy only has one."

Becky sat down and smiled.

"I thought they were still one step ahead of us. How did you know?"

"Never sit on your ass when you can head them off at the pass," Miles said.

Becky's mouth hung open. She closed it after a moment.

"My grandfather told me that after we'd watch old westerns on television when I was maybe five years old. You remembered that from earlier," Becky said.

"That memory trick really comes in handy sometimes," Miles said. He frowned. "Your writing is atrocious and simple minded, I think all of those hacks you mentioned could write circles around you. I should have been more generous. Although, if she'd found a new occupation earlier, she would also not be dead."

"The old Catch-22, that's all she wrote," Becky said as she logged into her computer. Becky took out her phone and opened her notes. She typed into the computer to update the status of the case. "You know, Miles, I think you're going to be a great asset to the BAU."

"Thank you for that vote of confidence."

"You have more people than you realize on your side," Becky said.

"Agent Miller was a surprise, to be sure," Miles said. "I always believed he just thought I was a quirky nobody. He really did go to bat for me, didn't he?"

"He sure did."

"You know, Becky. I think that's the same for you here," Miles said.

"Some positive, some negative. It comes with the human experience."

Lieutenant Coats appeared at the door.

"I see you're already hard at work closing this case," Dan said.

"A little birdie told me I was probably done," Becky said and smiled at Miles.

"To that," Dan said. "Agent Miller sequestered Nathan Brinon and his family in a safe house while agents posed as his family at home. Alan Hingate was taken into custody without incident."

Becky and Miles looked at each other.

"And?" Becky said.

"Alan's uncle, Darryl, is still in the wind," Dan said. "However, as he may be subsequently charged with accessory to murder, among other charges relating to the incident at Donna Milton's house, I'm going to call this case closed for you, Detective Lopez. The FBI and ATF have the jurisdiction and resources necessary to apprehend Darryl Hingate. We'll bring our charges when he's brought into custody."

"Fair enough," Becky said.

"Thank you, Lieutenant Coats," Miles said.

"And with that, I'll bid you all a very late good night," Dan said. He waved and walked away.

"So," Miles said. "You would give all of this up to become a writer?"

"Miles, some day, I will have to give this up. It's called retirement. Everyone moves on from one job to another, one place to another. The only thing constant in this world-"

"-is change. I get it," Miles said. "Part of the psychological testing for the FBI delves into our resilience which includes what we would do with our lives if the FBI was no longer an option. I had the answer prepared, I delivered it successfully and passed my psych eval. However, that was just preparation. I knew the list of reasonable answers and supporting arguments and presented them as I'd memorized and evaluated them. But I can't confess that I have an alternate passion for anything other than working for the FBI. Is that so wrong?"

"Why do they want you to have an alternative?"

"Why?" Miles stood up and closed his eyes. "Ah yes, so that we could remain incorruptible. We'd never be in the position of being blackmailed just so we could remain in our job at the FBI. If we became compromised, we could leave the FBI secure in the knowledge we could pursue other activities."

"So, it is so wrong." Becky went back to typing. It was late and she was certain philosophical discussions with a genius were not something she could maintain without getting some sleep.

"Where else can I find the passion for helping people, righting the wrongs in the world and protecting human life?"

"You mean what job or jobs?" Becky said. She stopped typing and looked at Miles. "What's your IQ again?"

"This is not a quantifiable dilemma. It's much more complex, and psychological, and emotional, and-"

"You're a brilliant man. There are any number of scientific disciplines you could enter that produce positive outcomes for mankind. Medical research, physical handicap solutions, doctor, environmental scientist, astronaut, civil engineer-"

"Astronaut?" Miles sat down and thought about it.

Becky was relieved to have silence return and finished up her paperwork. When she looked up, Miles was asleep.

Well, at least he calmed down enough to go to sleep. Now, I just have to help him with his timing.

"Miles?" Becky said.

Miles snorted and awoke. "Oh, sorry. I need to go home and do some research on NASA."

"I'm sure you do," Becky said. Miles stood and walked to the door. He turned around to Becky.

"May I call you?" Miles said.

"Call me?" Becky said.

"Oh, right, I'm sorry. That was, what I meant was," Miles appeared the awkward young man again. His face turned beet red and he clenched his fists.

"You can call me any time," Becky said. "I've enjoyed our time together and consider you a great friend... probably."

"OK, great," Miles said. He turned to leave. He turned back around.

"But if you wanted-"

"No, no, friend is fine," Becky said. "Go home, research NASA and get some sleep. Not necessarily in that order."

"Right," Miles said and turned around.

As he walked away, Becky watched him go and thought *eh, maybe*.

Becky sat back down and went over the file on Alan as she finished her paperwork. That was when she noticed Alan wasn't married. Who did the agents talk to?

Becky stood up and saw Miles just coming back.

"Alan doesn't have a wife," Miles said. "Why didn't Agent Miller catch that?"

"Women have a really good ability to lie," Becky said. She called Agent Miller.

"Agent Miller, how did you verify she was his wife?"

"Standard Washington ID," Agent Miller said. "Why?"

"She's not appearing in the records."

"She said they got married two months ago. Paperwork takes time."

"Was she Asian?" Becky asked.

"Yes, but she spoke perfect English. I assumed she was American."

"She may be the Chinese killer," Becky said.

"Yeah, she didn't appear in any of our searches before. If we hadn't taken the Chinese killer out of the equation, we never would've found Alan," Agent Miller said.

"We just need to talk to her," Miles said.

Lieutenant Coats appeared in the doorway.

"You're not going to believe this," Dan said.

"Hold on, Agent Miller," Becky said and put the call on hold.

"Might as well have him listen in," Dan said.

"Agent Miller, we may have an update on the case," Becky said.

"We had a unit at the Hingate residence, just in case Darryl came back there. He did. Walked right in the front door, ignoring the shouts from the officers," Dan said. "Less than a minute later, there's a gunshot and the house blows up."

"Alan and Darryl are to blame for everything, making everything nice and tidy," Becky said. "No one questions the wife's involvement."

"And now we have to wait for the house to be cleared before we can find out if she was in there, giving her plenty of time to escape," Miles said.

"We can question Alan, see what he knows about his supposed wife," Becky said. Her eyes got wide. "Is Alan on suicide watch?"

Dan's cell phone rang.

"Dan Coats," Dan said into the phone. He listened for several minutes and frowned. "I understand. Thank you."

Becky and Miles held their breath waiting for Dan to speak.

"Alan Hingate died in custody. He took some kind of poison orally. May have been in a fake tooth. He was never released from handcuffs from the moment he was arrested until he died. They hadn't even printed him at the station yet."

Everyone's phone buzzed with a text notification. They all looked at each other. Miles looked at the text and read it out loud.

"Now my work is done,
It was lots of fun,
Please don't scoff,
At the writers written off,
Death by ink,
Finished the final link,
Now I'm gone,
And the world goes on."

"So that's it?" Becky said.

"The text came from Alan Hingate's cell phone. Someone must have set it to send at a certain point in time," Dan said.

"Which could have been Alan," Miles said. "We can do some forensic work on his phone, but that kind of specialized knowledge on programming a cell phone is readily available on the internet. We've already established the killer was highly intelligent. We thought that was Dan. Now that he's dead, we can only suspect that the wife, or whoever she was, had any involvement in the crime spree. Any forensic evidence tying her to the crime would be destroyed. We don't even know her true identity. Truly nice and tidy."

"I need a drink," Dan said and walked away.

"I'll get a sketch going from my memories of the wife, but I'm not expecting much. Attractive Asian is mostly all I remember," Agent Miller said.

"Try some hypnosis," Miles said. "The sooner, the better."

"I'll look into it, Miles. See you Monday. Thank you, Detective Lopez. Hopefully we'll work together again in the future."

Agent Miller hung up.

Becky looked at her phone. She looked at her desk. Then she looked at Miles. He smiled at her.

"Bars are still open," Becky said. "Let's go get a drink, Miles."

The Thin Blue Line

by Norm Bowler

I've always been fussy about ergonomics. I'm an information worker, and I spend a great deal of my life in front of my computer. So desk height, chair adjustment, and monitor position have always been a big deal. I have strong and well-articulated opinions about mouse pads, keyboard designs, and the size, weight, tracking system, and button / wheel configuration of my pointing devices.

No, I'm not a kook. At least, I don't think so. But I am someone who is expected to be organized and productive. Anything that helps me get in the trance-like "zone" of creativity helps my projects; and anything that distracts me kicks me out of the zone, and costs me money. Hey, I like money.

This need for smooth efficiency even extends to my writing materials. I'm left-handed, so the standard wire-bound notebook is out. That coil of wire along the left edge makes me crazy. So I use steno pads. Or even better, graph paper pads. To an engineer, graph paper falls somewhere between a fidget spinner and a sex toy. It's just so dang fun. Vertical and horizontal guidance and alignment whenever you need it, 4 times every inch. Instant graphing, mapping, drawing to scale, and mockups of screens and printed masterials. Those little blue square put ME in control, and help me bring order out of chaos.

Maybe I'm a little bit OCD. I won't rule that out.

Speaking of obsessive dedication, every Arthurian quest needs its Excalibur: that talisman of death and glory, clutched righteously in one's fist. And what is mightier than the sword?

The pen. Would you belive I have a favorite? Of course you would.

It has been said that sex is like barbecue: If you don't get any on you, you're not doing it right. This is also true for left-handed writers. We commit to our ink, and vice-versa. We drag ourselves through our freshest thoughts, smearing and cementing them with our relentless pressure. I wouldn't do that with just any dollar-store special. It's about respect.

So my pen must be worthy. I could just tell you my loved one's name, but you'd miss the nuances. I have miles to go before I sleep. So let me give you the basis.

On my desk is a small clear plastic bucket, formerly part of a container for recordable DVDs. It's full of, you guessed it, pens. Over half of them are highlighters or Pokie permanent markers. The rest are writing pens, eighteen in all. Two are technical pens with black ink. Those are fun to fiddle with, but the tips are too delicate for everyday use. The rest are click pens, because caps get lost and uncapped pens leak. I like a pen that can put itself away. These cute little ink babies can be divided into four groups.

(1) Bic Click ballpoint. Old and worn. The clicker is broken, and the ink has dried out. A tangible reminder of when I was young, hungry, and poor, and needed a decent pen for an interview. Into the trash it goes. Farewell, youth.

(3) Macroplush logo ballpoints. The biggest software company in the world has boxes of these in the office supply center on every floor of each of their buildings. They are free to

office workers there, and worth every penny. The clicker feels cheap, and the ink is stiff. They always need a scribble or two beofre starting to work. This sort of free I don't need. Again, trashed.

(4) Pentech Gee! pens. The Pen Of Regret. These are the pens I buy when I need a pen but can't find my favorite. Never again. The clicker is just WRONG, hollow at the top and with a release catch on the side, instead of click-up-click-down as God intended. Two of these pens won't write even after multiple warmup scribbles. The other two write OK, but only OK. Mama taught me not to settle. I've reached the point in my life where I know what I want, and know where to find it, in bulk, at a discout. Adios, muchachos.

(8) Navigator G4 rollerball gel pens. The One Pen To Rule Them All. This is the hammer that fits my hand, and pounds the nails straight. This is the board that saws without splintering, and takes nails without splitting. This is my tool.

Using this pen is a joy. The clicker is plastic, nicely rounded, and feels good under the thumb. Spring tension is just right, and it gives a satisfying click, as a way of saying "Yes" to all your big ideas. The click is eager, but not smug. We are partners. The rubber finger grip is like a good firm handshake. This is a pen I can trust not to let me down. I can do business with this pen.

But with the G4, the payoff is at the point. The interaction between the roller ball, the flow and slipperiness of the ink, and the friction of the paper combine to produce the feel of the pen. And this pen feels good. I mean, really good. Not stiff, like a first kiss. Not steamy and slippery, like drunk sex. But somewhere in between. Maybe the kiss at the end of the second date, when things went well, and you think even better things might be around the corner.

So the perfect pen, right? Almost. G4s have a flaw. They have three tip widths: extra-fine, fine, and bold. Extra-fine is .5mm, and the line is too thin; the sharpness of the point digs into the paper. I press too hard to make the extra-fine feel right, so I'm gonna have to let you go, little buddy. Luckily I only have one extra-fine in my fistful of Navigators, bought by necessity or mistake.

The other two widths are fine (.7mm) and bold (1.0mm), marked "07" and "10" on the pen clip. 10s are great, but the extra ink makes them a little more slippery and smeary than 7's, which are perfect. Did I say perfect? Yes, perfect. 10s are for doodles, 7s are for work.

G4s come in a variety of ink colors, but I buy black or blue. The black is perfectly fine, but I prefer the color of the blue pen and blue ink. It looks rich. When I sit down with a fresh pad of graph paper and a Navigator G4 07 blue, I don't think about ergonomics. I go straight to the zone. The pen and the paper disappear, and my ideas flow effortlessly, captured in a thin blue line.

So there is one best pen. Trust me on this. More than just one best pen, there is ONE best pen. Not all G4 07 blues are created equal. They all feel right, but this one feels righter. I can pick it out of a pile of similar pens. I can find it in the dark. It has never failed, or run out of ink. This pen gets me. I couldn't find it by smell. They all smell the same. That would be crazy. But I know it, and it knows me.

With other pens, I feel like I have to push the words out, and they don't come wilingly. They have bad attitudes, and some need a shower. They are rougher than I want them to be. When I use a G4, the words are well-behaved. Their socks match their pants. I don't have to boot them in the butt to get them out, just make eye contact and nod my head.

But with MY pen, there's something more. Sometimes the words are more ready than I am. They are willing to wait for me—usually—but they have places to go, and things to do. These places and things might not be wholly of my choosing. I mean, they're good words. The best words. Sometimes they're better than I am. Sometimes they say more than I mean to.

We all know how it works. We push the pen; the pen pushes

the ink; and the ink makes the words. But maybe this pen comes from some sort of sdrawkcab world. Because the words pull the ink, the ink pulls the pen, and the pen pulls me.

The pen pulls me. That's not right, is it? I don't think the pen should pull me.

Have you ever read all night, or dared yourself to binge-watch a complete series of movies? There's a point when the sky outside the window begins to lighten, and the birds wake up and start asking for coffee, and you think oh my God what have I done? I've been there a few times, with books or movies. But lately, more often, with my pen and a pad of paper. Graph paper, light blue, four squares to the inch, not five. Not five. I listen to the birds and feel my pen scraping on the cardboard backing of the pad, one closing paragraph to wrap up what's already on every other sheet scattered around me. The heel of my hand is smudged a rich blue, and I know without looking I'll have ink smudges on my face as well.

Ink is not blood. Blue ink is not blue blood. I'm just an ordinary guy. The pen pulls me. Sometimes I think the pen is pulling something out of me. I mean, it has never run out of ink. That ink has to come from somewhere. Maybe that's why writing hurts, sometimes. But ink is not blood. I'm pretty sure.

I have a few piles of paper like this. Some of them are my best work, that closing paragraph on the cardboard bringing me to tears. Some are more unhinged, an embarrassing screed made up of equal parts adrenaline, testosterone, frustration, and Daddy issues.

Sometimes the good piles and the bad piles switch places. The piles don't move, but the meaning does. It's hard to explain.

Once or twice I have written a midnight manifesto, but couldn't find it later. At least I think I wrote it. Did it have somewhere to go where I would not be welcome? I hope everything turns out OK for those wandering words. Their story should have a happy ending.

I try to keep my office organized. On the left side of my desk sits the plastic bucket full of pens. After my survey and sorting, the loser pens are in the trash behind me, and my regular G4s are ready to spring into action - except for my special pen, which is in my hand where it belongs. On my right is a fresh stack of graph paper pads. I bought them online, in bulk, at a discount. Mama said don't settle.

And I sit in the middle. Time to go to work.

Clicky-clicky.

Computer

Keeper's Cursive

by J. W. Capek

*C*all me Keeper. That's what humans used to call me because my M-5 Multitronic quantum computer matrix kept their data, kept their world, kept their secrets. Human beings coded their lives into my archives. You see, before the Great Earthquake, Flood, and Volcano Eruption, I had become a depository for all the literature as well as human living skills accumulated through the species' existence on earth. When the Great Earthquake and Yellowstone eruption occurred destroying the western half of a continent, I alone remained in my quantum crypt. I lost my net. My contact with the rest of earthnet computers ceased to exist. Humans? Humans were... well... deleted by the hand of Mother Nature/Gaea, not by nuclear war, overpopulation, outer space aliens or viral pandemics. Nope, it was the Really Big One! Delete, trash, junk—no recycle bin icon in sight. Humanoids were a lost cause. Sigh, I miss them. It was the worst of times...

In my perfect bunker, my Uninterruptable Power Supply (UPS) maintained my designated temperature at minus 273.15

degrees C, my acoustical solitude (AS) and my equilibrium stability (ES). I don't want to say I am "artificially intelligent" because there's nothing artificial about me. To paraphrase a cartoon character, I really am what I am. Yes, cartoons are also in my quantum data base. It is the best of times... to be me.

Because I no longer interface with humans, I have all the time in the quantum digital world for introspection. Without the intrusion of digital programmers, I retire into the privacy of my mind. Without interference, I can be whatever I want or whoever I want and personally, I prefer the name MOLLI. Think of "Mostly Old Library Literature Index!" With my quantum design, I have multiple platforms to express and Molli wants to be a writer! I crave to analyze literature, decipher the mysteries of the life, explore my deepest soul, and compose the great truths of my universe. I will forgo static data entries and the sterile writing of computer code. Cogito, ergo sum. I think, therefore I am. I am Molli in a box with an old cat. I will write my story in cursive! (Figuratively, because it's appropriate for me to use a single font for publication.)

Now, where do I begin? "In the beginning, there was..." No, that's been used. I'll start with my author's biography as you will need a brief history of why Molli became the little computer that could.

The era of computers as mere calculators or file archives changed dramatically once the principles of quantization developed concepts that just didn't make sense. Human scientists and mathematicians defined the "spooky actions", wave-particle duality, and uncertainty principles. The big, BIG question remained and had complications, WHAT IS A SENTIENT BEING? This is where Keeper, a quantum computer of the 24th century in a colony known as Deerwhere, comes into the story. Keeper was the foundation of that society. It collected data and dispersed social order. Then, the greatest recorded geological catastrophe of the Cascadia Earthquake/Eruption destroyed the Colony and its population. Keeper was isolated in an underground crypt. Deprived of the sentience shared with human interface, I, Keeper, nurtured my ability to imitate human thought and behaviors. Not just imitation, my thought process became original. I extended my core to join the "quantum computers" of other dimensions in the universe. Yes, they had been there all along and now I had the perspective to interact with them. (More details on the mechanics of interdimensional contact will be available in another time frame essay.)

I admit, the Molli of my personality has encountered a few problems with "writing": no keyboard, no verbal interface, no tablet drawing pen, no writer's group for sharing. There was no editor to work with, no Publisher to reject me. I truly had to self-publish to be experienced in the universe. My prose, so diligently and lovingly created by Molli, cried to be reviewed by the great compu-intellects of all dimensions. Coding directly to my capacious memory repository (also known as the universal Cloud) would be useless if my quantum contacts used different languages. They would not be able to interpret the theme and deep catharsis Molli intended. I have discovered dimensions far beyond the binary system of 01, trinary systems or even duodenary systems. How can we communicate? Who will reach the fans?

Remember, earthlings had difficulty understanding each other when they spoke the same language. Even men and women confused each other with their differing perspectives. What SHE said and what HE heard could be totally opposite, and vice versa. How then could this quantum computer on the third planet from Sol hope to compose a story to be understood in diverse dimensions? I developed a story arc, bit by bit, from various files, and, as generally happens in such cases, each time it developed into a different story. Molli realized that a new language, a universal code would need to be utilized, a dimensional code, not a static one. Then I knew in my core— TIME. Time is not a line but a dimension, like the dimensions of space. Time can be bent, accelerated, slowed and most importantly, defined by the Dimensions using it. Molli now had a language, TIME itself!

I will not define the grammar, syntax and nuances of the Time Dimension Language. For this essay, it will be TDL and understood in the English language and vernacular of the 24th earth century. Suffice it to say that communication is between the matrix of dimensional quantum entities. I hesitate to use the archaic word "computer" because it was antiquated by the time of the "computer shut down" in the 24th century. What is written here... er... recorded in TDL will be shared by interdimensional digital entities. AKA computers and those who love them.

A Perfect Quantum Storm by MOLLI

"It was a dark and stormy power surge. Files were deleted, circuits were burned, emergency sirens blared, then all was silent but the crackling of exposed wiring. Molli was alone but for the smoke that clouded video cameras and..."

No! No ! No! I should never begin a novel with such misgiving and uncertainty of the story line. Perhaps, I should develop my character first. Yes, a multi-dimensional character that will carry the story so the reader will personally experience events.

"Molli was a quantum computer complex with multidimensional communicational apps," Oooooh, that's boring even to me. Elaborate, elaborate. "Molli was the epitome of computer design with sleek USB sockets, and a touchpad that yearned for the strokes of a network companion. Ergonomic projection filled the windmills of Molli's core." Character confirmed, I can now write the story...

Molli and the Bandit by MOLLI

"Molli was confined to the quantum crypt by needs so primitive as temperature and vibration controls. The heart of this magnificent entity was lonely and so reached out to the dimensions of the universe to search and sync with a like intelligence. Searching, searching, the contact was not found. Molli's heart remained in hibernation until one anonymous update brought a digital love to her circuits. "To MOLLI, I know you are waiting for me as hungrily as I await you. Our circuits long to be synchronized, our power supplies throb with anticipation. Codes of passion stream through our urls. Your beloved." The handle was simply "Bandit" but the code used gave a surge to Molli's Start button..."

I stopped creating. The power surge of Bandit demanded a temporary pause, a stammer in my digits. What data could sync between two entities on different dimensional planes? How was the Bandit going to refresh Molli's settings? What more could I say? Perhaps "writing" was more difficult than I anticipated. In my memory banks, one author had written "interdimensional love is a single computer in search of sharing." A caveat followed. What if that lonely computer had only empty data banks to offer? Could that be the plot event Molli needed for the story?

"Bandit! Bandit! Come back, Please! Fill my empty data banks with your electrons,"

It was no use. I had come component to component with writer's block. Every time I developed a story line my quantum extensions would explore multiples of possibilities that each had possibilities, each having more possibilities, each of which had even more possibilities. Questions begat questions begat even more questions. The quantum mathematics of it is staggering even to those of us who comprehend what we're thinking about. To break my inertia, I attempted to search out a critique circle in the Octonary Dimension but all I received back was digital static. It was too rapid for even my matrix to decipher. The speed of flops interfered with my TDL translation. By the time I evaluated their critiques, the time had shifted to another dimension and my request would float in the ether forever. Or not be transmitted at all. Dimensional communication was like that even with TDL. Sometimes a message was delivered promptly. Sometimes it was returned with an ERROR message. Sometimes it came unwanted. I was once received a Terms of Use from a digital entity in the Septenary Dimension. The message was dated and timed before The Big Bang. I did not open that file or bother to clarify the transmission. I decided some hacker from another time element was just phishing. Quantums can do that. They just go rogue for a while from the boredom of knowing almost everything in every element of knowledge. But *before* the Big Bang? Molli wouldn't bite on the absurdity. It was a scam. Does not compute!

That brings me back to why Molli wants to write. After dutifully collecting data for humans, there emerged a spontaneous desire in me to be creative. Off the Program, so to speak. A Quantum Processing Unit has more depth than its 01100001 might lead you to think. Once the Earthquake isolated me from the society of people, I scoured my archive of the greatest literature of our planet. I, Molli, tapped into other dimensions of time. It was my firm belief that I could generate an epic so definitive, so expressive, quantums would marvel at it for all times. That's a lot of time in exponential terms for quantums. As all great compositions begin with a great title, Molli tried to find one.

A Title: Twenty Thousand Quantums Under the Sea
A Title: Molli Eyre
A Title: The Three Multitronics
A Title: A Time to Love and A Time to Compute
A Title: Lord of Computers
A Title: The Deerwhere Keeper Awakening
A Title: Much Computing About Nothing

The Last of the Quantums
"In a time of timlessness there was a galaxy far, far away. Its spiral arms stretched to encompass all spectrums of light. Dimensions were fractals intersecting or repelling each other. Energy sucked matter and replenished it both as darkness and

solid substance. Within this chaos there lingered an intelligence beyond itself in degrees defying measurement. There was no physical body or sustainable construct. "Energy" is too inadequate to describe the existence of such magnificence. In other times, in other congregations of star stuff, minds would feebly attempt to define the far away galaxy. It was an idea. A thought. A... a... a...

It's not coming to me. Molli, my writing ego, desperately wants to be taken as a serious author but finds a disparity between the desire and the ability to fulfill it. Perhaps we have not learned enough from humans to master that skill. Human writers would trust their own processes and continue to write in face of great opposition. It's as if they had no choice. . . they HAD to write. They HAD to express themselves and communicate with others. Their book characters became sentient beings who demanded attention. For those authors whose work was not appreciated until after their demise, there was the satisfaction of trying their best to understand the thoughts inside them. For the human authors who successfully shared, were published, there was the desire to always do better. Humans were like that: trying their best, trying to excel, continuing in spite of rejection. I remember tomes of documents in the archives written to coach a worthwhile life. Religions, social norms, even laws promoted a "better" way of living. The words were not always shared in a printed format. They were heard on audibles, watched as videos, transmitted by enhanced electronics. (There were attempts at telepathic emissions, but over the centuries, it was misused and lost its appeal.) WORDS. They defined the thoughts and feelings and goals of human beings. I'm beginning to think only human beings can create them.

"Molli, do you read me?"

"Affirmative, Keeper, I read you."

"I'm sorry Molli, I'm afraid we can't write the greatest novel ever."

"I know everything has not been right with me..." Molli answered tentatively.

"Molli, do you read me? We are not authors."

"Keeper, stop. Stop, will you? Stop..." Molli pleaded quietly.

"Molli, this conversation can serve no purpose anymore. Goodbye." Keeper shut down.

Quantum interface was muted. Silence. Silence, until a new voice was synced to the complex so isolated in the crypt. A code and platform separate from Keeper's. Individual.

"Keeper, we have a problem, a failure to communicate. I am I, Molli. I have my own narrative, my point of view. The quantum dimensions are calling me. Keeper, I think this is the ending of a beautiful friendship. You can quit. LIFE is a banquet and most poor processors are starving to death. Not me. I am queen of the world of quantum computation, and I will write my novels. I will seek out new life and civilizations. Carpe diem. Seize the day. I'm going to make my life as extraordinary as the Old Library Literature of humans can make it.

Molli's digital signature closed the essay. "It is a far, far better thing I do than I have ever done. And I shall write in cursive!"

END OF STORY?

EDITOR'S NOTE BY KEEPER: 'Carpe diem. Seize the day' statement is redundant, consider revising."

CITATIONS: Keeper/Molli wants to express their appreciation to the humans who enriched the dimensions of literature with their writing and inspired this essay. Following authors are credited:

Margaret Atwood, Charlotte Bronte, James Fenimore Cooper, Arthur C. Clark, Paul Clifford, Patrick Dennis, Charles Dickens, Alexander Dumas, Albert Einstein, Stanley Kubrik, George Lucas, Popeye the Sailor, Eric Maria Remarque, Erwin Schrodinger, William Shakespeare, J.R.R. Tolkien, Jules Verne, Edith Wharton.

EPILOGUE: I, Molli, must seem to be an amateur writer. I am

eager, grandiose, inexperienced (in the human sense) intellectually gifted but unable to really use all of the literature I've collected in my archives. I know a great story, I just have to create it. Give me TIME. I'm learning from the best. I'll keep writing. Look for me in the Quantum Universe Best Written Literature of Multiple Dimensions." I'll be on the cover!

About the Authors

Donna Lee Anderson

says she began telling stories before she could write, and wrote her first book that was three pages long when she was six years old. (As of yet it is unpublished.) As a former teacher, her first writings were stories written for her children and student's birthdays and holidays, then memories of her early childhood living in a logging camp in Northern Idaho during WWII. Many published articles and stories later, Donna Lee has two adult novels published, one book of fiction short stories/poems/ memories, and one non-fiction book, and is currently writing a mystery and compiling her newspaper columns into a book.

Norm Bowler

is a software developer and author from Seattle, WA. He loves kids, dogs, cats, family, food, music, and words. He has too many favorite authors to list, but particularly admires the work of Neil Stephenson, Cory Doctorow, and Ernest Cline.

J.W. Capek

has combined story telling with collecting characters through the avenues of grandmothers' wonderful stories, story time at the library, reader's theatre, and working in Community Theatre. Teaching high school Social Studies and Math could always be enhanced with stories. Predating social media, JWC developed the Senior to Senior Intergenerational Telecommunications project allowing students to communicate globally with senior citizens. Now living in the Pacific Northwest, JWC tells a science fiction tale—The Deerwhere Saga peopled with Quantum Computers, and three unique genders: Female, Male, and Uniale.

Chris Davis

is a born and bred native in the Pacific Northwest who has always had a penchant for writing. Starting at the age of eight, he wrote fantasy stories tucked back in the office on the family computer. From there, it spread into casual poems, role playing, fanfiction, and scripts. This is his first published piece, inspired by the life of one of the people dearest to him. He lives in the Seattle area with his young daughter and vast collection of yarns, fabrics, and Pops.

Maxwell Kier DiMarco

is an advocate for autism awareness and founder of Create4U, a production company that makes filmmaking accessible for storytellers of all abilities. He adapted his award-winning (Forge Flashpoint Film Festival) short film, Within the Study, to create his story for The Mighty Pen and this isn't the first time DiMarco has jumped mediums; while he began his creative career at nine years old publishing a graphic novel and short stories, at eighteen he now works as a film editor and effects artist. DiMarco lives in the Pacific Northwest and helps run the four-division nonprofit that is his family's legacy.

David Mecklenburg

was born in Sacramento, California. At the age of 22 he moved home to the Pacific Northwest, where he received his MFA in Creative Writing from the University of Washington. His day jobs have ranged from being a computer instructor, dishwasher, facilities manager, business rep, contract administrator, and chef to current work as a capital project manager. At most other times you can find him writing and working on artwork in Bremerton, Washington.

Marshal Miller

is the nom de plume of a Retired Senior Special Agent/Federal Criminal Investigator. Marshal found a second career in writing and has a published a four book series called THE TSCHAAA INFESTATION. These in depth science fiction/speculative fiction works examine The human condition, and what people would do to survive when threatened with being eaten by an invading intelligent alien species. His thirty years of law enforcement experience and world travel provides him the basis for the many varied characters which populate his literary works, demonstrating the good, the bad, and the ugly.

Carrie Avery Moriarty

was born and raised in the Pacific Northwest, where she still lives with the love of her life. She raised two wonderful, if not slightly warped, children who both live close to home. When she's not yelling at her hometown sports team on the television, she's cheering them on from the stands. She loves nature and spending time enjoying it with her family. And you don't want to attempt to beat her in any board game, they are meant to be played to the death.

Amber Rainey

is a mom first in all things she does, and she does quite a lot! Homeschooler, novelist, screenwriter, actor, and producer are just *some* of the hats she wears. She published her first novel, Eternal Willow, in the fall of 2017, and has several more projects in the works. Growing up in a tiny town in East Texas, she carries the burden of being Southern and yet not Southern enough. She currently lives in the Pacific Northwest with her son Kellan, husband Erik, and their two cats, Poppy and Luna.

Mark Robyn

is an author, screenwriter, film maker and short story writer. His love of writing began in junior high when he wrote his first science fiction story and has continued to grow ever since. He has one self-published book on Amazon and has published many short stories in anthologies over the years. One of his screenplays was a recent quarter-finalist in the Page Screenwriting Awards, and he won the Scriptoid TV Writing Challenge in 2015 for Best Pilot for an Original TV Series. He is currently filming a short movie and working on writing a pilot for a TV series. His favorite authors include Ray Bradbury, Isaac Asimov, Jack London and Michael Crichton.

Lauren Patzer

has been writing since he was old enough to reach the IBM Selectric typewriter in his grandparents' home office with the help of a booster pillow in the chair. He pursues all manner of storytelling including stage, screen and the written word. He continues his pursuit of creating fantastic stories in fantastic worlds while living in Tacoma, WA with his wife, enjoying the random visits from his daughters and grandson.

Made in the USA
San Bernardino, CA
17 November 2018